FIVE OF CLUBS

THE TRENT RIVERA MYSTERIES
BOOK 5

BLAKE VALENTINE

FIVE OF CLUBS

First edition. October 14th, 2024.

Copyright © BLAKE VALENTINE, 2024.

Written by BLAKE VALENTINE.

CRED Productions.

All rights reserved. No portion of this book may be reproduced in any form, stored in any retrieval system, or transmitted in any form or by any means – electronic, photocopying, mechanical, recording, or otherwise – without written permission from the author.

This is a work of fiction. All characters in this book are fictitious, and any similarities or resemblances to real people living or dead is entirely coincidental.

Contents

1. Lancashire, UK. — 1
2. Chapter 2 — 20
3. Chapter 3 — 25
4. Texas, USA. — 31
5. Lancashire, UK. — 36
6. Chapter 6 — 39
7. Chapter 7 — 44
8. Chapter 8 — 49
9. Texas, USA. — 53
10. Lancashire, UK. — 59
11. Chapter 11 — 67
12. Texas, USA. — 71
13. Lancashire, UK. — 77
14. Texas, USA. — 81
15. Chapter 15 — 84
16. Chapter 16 — 87
17. Chapter 17 — 92
18. Chapter 18 — 96

19.	Chapter 19	100
20.	London, UK.	105
21.	Lancashire, UK.	111
22.	Chapter 22	115
23.	London, UK.	118
24.	Lancashire, UK.	124
25.	Chapter 25	135
26.	Chapter 26	139
27.	Chapter 27	145
28.	Chapter 28	148
29.	Chapter 29	152
30.	Chapter 30	156
31.	Chapter 31	163
32.	London, UK.	169
33.	Lancashire, UK.	173
34.	Chapter 34	178
35.	Chapter 35	183
36.	Chapter 36	187
37.	London, UK.	191
38.	Chapter 38	195
39.	Chapter 39	198
40.	Lancashire, UK.	202
41.	Chapter 41	205
42.	London, UK.	210

43.	Chapter 43	215
44.	Lancashire, UK.	220
45.	Chapter 45	231
46.	Chapter 46	236
47.	Chapter 47	242
48.	Chapter 48	246
49.	Chapter 49	251
50.	Chapter 50	259
51.	Chapter 51	266
52.	Chapter 52	269
53.	Chapter 53	275
54.	Chapter 54	288
55.	Chapter 55	292
56.	London, UK.	295
57.	Washington State, USA.	302
58.	Texas, USA.	307
59.	Next Novel Excerpt.	312
60.	TRENT RIVERA NOVELS.	321
61.	Get Exclusive Blake Valentine Material.	322
62.	About the Author.	322

Chapter 1
Lancashire, UK.

Precisely seventeen minutes after the Talbot Express departed the Foulmile camp, it appeared on the large screen which dominated the basement office of LD Chopper Tours. An instant later, a pre-programmed alert pinged loudly, drawing Sanderson's attention to the moving vehicle. The man had been dozing in a gamer's chair, but sprang into wakefulness.

'Trout!' he called out gruffly, his voice echoing through the basement office.

'What?' an irritated reply from the adjacent room enquired.

'Get in here!' Sanderson called out more urgently. 'I think we've got a bogie.'

As the other man stepped into the office, he squinted at the same screen as the other man. The grainy outline of an old RV was crawling slowly up the steep slope towards Black Fell Beacon on the road towards Brynworth. The image was wide-angled and jumped slightly; it was fuzzy at the edges where the headlights danced across the uneven tarmac. 'Is it one of theirs? The fucking crusties?' Trout enquired.

'We'll know in a minute.' Sanderson tapped at his keyboard. 'If it is, then it's in the right zone.' He paused. 'And there's no other traffic – not by the look of things – no headlights for miles.'

Silence.

'You think it might be a Sierra Bravo job, then?' The other man spoke a little hesitantly, raising his eyebrows.

'Maybe. We'll have to see what her ladyship says, won't we?'

'Shit!' Trout sighed, the hint of a smile appearing on his face. 'Fucking death from the skies or what?'

Sanderson scoffed, but couldn't help smiling himself.

Fifty thousand feet above, Big Bird - the military-grade drone procured for the two men - responded to the string of numbers Sanderson inputted on his keyboard. It turned sharply and angled its nose downwards, its focus now firmly on the moving vehicle. At that altitude, the temperature was below minus fifty degrees Celsius; the two laser-guided Hellfire missiles the drone carried were coated with a delicate frosting of ice. It was – as the men knew – invisible to anyone on the ground; the darkness cloaked its vapour trails.

Such weapons were highly illegal in almost all countries. The reason was simple: a drone manufactured to such specifications had no place outside a combat zone. And there was no way a craft of such deadly potential had any reason to be in the location it was – high above northern England.

Especially not when it was being piloted by civilians. Particularly when those civilians were the calibre of Trout and Sanderson.

But the drone didn't belong to Trout or Sanderson. Their role was simple: in return for close to twenty grand a month each, they launched the fully-loaded craft when they were instructed. They flew it in a holding pattern within the confines of very specific coordinates. And they waited. Orders came from a faceless source – Sierra Bravo. A well-spoken woman who'd made them her operatives. They'd never met her – they'd only ever heard her voice. Any business conducted with the pair was done through Foxtrot Delta – a man their mistress described as being a handler.

Neither Trout nor Sanderson ever questioned the legality of what they were doing. It wasn't that they were unintelligent – rather the way it was sold to them made the righteousness of what they were doing irrefutable. They didn't ponder the connection between illegal drones, devastating weaponry, and a list of civilian targets. And, anyway, the money blinded them to any moral worries they may have had.

When it came down to it, they believed they were doing good. They believed the few they were sacrificing would save many more in the long term.

On the rare occasions Sierra Bravo addressed them, she described them as being assets. They were under her protection. And, under the tutelage of Foxtrot Delta, Trout and Sanderson were no longer simply tourist pilots.

They were agents.

***

Earlier, Mohawk and Nomad had punched the air in celebration. The diesel engine of the bruised and battered Talbot Express spluttered into life at the first time of asking. It was a minor miracle: a plume of dark blue smoke emanated from the exhaust and the vehicle's side panels rattled vigorously as Mohawk revved its engine. The RV was thirty-five years old – older than either of them.

Gently slipping the Talbot into gear, Mohawk depressed the clutch and eased the RV over the boggy, broken ground at the edge of the Foulmile Protest Camp. The camp – an ever-growing collection of tents, yurts, cabins, and campervans – clung to the edge of a hillside in rural Lancashire. Its inhabitants were a loosely organised collective led by the shady figure of Daltrey – a veteran of such environs. Their cause was an environmental one: experimental fracking had been started by what was rumoured to be an international conglomerate. Permission had been granted with the understanding that drilling was being done on a trial basis. But Daltrey and his acolytes knew what that meant: the moment Westminster approved it as being safe, the operation would be entrenched. And fracking would spread to the dozen or so other sites earmarked for further experimentation.

Deep down, the protestors knew that once the money began rolling in, there would be no way back for them, or the planet.

The hillside opposite Black Fell had been ravaged. Though the fracking organisation claimed its work would be done underground, the scarred landscape was clear evidence of the truth. Verdant greenery had been stripped back, and heavy drilling and pumping equipment littered the incline. At all times of day and night, the earth reverberated as high-pressure jets of water and sand were used to drive valuable shale gas out from the broken bedrock where it had remained undisturbed for millions of years. What had once been a spot deemed an area of outstanding natural beauty now looked like a giant industrial wasteland. Beyond the barbed wire of the perimeter fence, hard-hatted men in fluorescent uniforms continually moved vehicles back and forth, and laid mile after mile of thick piping and cabling. It didn't take a qualified environmentalist to appreciate the damage being done; the Foulmile protestors had significant support among naturalists and ecological action groups. And a petition launched on social media had gathered close to three million signatures in support of its cause.

But Westminster wasn't listening. At least, that was how it felt. The protest group had sent three delegations to present its petition.

Three times they'd been turned away. But – thanks to a groundswell of support – they'd become a thorn in the side of the fracking efforts. A nuisance. Operations were continuing near Brynworth, but drilling had been stalled at the other proposed sites. And the movement was being kept afloat by regular donations.

***

'Is it on the list?' Trout enquired.

'It is,' Sanderson nodded. With each tap of the keyboard, the drone camera zoomed in. For a split-second, the image was blurred; pixelated. Then, its focus sharpened. Once the registration plate was visible, Sanderson checked it against the numbers he'd been provided with. 'Yeah. Fucking bingo! It's one of them. One of the crusties,' he nodded.

Trout sighed and leaned back against the wall. The basement office was built with bare brick surfaces, but it had been modified; it bore the kind of shabby-chic fashion one might expect to find in a converted wharf warehouse in a well-to-do former industrial town. Their office space was located twenty feet below the ground. It was a location few people ever saw, but it was decked out with the type of toys one might expect to find in the offices of a profitable software start-up.

The two men had come into a great deal of money. And they had to spend it on something – it wasn't as if they could bank the cash that Foxtrot Delta regularly provided. A full-size snooker table; a collection of pinball machines, and an indoor VR golf range were among their purchases.

Operating the drone hadn't been their idea when they'd first arrived just outside of Brynworth. They'd purchased the Goreton Hall site cheaply. During World War Two, the RAF had begun building a runway there. Construction had commenced in early 1943, but had ceased shortly afterwards; the course of the conflict had altered by then, and there was no need for a Bomber Command squadron to be stationed so far north.

So the ageing concrete had been left to crack and deteriorate. Nature had reclaimed much of the cleared surface, and the hangars had fallen into disrepair. The foundations, though, remained solid. It was a simple enough job for Trout and Sanderson to freshly concrete a small section of the runway; their helicopter didn't require a huge space to take off or land. And although the hangars weren't worth saving, a new, inexpensive one was quickly erected on the existing site.

And then they were in business.

It was nearly a year later when the call had come. The deal was simple – the drone would be able to operate from the LD Chopper Tours site. It would be stored in the hangar alongside the helicopter. They were to become deep cover operatives and would be extremely well-paid for their trouble.

And that was that.

***

The Foulmile site was located close to Brynworth – the Lancashire county seat centuries before. On a map, it was simply a dot between Blackpool and Preston: a name etched against a wash of green. It was a place that – prior to the fracking operation propelling its name into the media – few people had ever heard of.

It was Brynworth to which Mohawk and Nomad were heading. The collective pooled resources like food and fuel; people paid into a central budget, and responsibilities for cleaning and cooking were divided accordingly. The rota meant that it was the pair's turn to visit the supermarket on the edge of the nearby town. Such excursions always took place in the evening – it increased the chances of securing purchases whose prices had been slashed at the end of the day. The protest camp had a vegetarian policy – that way the stews and soups cooked up in giant vats could cater for everyone.

The more the merrier.

Mohawk had a shaved head and a thick beard. Once upon a time, as a dedicated punk rocker, he'd sported the haircut that had given him his nickname. An array of home-grown tattoos with the logos of various bands of yesteryear covered his arms, attesting to his years in the counterculture. He was a dedicated revolutionary: he'd been arrested on numerous occasions; had been evicted from protest sites; had been forcibly removed from forests to whose trees he'd chained himself; had been dragged down from buildings while dressed as a variety of superheroes; had been dug out of underground tunnels where he'd railed against the building of bypasses, and he'd marched more miles holding banners and bullhorns than he cared to remember. Mohawk had never held what would have classed as a regular job. Instead, he'd crossed the country, moving from one protest camp to another, fitting in with whoever lived there and hooking up with the loosely affiliated groups of people who trod a similar path. Along the way, he'd fathered several children – some of them he saw occasionally, but most he didn't. The traveller's brother worked in the city. He was a senior partner in an investment firm and made a salary so large it resembled a telephone number. He was Mohawk's antithesis. The two only met occasionally; usually while attending family funerals. Mohawk believed himself to be a free spirit. His brother thought he was a loser.

Nomad had a PhD in Geological Sciences and a further degree in Ecology. As a career student, he'd only recently strayed from his white tower of academia. Where Mohawk was sharp, streetwise, and gregarious, Nomad was quiet, withdrawn, and naïve about matters of the world. He spoke with a soft lisp and wore his long hair in dreadlocks. The experienced traveller had taken him under his wing upon his arrival. There was a mutual respect between the two men: Nomad admired the other man's survival knowledge – it was from him that he'd learned about how life in the camp operated. Mohawk, meanwhile, used the other man's scientific knowledge to bolster any arguments he was making. If he was the voice, then Nomad was becoming the brains. Before his arrival at the camp, he'd been known to the world as Barnabus Hoffman-Gates. It had been Mohawk who'd renamed him. It had been Mohawk – too – who'd engineered him getting laid for the first time in his life. After three celibate decades, the academic had finally lost his cherry to an ageing earth mother called Alice, who had extremely low standards when it came to members of the opposite sex. Nomad's new friend didn't mention the twenty-pound note and bottle of vodka he'd proffered to sweeten the deal. Instead, he'd seen it as a worthy way of securing the other man's undying loyalty.

'Have you got the list?' Nomad asked, looking at the driver.

'All up here,' Mohawk tapped at his forehead. 'I could make veggie shepherd's pie in my sleep, mate!'

Nomad nodded. As the pair drove along the perimeter of the fracking site, he looked out at the stationary diggers, JCBs, and pumping trucks. Under the garish glow of security lights, the area was eerily silent – at night, most of the crew were housed in hotels on the Brynworth industrial estate, or further afield in Preston. At one point, Daltrey had planned night raids on the site where the protestors might damage the fracking equipment. But shortly after drilling had commenced, the perimeter fence had been strengthened, and a private security firm had been brought in. Nomad perceived the pinprick lights of some of the night-watchmen's torches high up on the hill. In recent weeks, they'd brought in further reinforcements.

'Bastards!' Mohawk hissed, angrily grinding the Talbot's gears as the incline increased. The pale beams of the RV's headlights raked across the edge of the industrial wasteland before them as the vehicle swung round onto the steep road that led up to Black Fell Beacon.

'You think we'll be able to stop them?' Nomad asked the other man, for what felt like the thousandth time, nodding at the space beyond the wire.

'Yeah,' Mohawk nodded. 'They might win a battle here and there, but we'll win the war.' He paused. 'Don't worry. We've got the people on our side. You can't buy that.' He narrowed his eyes and stared fixedly ahead as the RV began to climb.

***

'So – do we do this?' Trout looked hard at the other man. 'Call it in, I mean?'

Sanderson nodded. His jacket was a Vietnam War-era replica. It had been purchased from a boutique seller online and had arrived in a state of fashionable distress. He had a large pair of mirrored Aviator sunglasses perched on the black hair that was swept back from his forehead. Trout was similarly attired; both men wore jeans and motorcycle boots. Each of them was the wrong side of fifty. They'd managed to keep most of the spread of their middle-aged paunches at bay, but they still looked heavy. Slow. Their jowls and pock-marked complexions spoke of too much time indoors. And a propensity for booze.

The pair had founded LD Chopper Tours when they reunited a decade after they'd last seen one another. Sanderson had worked for years in Arizona, where he'd spent his days flying tourists over the Grand Canyon. Trout had been employed by various different companies in Dubai. Sometimes he'd flown guests on chartered flights, acting as a rich person's taxi service. At other times he'd given tours, flying high over the city's rapidly ascending skyline.

But then Covid had struck. And, suddenly, neither man's services were required.

After successive lockdowns, they'd both wound their ways back to Lancashire, moving like homing pigeons. They'd run into each other on the first evening restrictions were lifted. Standing in line in the pub they used to drink in, they'd renewed their acquaintance. The idea for LD Choppers was simple: people liked the Lake District, and what better way was there to see it than from the air? Founding the company had been a formality, and securing funding for the lease of a helicopter had been relatively easy. Within three months, they were turning a profit, and – after two years – they were ready to expand. That's when they brought in Granger, an ex-Navy helicopter pilot who'd fallen on hard times. He'd drunk his way through three divorces in under a decade, and was desperate for any kind of job that would keep him on the straight and narrow. His estranged family had all but given up on him. LD was his last chance.

Granger had fitted in fine. He'd been more than happy to go along with the demands of Sierra Bravo's deputation that had arrived at the Goreton Hall site too. The instructions they gave were easy to follow. They simply had to fly the drone within specific coordinates; the film footage it captured would then be conveyed to Upavon where British Military Intelligence would scrutinise it – at least that's what they were told. The deputation had described the fly-zone as an aeronautical blind-spot; as long as the controllers kept the craft within it, they would be able to ensure it remained invisible and able to do its vital work.

'Why the need for weapons?' Sanderson had pressed.

His question had been met with a cold, hard stare. 'National Security,' Foxtrot Delta had shrugged. 'When we need you to strike, you strike.' He'd paused. 'Otherwise we could have another 9/11 on our hands.' The man had let his statement hang in the air.

In the silence, Sanderson had nodded, grimacing. He'd puffed out his chest, feeling a strange tingle of patriotic pride.

'You men have no idea how important the work is that you're doing here,' Foxtrot Delta went on. 'The country will owe you an enormous debt of gratitude. And I mean the *entire* country. We're talking medals, gentlemen. I mean it – that's exactly what Sierra Bravo would be telling you if she was able to be here in person.'

Buoyed by a sense of responsibility, the men had approached their task with gusto. The only issue was that, one night when he was supposed to be monitoring the drone, Granger had started drinking. And, once he started, he was the kind of man who didn't stop until he fell off his chair.

By the time Granger woke up, Foxtrot Delta had arrived at LD with three other armed agents. They were polite; pleasant even, and Trout, Sanderson and Granger answered their questions truthfully. Once they'd ascertained who was to blame, Trout and Sanderson were asked to wait in another room.

Twenty minutes later, they were marshalled out onto the tarmac where Granger was positioned. He had been made to kneel – a brown hessian sack covering his head. His hands were bound behind his back. Two men pointed pistols at him, while another held up a phone, filming proceedings.

'What the fuck's this?' Sanderson demanded, bullishly, rolling his shoulders as he strode forwards, attempting to portray a confidence he didn't feel.

'Heads or tails?' Foxtrot Delta asked, ignoring his question.

'What?' Trout frowned.

'Call it,' the handler pressed, flipping a coin.

'Heads,' Trout shrugged.

'Tails it is,' Foxtrot Delta announced, peering down at where the coin had landed.

'So fucking what?' Sanderson growled.

'So, this is what happens when grubby little drunks fuck up matters of national security,' Foxtrot Delta replied. He spoke in a clipped, unemotional tone. 'We can't take such chances.' He withdrew a Beretta 92SB and slid out its magazine. Then, using his thumb, he flipped out the bullets one-by-one until there was only one left. Sliding the bolt, he then chambered the final round. Before handing the gun to Sanderson, he removed another Beretta from his pocket and levelled it at him.

Sanderson frowned. 'What...?' His voice had lost its earlier bravado.

'It's graduation day,' Foxtrot Delta announced, holding out the handgun for the other man to take. 'We take your commitment to our cause as a given. We didn't make you swear an oath - your flying of the drone made it unnecessary. But this is a step up.' He paused and spoke heavily. 'Sometimes just monitoring threats isn't enough. Sometimes we have to eliminate them. It's as simple as that – for the greater good.'

Sanderson nodded.

Silence.

'It's time for you to grow a set of balls,' Foxtrot Delta announced. 'Anyone not with us is against us. Understand?'

Sanderson nodded once more, his jaw set firm.

***

'Dangerous bit of road this,' Mohawk announced. He was rolling a cigarette one-handed as he rested his other hand on the wheel. 'If you don't know what you're doing, I mean!' He grinned and turned the wheel slightly. The Talbot wasn't going quickly enough to swerve, but Nomad gripped at the dashboard, nonetheless. Mohawk laughed. 'Nearly had you there!' he grinned.

'Is it, though...?' Nomad asked. 'Dangerous, I mean?'

'Maybe,' Mohawk shrugged, yawning. 'Although you're probably in as much danger from sheep and bloody potholes as anything else. The fluffy little bastards just come wandering out like they don't give a shit.' He laughed. 'Here. Hold the wheel a minute, will you?'

Nomad reached across and took control, holding the vehicle on its juddering course as Mohawk lit his cigarette.

'Cheers,' the driver said as he grabbed the steering wheel once again. He exhaled a lungful of smoke and then squinted into the pools of yellow cast by the headlights. 'Now this bit *is* more dangerous,' he explained, his tone growing more serious. 'Black Fell Beacon – it's a bit bloody precipitous for the next couple of miles.'

Silence.

'Yeah,' Mohawk nodded to himself. 'I've driven it in the snow before and it was fucking lethal – you leave the road and you *really* leave it. Know what I mean?'

'Long way down, huh?' Nomad said, trying to affect a tone of nonchalance.

'Damn right!' Mohawk replied.

Both men jumped slightly as the ancient hulk rattled over the bars of a cattle grid. The vibrations made the sun visor above Mohawk fall down. The shredded remains of a long-forgotten spliff cascaded into his lap as it did. He laughed as he pushed the visor back up and brushed the mess of tobacco strands, buds, and yellowed cigarette papers onto the floor. 'Not sure we're going to need the sun blinds tonight – we're going to Brynworth, not fucking Bikini Atoll!'

Nomad chuckled.

'Anyway – how about you and that Alice?' Mohawk continued. 'Fancy going in there again? She'd be up for it, I reckon…'

Nomad blushed.

'What?' Mohawk laughed. 'You're a man of the world now, mate! Might as well start putting some notches on the bedposts of that doctoral thesis of yours, right?'

'I thought this was a serious business – protesting,' Nomad replied, changing the subject.

'It is mate. It is. But every soldier has to have a little rest and recuperation from time to time, don't they?' The man paused. 'Even God had a day off, right? I bet even Elvis put his feet up once in a while!'

Nomad laughed. The two men stared ahead as the insipid yellow headlights of the Talbot cut through the pitch blackness towards Black Fell Beacon.

***

The drone's lithium-ion battery meant that it could remain airborne for almost all the hours of darkness. Sierra Bravo had informed them that its main purpose was data collection, but she'd also warned them there would come a time when the missiles might need to be deployed in order to save giant swathes of the population. So, night after night, Trout and Sanderson had launched it, piloting it in concentric circles miles above Brynworth. And, after each flight, they'd dutifully disarmed its ordnance. Once uncoupled, they'd wheeled it to a makeshift silo in a hangar that looked – to all the world - as though it hadn't been touched since the 1950s. As ever, they'd ensured the Hellfires were armed prior to the drone taking off. Deploying the weapons had always been an abstract concept, though; something that would possibly happen somewhere in the distant future.

Until it wasn't.

'Well?' Trout enquired, looking up. 'What do we do?' His expression was slightly drawn.

'It's go-time,' Sanderson answered.

'Yeah?'

'Yeah,' Sanderson nodded, forcibly. 'It's going to have to be – we don't want to risk her ladyship pulling the purse strings back up. Make the fucking call.' He clicked a couple of keys; white crosshairs appeared on-screen. A further couple of clicks turned them into a green roundel.

'What does that mean?' Trout asked, squinting as he waited for his call to connect.

'We're locked and fucking loaded!' the man at the keyboard replied, turning to face his colleague. He theatrically lowered his sunglasses over his eyes and grinned broadly. 'I...'

'...Lima,' Trout announced into the phone's receiver, holding up his hand to silence his colleague. 'Fifty-three point seven eight seven five North. Two point eight nine five three West.' He frowned, listening intently to the voice on the other end of the line. 'You're sure?' he pressed. 'Do I have confirmation?'

Sanderson stared at him, raising his eyebrows.

'Can you confirm th-that I have confirmation?' Trout stuttered. He turned and shrugged, lowering the receiver. Then he gave Sanderson the thumbs up.

***

'Well, fuck me!' Sanderson announced under his breath. 'I wasn't expecting that – whoever it is in that van must be a proper big shot. Who's driving it – Bin-fucking-Laden?'

Trout's brow furrowed. 'Yeah... How the hell are they going to square this? I mean, it's going to blow a hole in half of fucking Lancashire, isn't it?' He shook his head in bewilderment. 'And this order is straight from Sierra Bravo, right?'

'Yeah – I mean, it must be, mustn't it?' Sanderson nodded. 'She's the only one with the authority. Right?'

Trout puffed out his cheeks and exhaled slowly. He looked hard at the other man. 'So, how do we do it?'

'We press the button,' the other man shrugged. 'Ready?' Despite his usual bullishness, a slight hint of doubt had entered his voice. 'Both barrels?'

'I guess,' Sanderson replied, unconvinced. He hesitated again. The vehicle on the screen hit a point where the road rose and turned to closely follow the contour of a ridge. It slowed; a steep fall bordered each side of the asphalt. 'Fuck it!' The man hit the button, slamming the keyboard several times harder than was necessary.

The green crosshairs turned red.

***

Fifty thousand feet above Brynworth, an electronic pulse bounced off the underside of the drone. The sensors built into its operating systems triggered, setting into motion a chain reaction. Within the space of half a second, the two Hellfire missiles – already locked onto their target – were launched. The drone rose in the air slightly as it was relieved of its two-hundred-pound payload.

An instant later, the missiles' burners ignited in fabulous fingers of flame that spat and streaked across the blackboard of the dark. Had anyone been looking upwards, they would have seen something akin to the wrathful arc of an amphetamine-fuelled comet.

But nobody was watching.

Indeed, the only indication anyone on the ground had of anything untoward was the sonic boom as the missiles broke the sound barrier. From then on, it was a simple case of mathematics: each missile accelerated to its top speed of just under a thousand miles an hour. They were locked onto their slow target, closing the distance with every passing heartbeat.

It was only a matter of seconds before the path of the vehicle and the trajectory of the missiles would intersect.

***

'Have you met Geordie?' Mohawk enquired, scratching at the stubble on his neck.

'No – I don't think so,' Nomad replied.

'Nice guy,' the other man explained. 'You'd like him – he's an intellectual. Just like you.'

'Yeah?'

'Yeah – he's done all these studies on badger habitats. And some nights he goes out and catches bats – the mad bastard! He counts them and studies their populations – shit like that.' Mohawk paused. 'Anyway, I was thinking he could be useful. The pair of you could write a paper or some shit. You know – figure out how much fracking is fucking up the local wildlife.' He grinned. 'The public loves stuff like that. Science and the like. You never know, you could get Attenborough involved. And...'

***

'Wow!' Sanderson slammed the palm of his hand onto the desk. 'Did you fucking see that?'

In response, Trout laughed in exhilaration like an over-excited school boy.

Once the crosshairs had turned red, the on-screen picture had juddered a little. For a moment after the launch, the display had turned blinding white as the burners ignited.

After that, the pair lost sight of the missiles; they simply kept their eyes fixed on the Talbot as the red roundel in the centre of the screen remained locked upon it, pulsing.

The room was silent. Both men were conscious of the sound of their breathing; aware of the thudding of their heartbeats.

And then the missiles impacted.

One moment the vehicle was there, and the next it wasn't. The night vision of the drone's camera showed the scene to be nothing more than a giant smoking cloud of dust, debris, and destruction.

'Sierra Bravo's going to be fucking delighted!' Sanderson grinned.

'Yeah – I'll take a CBE,' Trout smiled. 'I might even settle for an OBE.'

'You'll be lucky! It was me that hit the button. So, I figure I'll be outranking you any day of the week.' He paused. 'You'll have to salute me and call me sir, I reckon.' He laughed. 'Beer?'

'Abso-fucking-lutely!' Trout nodded. 'Actually – sod that! Let's land Big Bird and crack out the champagne, no?'

Chapter 2

Mark Garner ran his hand through what remained of his receding red hair and frowned deeply. He peered once again at the data printed on the various pages tacked to his clipboard. Shaking his head, he looped the notes back onto the hook at the end of the young patient's bed. The child's address had been recorded as *No Fixed Abode*. What that meant – as other staff had explained – was that they were a resident of the Foulmile Protest Camp.

Garner sighed, exhaling slowly as he noted down new medication for the patient. Summoning a nurse, he asked him to put the patient on an intravenous drip; if nothing else, she was severely dehydrated. But it was the kind of dehydration the locum doctor had only seen in India and in Cameroon, where he'd worked in rural communities with various aid agencies. It certainly wasn't the kind of thing he'd expected to find in Lancashire. Fixed abode or no fixed abode.

The nurse wheeled over a trolley with an IV bag hooked up to it. He then began to sterilise the patient's forearm, swabbing it with cotton wool. Garner nodded his thanks and then moved away down the ward to continue his rounds. He was certain the injection of fluids would solve the issue, but something about the patient's condition still bothered him. After all, this was Brynworth. It wasn't the developing world, and yet the symptoms he'd seen resembled those he'd encountered in makeshift aid stations where death walked close, stalking the weak and malnourished like a cold-hearted hyena.

As Garner exited the ward, he spotted Mister Alexander. The consultant was big news in the local area and oversaw a number of hospitals within the trust. Ordinarily – as a locum doctor – Garner would have been invisible to such a man. There would have been no real reason for their paths to cross. But the younger man was peripatetic; he split his shifts between Brynworth Health – a private facility housed inside a converted municipal building in the centre of town – and Lancaster West, where the dehydrated patient had been admitted. The latter hospital was a crumbling tower of brutalist 1960s architecture. Three of its wards had been temporarily closed due to RAAC, and teams of surveyors were scheduled to investigate how much of a threat the aerated concrete posed. Elsewhere in the facility, the effects of chronic underfunding were clear to perceive: patients were positioned in corridors as wards ran out of space; refuse bins remained unemptied, and paint peeled from brickwork in a fashion that made the place look more like a Soviet-era shell than a first world facility.

Garner's return from Africa had been prompted by an administrative issue. In order to remain registered with the Medical Council, he had to fulfil a mandatory number of hours within the National Health Service. He'd submitted a general application and had been posted to Brynworth. Flying over the red and yellow hues of the Sahara, he'd imagined that coming back home would see him conveyed down alabaster corridors of clean perfection.

The reality, though, had been rather different.

Mister Alexander was a man Garner had already run into several times in his short tenure. He always appeared haughty; always dismissive. His attitude towards locums – it seemed – mirrored his perception of cleaning staff. But the younger doctor felt compelled to approach him, nonetheless.

'Mister Alexander,' Garner called out, clearing his throat.

The consultant turned, frowning. The two men were in a vestibule whose floor was tiled in a black and white chessboard pattern. Garner felt like a vulnerable black pawn approaching a vengeful white queen.

'Well?' the other man demanded.

'It's about a patient, sir,' the locum began. 'They have dehydration.'

'And?' Alexander looked hard at the other man.

'Well, sir, it's severe – *really* severe.' He paused. 'In fact, I haven't seen a case so bad outside of Africa or the Sub-Continent.'

'Hmmm,' the consultant scratched at his hairline with the end of his biro. 'And you've put said patient on a drip, I assume?'

'I have,' the locum nodded. 'Forty-two over twenty.'

'Then the matter's in hand,' Alexander announced. He turned and began walking away, approaching the door that led to another ward.

'I wonder if it's more than that,' Garner continued.

Alexander turned once more. 'Come again?' he demanded.

'The patient – they're resident at the Foulmile Protest Camp. The place opposite where the fracking is happening.'

Silence.

'I wonder if there's something in the water,' Garner went on. 'Some kind of pollution or something?'

'I doubt it.'

'But these symptoms are consistent with what I've seen in the Developing World,' Garner protested. 'The kind of places where people don't have access to clean drinking water. And...'

'...poppycock!' Alexander cut in. 'Any drilling or fracking in this country has to have clearance at the highest level. We're not talking about the kind of banana republics you've been plying your trade in here – this is England. The safety protocols are endless. Exhaustive. And the cleanliness of the drinking water supply is always prioritised.' After emphasising his utterances with jabs of his pen in the other man's direction, the consultant folded his arms.

'Well, that's what they *say*,' the locum answered, acutely aware of the other man's piercing stare. 'But what if there's been an issue – contamination, I mean?' He paused. 'Look – this probably isn't my place. I'm a locum doctor, but it means that I get to see a few different facilities. And I'm posted on different wards.' He cleared his throat, uncomfortable. 'What I'm trying to say is that this isn't the first patient I've seen admitted with these symptoms.'

The consultant frowned for a moment. He then smiled gamely at a female nurse who walked past the pair, wheeling a trolley before her. 'You're right – er...'

'...Garner.'

'Yes, Garner,' Alexander frowned. 'You're absolutely right.'

'I *am?*'

'Yes. You're a locum.' The consultant paused. 'It isn't your place to speak out. Your job is to treat patients. That's all. Your job is to do what you're told to do by those above you, and to do so in a timely fashion. That's all. Nothing more; nothing less. I'd like to remind you to keep your mind on the job in hand - it's certainly not appropriate for you to distract yourself by digging into the protocols of a fracking organisation. You would do well to remember your remit. Do I make myself clear?'

The locum nodded. 'But I run a clinic there once a week – a pop-up.'

'A what now?' Alexander frowned.

'Yes, sir – community medicine. It's part of a wider charitable obligation. It's written into my contract.'

The consultant narrowed his eyes. 'So, you're telling me that you spend time at the Foulmile Protest Camp?'

'I do,' Garner nodded. 'In a professional capacity, of course.'

Alexander frowned. 'Take my advice... Steer clear of that place. And don't go spouting any bloody communist conspiracy theories, either. You start siding with the protestors there, and people will get suspicious. They'll wonder if you have a conflict of interest.'

'I'm not sure I understand, sir...'

'Forty-two over twenty, you said?'

'Yes, sir.'

'Then, as I said, the matter's in hand,' Alexander announced in a clipped tone. 'Now, if you'll excuse me.'

The consultant walked away.

Chapter 3

'Can you hurry it up, please?' The voice that came from the surgeon on the other side of the counter was harried. Insistent. The utterance turned into a string of invective muttered under the breath.

Trent Rivera turned to look at the man who'd addressed him. He was dressed in blue scrubs and was idly scrolling through his phone. Rivera opened his mouth to give a sarcastic answer, but then thought better of it. Customer service wasn't one of his strong suits, but his circumstances were somewhat straitened; he needed his pay cheque. 'I'm going as fast as I can, sir,' he announced politely. 'Two more minutes, maximum – I promise.'

The customer nodded and then returned to muttering beneath his breath as he continued to distractedly scroll through the news feeds on his phone. Rivera turned back to the grill and flipped the two burger patties over once more. They sizzled and spat as licks of flame rose from beneath to greet the dripping fat. His official job title of chef seemed disingenuous: burger flipper would have been more apt. He peered up at the rotating spindle to which the orders were tacked with pegs. There were only three more slips of paper remaining; the lunch rush was coming to a close.

Club Med Café was located next to Lancaster West. Whenever the hospital disgorged its staff, they invariably made their way to it - the establishment's nearest eatery. The café had two large seating areas where plastic and metal chairs were clustered around Formica-topped tables. In the central area, four cash registers were located at pay stations; the stations were like islands in the midst of a shiny plastic floor. At mealtimes, queues of customers snaked around the room. Ninety percent of those who crossed the threshold were medical employees, and - to meet the demands of the hospital's shift patterns - breakfast was served all day, as were lunch and dinner. Rivera sometimes felt as if working there was like living a life seen through a slow-exposure lens – the same cast of characters seemed to roll across Club Med's threshold on a continual loop, albeit at different times each day.

Rivera knew how to cook. His mother had taught him back in West London years before. It was a skill he'd honed in the Army, and – since leaving the service in less than auspicious circumstances - he'd occasionally been employed as a short-order cook. It was a level of experience that seemed to satisfy his new employers, but he didn't claim to be gourmet. Indeed, he didn't really claim to be anything. These days, he didn't have a trade to speak of – he simply seemed to become embroiled in saving people who needed saving; he felt drawn to the very trouble he tried so assiduously to avoid. Lancashire had just been somewhere he'd ended up after a last-ditch attempt to patch things up with an old girlfriend. His amorous efforts had come to naught; he'd simply driven to the first place where he'd seen a job advertised and plumped to stay there.

Brynworth.

***

At the end of his shift, Rivera sat alone at a table and slowly ate the burger he'd cooked himself. He'd fully loaded it, pretending to himself that it negated the need for salad. As he chewed, he read a novel by Walter Mosley – the novelist was the latest in a long line of writers he'd become hooked on. He loved the setting of 1950s and 1960s Los Angeles, and the way that reading about the exploits of its hard-boiled detective seemed to transport him away from wherever he was. Ever since leaving the Army, Rivera had been on a literary mission; he'd worked his way through a whole host of classics that he'd found through forays into charity shops. Along the way, he'd taken various diversions – the Mosley avenue was the latest.

Looking up from his book, Rivera rubbed at his right shoulder. The bullet which had made the wound had been dug out, and the rest of the damage had been stitched and patched. He still sported a significant scar, and, beneath the surface of the skin, he was sure things hadn't quite knitted back together properly. Sometimes he awoke in the night, replaying the moment the wound was inflicted. Rivera wasn't a proud man, but he still rued the way he'd not seen the attack coming. Massaging the area, he caught a glance of his reflection in the glass of the café's window. Two months had gone by without him shaving, and his hair was now beyond the length of his shoulders. He would be – he mused to himself – unrecognisable to those people he'd served with in the military. Various beads, piercings and other accoutrements added to his look. He looked more like a San Francisco hippie from Haight-Ashbury than a man who'd spent several years in combat.

But looking that way suited him fine.

These days he tried not to think too much about his days in uniform, but memories of his exit from the forces remained raw. Towards the end of his time in khaki, the Army had put him on several intensive courses to learn Pashto and Dari. Though he'd never become fully fluent, he'd grown into a capable enough linguist to act as a translator. And so he'd been deployed to Afghanistan in that capacity. He'd presided over meetings in rural hamlets all over Helmand province, mediating between tribal elders and senior officers. Most of the time, he'd held things together. He was organised. Competent.

It was only when he arrived back at home that he fell apart. Suddenly, all the tension and fear he'd been bottling up erupted in a volcano-like stream of horror. After a week-long drink and drugs bender, he'd finally flipped, and smashed up the flat he shared with his then girlfriend. Terrified, she'd called the police. The next morning he'd been bailed out of the cells by two Army liaison officers. They'd been courteous but firm. The pathway they planned for him was simple: they used words like options, but he wasn't really given any choice at all. Instead, it was a simple case of selecting between a medical discharge and a court martial.

After being discharged, the now ex-soldier had drawn early on his military pension to purchase Iris – his campervan. The Volkswagen T2 Silverfish had been standing on the forecourt of a backstreet garage in Hammersmith. A flash of yellow and purple flora was sprayed on the driver's side door – it was this that had inspired her name. And it was this vehicle Rivera was living in now. She was currently parked in between two broken-down ambulances in an underground parking lot reserved for staff. He'd known better views than that of the orange-lit bunker he now woke up to each morning, but he reasoned that Brynworth wasn't forever.

Forever wasn't really how things worked out for Rivera. Most of the time, he was satisfied with staying in a place long enough to settle a while before trouble caught up with him.

Upon purchasing the Volkswagen, the ex-soldier had driven away and then parked in the shadow of the Westway, trying to work out if he'd done the right thing. It was then he realised that Rosie – a mackerel tabby cat – came as part of the package. For a moment, he'd considered ditching her. But then he'd thought better of it; it was as much her van as his. So she'd stayed. The pair of them had travelled around the country, moving from campsite to campsite. Though the Army liaison officers who'd spoken to him hadn't termed it in so many words, the ex-soldier knew it was his breakdown, which was the elephant rampaging through the rooms of his mind. Rivera credited Rosie with stilling it. With dragging him out of it.

Brynworth had begun with him being reasonably buoyant. In recent weeks, though, he'd felt himself slump once more. He'd brought a cavalcade of co-workers and horny nurses back to Iris after his shifts at the café. The liaisons were rarely memorable; he was increasingly certain that Rosie regarded any such actions with disapproval. The women he worked his way through didn't seem to resent the cat's presence, but the cat definitely seemed to resent them trespassing upon *her* territory; she regarded them imperiously.

One morning, after bidding goodbye to a nurse whose name he'd already forgotten, the ex-soldier considered moving abroad once more. It wouldn't be the first time he'd taken Iris and Rosie overseas. What he'd liked most about leaving the Army was the way his time was no longer dictated to him. At first, a world of possibilities had seemed to present itself. Now, though, it felt like he was in an endless cycle of burger flipping and joyless sex. Any sense of him playing a significant role in anything or having a sense of purpose seemed to evaporate. He was still managing to limit himself to two hand-rolled cigarettes a day and a couple of pints of beer per week, but the temptation to exceed his allotted dose told him he was existing rather than participating in life.

Simply put, Rivera was in a rut.

Chapter 4
Texas, USA.

Ten minutes after landing at George Bush Intercontinental Airport, Houston, the Airbus A330 had taxied to the end of runway five. British politician – Stella Cowerman, having changed into business wear and touched up her make-up – stepped out into Terminal E. Her first-class ticket meant not waiting in line, and her diplomatic status meant she was waved through immigration with the most disinterested of cursory glances. Homeland Security was known for its diligence, but it was a thoroughness that rarely applied to the more well-heeled traveller. In a land where the dollar reigned supreme, being faced with moneyed arrivals lent a distinct lassitude to passport officials.

Where many public figures are able to flash dazzling-press-friendly-ivory-toothed-photogenic smiles at the click of their fingers, some aren't. Stella Cowerman was one such Member of Parliament. In truth, the Honourable Member for Winchcombeshire West struggled to smile at all. Years before, her mother had suggested it was a genetic predisposition – she'd even had physicians investigate. But nothing had come of it, and her ability to look anything other than disdainful had remained in a state of arrested development. At best, her attempts to smile resulted in a supercilious sneer; her olive-skinned complexion puckered up in an expression akin to a rodent sniffing citrus. Stepping into the terminal, she proffered one such approximation of delighted happiness to the sole photographer who was waiting to greet the arrival of her flight.

In truth, Cowerman saw her position in Westminster as more of a hindrance than anything else. Having to go through the machinations of debates in the Commons and being forced to turn up to vote when a three-line whip was applied had swiftly soured. She rarely held clinics for her constituents in Winchcombeshire. In truth, she loathed the people who'd voted for her. They were either old, dyed-in-the-wool Tories, or they were second or third generation unemployed. Surprisingly, it was the latter who'd seen her – the daughter of a Hungarian father and an Iranian mother – as inspirational. There was a sense that if she'd been able to drag herself up to the status she'd attained, then so could they. They would come to her cap-in-hand, pleading for assistance and welfare handouts. None of it ever amounted to anything, though. She saw poverty as a choice; public healthcare as simply encouraging people to call in sick, and unemployment benefits as encouraging laziness. The outspoken views she spouted from the back benches made her a darling of the right wing press. She already supported many of the policies they held dear: the fiction of climate change; the all-consuming danger of immigration, and the urgent need to dismantle the welfare state. If there were other issues where her allegiance hadn't yet been declared, she was Machiavellian enough to change tack and align herself with whichever standpoint would generate the most column inches. Moderates and left-wingers despised her, satirising her as vile. But, within the enclaves of her populist echo chamber, her popularity kept on growing.

It was a position that suited her very well. While she enjoyed being chauffeur-driven, and took full advantage of opportunities to claim back any and all expenses, she regarded herself as deserving more. *Far* more. Though her politician's salary was easily double that of the national average wage, she regarded it as paltry. Since marrying, her husband had been the breadwinner; the provider – she'd relied on him for the finer things in life. But her political influence meant that she'd begun to carve out opportunities for herself.

Big opportunities.

And suddenly she was presented with chances to make more money than she'd ever thought possible.

***

The call to Cowerman had come eighteen months before. Even as she heard the plan outlined, she knew it was her key to the big leagues. Her role was relatively straightforward: she was given directorship positions on the boards of four different companies. Three of them had a sizeable salary attached, but none of them required her to do anything. Instead, they were simply tokenistic postings. The fourth was the one that mattered – its remuneration dwarfed that of the others. When it came to Green Fuel Prospects - or GFP, as the company logo had it - rather than simply having a seat at the table, she was the managing director. With capital injections from its American benefactors, the company had swiftly expanded, purchasing a dozen sites across the UK for experimental shale gas drilling. The aim was straightforward: once large-scale fracking was approved, GFP would move in and dominate the market.

To massage public opinion, Cowerman had founded the Carbon Reduction Committee. It had risen to a position of prominence and had become one of Westminster's most powerful lobby groups. Though moderates decried her involvement as an abuse of her power, various parliamentary commissions had cleared her to continue. It was

– as her US partners intended – a case of hiding in plain sight. Cowerman had no desire to reduce carbon emissions; with the fracking operation, she planned to do the exact opposite. But the lobby group's claims were enough to sow doubt in people's minds. And doubt – as her financiers had explained to her – was all they required. It was the same approach that big tobacco had used in the face of anti-smoking legislation; it came out of the same playbook used by flat-earthers and climate change deniers against a tide of overwhelming scientific evidence.

From seeds of doubt, clouds of confusion could be conceived.

It was on account of how well she'd done in this regard that Cowerman was now in Texas. Houston held no interest for her. Instead, the waiting limousine was set to spirit her away to the town of Juniper. She'd been told that the outlining of the GFP's next stage of operations needed to be done in person.

By her.

Cowerman was fine with that. She'd manoeuvred herself into a position where she believed she could deliver on most of the promises she'd made to her business partners. The only niggling doubts she had surrounded the Bolsheviks in residence at the Foulmile camp. Despite stories planted in the press and the stepping up of security operations, they were still persisting. More than anything, the way public support seemed to be mushrooming for the protestors concerned her. It had come time to take a more direct approach.

As the chauffeur closed the door of the limousine behind her, Cowerman's phone pinged. Glancing at the screen, she saw it was from a number she didn't recognise – the kind of number she'd rarely seen before. One that bore no resemblance to how phone numbers usually looked. She frowned and clicked the link it contained, wondering if the encryption would permit her to access it.

It did. For an instant, the screen displayed a single icon: a green tick. Then the image faded into nothingness.

It was a thumbnail of correspondence that could have meant anything. But it was significant to her – it told her that direct approaches were beginning to bear fruit.

Cowerman screwed her face up into a facsimile of a smile as her driver joined the flow of traffic on the Will Clayton Parkway.

Chapter 5
Lancashire, UK.

As Mark Garner peeled the rubber strip back to reveal the gummed lip of the plastic envelope, he paused. The samples he'd taken from the young patient from the Foulmile Camp hadn't been officially sanctioned, and Mister Alexander's warning chimed in his mind. The locum physician pondered the other man's words for an instant before disregarding them once more. Garner had been around long enough to know when he was being fobbed off. He also had enough of a sense of morality to know that he'd plough his own furrow, no matter what anyone else told him.

Especially in a case like this.

He shrugged and sealed the envelope before approaching the slot on the wall for internal mail. The sample would be couriered to the laboratory for analysis, and if the staff there found anything untoward, they'd raise the alarm. And if not, the sample would simply be destroyed. In the event that any findings came out, Alexander would doubtless demand answers. But it was a battle that Garner was willing to fight. If the lab *did* turn something up, then he'd have to act, anyway.

Garner let go of the package and heard it land with a soft thud on the other side of the slot. He was reconciled; despite the IV drip, the patient's condition was worsening.

The locum doctor was convinced that the official diagnosis was false. He believed the symptoms he was seeing were nothing to do with a bacterial infection – he was convinced they had more in common with cholera. And if that was proven, there was no way Alexander would be able to hush it up.

Garner looked around as he stepped away from the mail slot. Save for a cleaner pushing disinterestedly at a broom, there was nobody around. And certainly nobody who was interested in watching him. He didn't class himself as an environmentalist necessarily, but he had far more sympathy with the residents of the Foulmile camp than he did with those doing the fracking. On his weekly visits to run his clinic, he'd seen just how much damage had been done to the local landscape. He also knew that cholera – if it *was* cholera, had no respect for class; it would kill wealthy people just as happily as it would bring death to the poor. There would be an outcry as a result.

And the few representatives of Green Fuel Prospects with whom he'd crossed paths had been out-and-out bastards.

Garner was aware of the bigger picture. Daltrey – the strange, de facto leader of the protestors – had informed him that dark forces were at play; big money was being deployed to push through the conglomerate's agenda, and to curry favour with those figures in government who had the power to approve their schemes. Though they had plenty of support, they weren't bankrolled by the kind of forces that the fracking company had behind them. It felt like they were doomed to fail.

Of course, just so long as their people didn't perish of it, cholera would be like manna from heaven to the Foulmile travellers. They could publicise its presence, safe in the knowledge that local residents wouldn't take too kindly to a Victorian-era disease cropping up in their midst. The flip-side, as Garner was well aware, was that it wasn't in the interests of the money-men or the money-women bankrolling the fracking to let the emergence of such news derail their plans. They would do everything they could to suppress it – at least until the bill permitting them to expand operations had passed.

And their reach was broad.

Looking out of the window, Garner spotted Alexander. The consultant was making his way across the parking lot. In the twilight, he watched as the doctor clicked the button on his key fob. The lights of an immaculate Mercedes EQS with that year's plates blinked twice. Garner didn't know how much such a vehicle cost – only that it cost a lot. Mister Alexander was clearly a wealthy man.

'Bastard!' the locum doctor whispered, shaking his head at the unfairness of the world.

Chapter 6

'Can I help you?' Rivera was leaning on the counter with one arm. His other was idly mopping at the stainless steel surface during a lull in service. He looked up at the dazed figure before him, whose head had been bandaged. Strips of gauze covered one of his eyes. The man's visage -- where it could be seen – wore the grey pallor mask peculiar to so many of the patients who crossed the restaurant's threshold.

It was early evening; the dinnertime rush hadn't started yet.

Sergeant Hoode was wearing his police uniform, just as he had done when he arrived at Accident and Emergency. He had no recollection of the blow that had felled him. His memory only came into focus while he was waiting to be examined. Prior to being seated on a row of green plastic chairs bolted to the wall, he remembered nothing. Despite his pounding headache, he'd been told he was free to leave. After checking his stitches and assessing him for concussion, the paramedic who'd administered to him declared him fit and discharged him. Hoode didn't feel particularly fit; he was woozy and blurred lines danced at the edge of his vision. 'What?' he asked, confused, struggling to focus on the figure behind the counter.

'Are you OK?' Rivera enquired. He narrowed his eyes. 'Don't take this the wrong way, officer, but you kind of look like shit...'

Hoode let out a rasping laugh. 'Yeah – I guess that about covers it.' He grinned. 'Maybe they'll give me a biff chit if I'm lucky.'

'Yeah?' Despite his concerns, Rivera smiled at the casual use of military slang.

'Yeah – you have any coffee?' the Sergeant asked.

Rivera nodded. 'We do.' He looked over at Cindy - his supervisor - and announced he was taking his break. She nodded, disinterested. 'Come on,' the ex-soldier said, turning back to the policeman and taking hold of his arm. 'Let's get you sorted out. I'll grab you a drink.'

***

Five minutes later, the two men were sat facing each other across one of Club Med Café's Formica-topped tables. A steaming cup of black filter coffee sat before each man. The policeman tentatively explored the area around his wound.

'Leave it,' Rivera counselled.

'What?'

'The bandage – you'll only have to go back if it comes off.'

Silence.

'What branch of the service were you in?' the ex-soldier asked.

'I'm a copper,' Hoode replied, pointing at his stripes.

'Yeah – I know that,' the ex-soldier nodded. 'But I've never heard anyone talk about a biff chit who hasn't been in khaki at some point.'

'Ancient history,' Hoode announced eventually, shrugging. 'I flew Lynx helicopters in Bosnia. Several lifetimes ago.' He shook his head. 'It wasn't my scene to be honest – there's only so much death and destruction a man needs to see on a day-to-day basis.'

Rivera nodded. 'Yeah. Roger that.'

Hoode blew steam from his coffee, sipped at it, and peered at the man opposite. 'You've served, I take it?'

'A while back now. I guess it's ancient history with me, too.'

Hoode nodded. An uncomfortable silence descended for a moment. Neither man wanted to uncover the ghosts of their military past, but they'd run into a conversational rut.

'Well, thanks for the coffee,' the Sergeant said. 'Appreciate it.'

Rivera nodded.

'So, what brings you to Brynworth, anyway?' Hoode enquired. 'This is my patch, and I've not seen you around. I mean – I don't know *everyone* here, but I know a lot of them by sight. And you're fairly memorable...'

'I'm just travelling around,' Rivera shrugged. 'You?'

The Sergeant smiled, sighing. 'After the service, I wanted a posting in the quietest place I could find. I wanted to do good. To know my flock – protect them. Look after them. All of that idealistic bollocks. Know what I mean?' He paused. 'And I had that – for a while, at least. But then things changed.'

'How so?'

'You know the fracking site over at Foulmile?' Hoode asked.

'Yeah. Vaguely. Why?'

'Because that – that happened.'

***

Rivera frowned. 'So, you're telling me you have no jurisdiction around the site at all?'

'Exactly,' Hoode nodded, warming to his subject. The coffee had revived him, and his anger towards the topic he was explaining fuelled his words, making him more demonstrative. 'I get to police the protest camp and Brynworth itself, but the fracking site's like a black hole.'

'I don't get it,' the ex-soldier shook his head.

'Yeah – you're not the only one.'

'But surely that's not possible?'

Hoode shrugged. 'The powers that be... It was an overnight thing – like building the Berlin Wall or something.' He paused. 'One moment I was a rural policeman with a real sense of who was doing what, and the next I was being given the cold shoulder.'

Rivera nodded. 'Is that even legal – forcing you out, I mean?'

'It is,' the Sergeant replied. 'Or at least, it *seems* to be. The way I see it, whoever's pulling the strings behind Green Fuel Prospects has got some serious clout. They're the company that's running the show up there. I know they have politicians on board, but I think it goes beyond even them.' He paused. 'And whoever it is has been able to turn it into a city state. It's almost like a sovereign base or something – it's crazy!'

'So they've declared it off limits? I still don't get how it works,' the ex-soldier pressed.

'Me neither,' Hoode shrugged, sipping at his coffee once more. 'But, let's just say this: before they arrived, Brynworth was a spot of natural beauty with virtually no crime. And here we are, not long later, and... it's not.' The Sergeant's expression clouded. 'They've fucked up the landscape, and the security firm they've brought in are a right bunch of Nazis.'

Rivera nodded. 'And what about your injury?'

'What about it?'

'Who did it?' the ex-soldier enquired.

'Who knows?' Hoode shrugged. 'I've no clue. Hopefully, it'll come back to me. In the meantime, all I know is that there've been plenty of strange things happening on my patch of late.' He paused. 'And this just feels like another addition to a long list.'

Rivera pursed his lips and nodded slowly. 'You going to be OK to get home, Sergeant?'

'I am,' Hoode nodded. He stood up and proffered his hand. 'Thanks again, Rivera,' he said as the two men shook hands. 'Talking with you feels like the first sane conversation I've had in weeks.'

The ex-soldier watched as the Sergeant shuffled away across Club Med's polished floor. As he approached the door to the car park, he still looked as though he was moving unsteadily on his feet. He reached one hand up absent-mindedly to touch at his bandaged wound and leaned hard on the door handle with the other.

Turning, Rivera caught Cindy's eye. She looked at him disapprovingly, tapping at her watch. 'You owe me ten more minutes, Rivera. And you're taking the piss with your break times. You get me?'

'Just thought he needed to talk.'

'Ten minutes,' Cindy repeated. 'The only reason I didn't interrupt is because I thought he was here to nick you.'

Chapter 7

'You look like a man who could use a drink!' Rivera announced good-naturedly as he made his way from empty table to empty table, cleaning the surfaces.

Mark Garner looked up and grinned, weakly. 'You'd need a bloody drink too if you'd seen what I've seen this afternoon.'

The two men had a passing acquaintance. They'd talked football and touched on travel. Garner invariably ate at Club Med during quiet times, and so the two had a distant familiarity.

Rivera frowned. 'But it's top secret, right? Confidential?'

'Yeah,' the locum doctor nodded. He was pushing about morsels of beef stew on his plate. 'Something like that. But I'm not sure it makes much difference – nobody bloody listens anyway, confidentiality or no confidentiality.'

'Try me.' The ex-soldier sat himself down at the table. 'I'm bored out of my brains here. This is the graveyard shift, anyway. I could use a little distraction.'

Garner nodded. 'You're not after a career in the catering industry then, I take it?'

'No – not so much. I guess these days I'm not after a career in anything, really.' Rivera paused. 'This is just a stopover really – I'm on the way to somewhere. I just haven't figured out where. All I know is that there are only so many dinner services I can do here without losing my mind.'

'Yeah. I know that feeling - I'm not long back from Africa. I've been out there doling out polio vaccines and looking after Aids orphans. This doesn't quite have the same sense of purpose, really.' Garner paused. 'To be honest, Brynworth has been a bit of a shock to the system.' He grinned. 'Round here, everyone looks at me like I should be putting down roots, but it's not really my scene. Mortgages. Pension plans. Golf club memberships.'

'I know what you mean.' Rivera nodded. 'I live in a T2 campervan...'

'...nice!' Garner interrupted.

'Yeah. It's partly in an effort to cut down on accumulating stuff. But mainly because I can't afford anything bigger!'

The locum doctor laughed. 'Amen to that! You get on that hamster wheel and you don't get off it!' He paused. 'We're only ever custodians of stuff, after all. And when people pass, that stuff just ends up getting ditched, anyway. When I compare what we have to what folks had in Sierra Leone, it's kind of shocking.'

Rivera nodded, recognising a kindred spirit. 'So how come you're back in Blighty? You sound like you should be on a crusade through the Developing World with an attitude like that.'

'Yeah,' Garner replied. 'I'll get back to that soon enough. Being back here is just to keep up my licence to practise medicine. It lapses otherwise.' He paused, lowering his voice. 'Mind you, I sometimes feel like we're not a million miles away from some of the stuff I was used to seeing there.'

'How so?' the ex-soldier enquired.

'Nothing.' The locum doctor shook his head, and then nodded at a couple of his colleagues who'd just entered the room. 'It doesn't matter.'

Silence.

Rivera sniffed and looked around the room. He watched as the newly arrived doctors made their way over to the counter. Scot – the obese deputy manager – greeted them with the sour, contemptuous expression that was his resting face. 'I'm no agony aunt, my friend,' the ex-soldier continued, looking back at Garner, 'but I know how to keep my mouth shut if that's going to help you. It sounds like you want to get something off your chest, no?'

Garner looked around a little furtively. He then lowered his voice to a whisper. '*Vibrio cholerae bacteria*. You familiar?'

'The Court for King Cholera.' The ex-soldier frowned and looked hard at the other man. 'That right?'

'John Leech,' Garner nodded. 'Punch Magazine – Eighteen Fifty Something.' He raised his eyebrows. 'You know your history, then?'

'Some – I read when I can. And I guess my memory's OK – despite one too many knocks to the head on active duty.'

'So...' the locum doctor went on. 'Have you encountered it? Cholera, I mean?'

'Yeah,' Rivera nodded. 'Back in Helmand. And a couple of places in the Hindu Kush.' He paused. 'It's a terrible thing - not very Lancashire, is it?'

'It's not.' Garner shook his head. 'Army?'

'A while back now.' He paused. 'Anyway...'

'Yeah, that's the problem. Or at least I think it's the problem. It shouldn't be here at all.' He sighed. 'To be honest, I think it has something to do with this fracking thing that's going on over at Foulmile – that's where the patient's from.' He frowned. 'This is between you, me and the wall, though, right? I shouldn't be breathing a word about any of it.'

'Scout's honour,' the ex-soldier nodded. 'But how come I haven't heard of this? This is big bloody news. An outbreak could be catastrophic.' His brow furrowed. 'What the fuck's going on?'

'I wish I knew,' the locum doctor shrugged. 'But I smell a cover-up of some sort. And I can't do anything about it – my hands are tied. The head honcho wasn't amenable when I outlined my suspicions; let's just leave it at that...'

Rivera exhaled slowly. 'Why are you telling me this?'

Garner puffed out his cheeks in resignation before answering. 'Because nobody else wants to fucking listen, mate.' He sighed again. 'I don't know anyone around here, really. It's not like I'll be in town long. Really speaking, I should just be keeping my head down. Not rocking the boat – that kind of shit. But...' His voice trailed off. 'You should check out the protest camp if you get a chance – see for yourself. I run a pop-up clinic there once a week.' He smiled. 'I've never been political really, but I've kind of come round to their way of thinking – the crusties. I mean.' He chuckled. 'And with a T2 campervan, you'd fit right in!'

'Yeah? Maybe.' Rivera shrugged, standing up. He glanced at the other man's half-finished food. 'Are you going to eat that?' he enquired, nodding at the congealed globules of gravy-covered gristle on the doctor's plate.

'No – I'm not.' Garner grinned. 'Compliments to the chef and all, but I think I'll pass.'

'Roger that,' the ex-soldier nodded. 'What was your name?'

'Garner. Mark Garner. You?'

'Rivera. Trent.' He proffered a hand. 'I'll see you around, doctor. And I might just check out Foulmile. Weirdly enough, you're the second person in less than two hours that's mentioned it to me. Most people would put that down to coincidence.' He paused. 'But I don't believe in coincidence.' He picked up the other man's plate and moved away.

Chapter 8

'Thank you for seeing me at such short notice,' Mister Alexander began.

Garner nodded. The early morning sun streamed through the window of the consultant's office. The younger man had almost finished his shift when a message came over the public address system, summoning him to meet with Alexander.

'I've been thinking... You were right to raise the state of the patient with me.' He paused. 'I concede that now.'

The locum doctor nodded once more, somewhat unnerved by the consultant's change in attitude. He opened his mouth to reply, but said nothing.

'You see, there were anomalies,' the consultant went on. 'But there's an explanation.' He paused. 'There always is. Anyway, I decided to review the patient's notes. I wanted to let you know that – as a matter of professional courtesy. And to – er – avoid any misunderstandings. In the future, I mean.'

Silence.

'Oh, come on Garner!' Alexander implored, a hint of irritation creeping into his voice. 'You're a locum doctor - the medical equivalent of a supply teacher. You should be honoured that I'm giving you an audience like this. I don't recall ever letting anyone like you into this office before.'

'Anyone like *me*?'

'Yes. So, don't get all high and bloody mighty.' Alexander cleared his voice. 'It's uncouth. And, anyway, if you'll do the decent thing and actually listen for a moment, you'll see I'm actually trying to apologise. We all make mistakes sometimes – and this was mine. A small one. Infinitesimal, really. A clerical error, if you will.'

'Very well, sir,' Garner nodded, unsure.

The consultant drummed lightly on his desk. 'I get to read all the bulletin reports, you know?'

'And?'

'And, I heard a certain someone sent away some samples for analysis.' Alexander narrowed his eyes.

Silence.

'This, despite the fact I expressly forbade you to pursue your inquiry. And...'

'...well, you didn't sir,' Garner cut in. 'Not in so many words. But...'

'...don't bloody interrupt me, man!' Alexander shouted. 'My word is *the* word here. Don't go fucking forgetting it.'

The locum doctor frowned, taken aback by the vehemence of the other man's words. He folded his arms, feeling vaguely combative, and stared directly at the consultant.

Alexander sighed. 'Look - what I'm trying to say, Garner, is that you were right to do what you did.' The consultant paused. 'We're all duty-bound to do everything we can to assist the wellbeing of our patients. It would do some of us well to remember that sometimes.'

'I stand by my actions,' Garner replied, indignant.

'So you should,' the consultant nodded. 'Anyway,' he sighed. 'I've looked at the lab reports. And there's no further action that needs taking.'

'Really, sir?' the locum doctor replied, incredulous. 'But ... it's cholera, I'm sure.'

'Yes – that's what the lab said.'

'It is?'

'It is,' Alexander nodded. 'But then I had a panicked phone call from them.'

'They'll want an isolation ward, I shouldn't wonder?' Garner nodded.

'No, no. Nothing like that.' The consultant shook his head. 'There was cross-contamination of samples.' 'Amazing how such things can still happen in this day and age, but there we have it.'

'And?'

'And there *was* a cholera sample, but it had been mixed up with ours. The positive result came from the College of Infectious Diseases.'

'Really?' Garner narrowed his eyes.

'Really,' Alexander nodded.

'Can I see the report?'

'Er – no, I'm afraid not. You see, in cases like this where there have been issues with paperwork, the paperwork gets sent back to head office to be securely disposed of.'

'Head office?'

'Mmmm. We should have electronic copies soon, but there'll be an investigation first of all.'

Garner frowned. 'So what's the story with our patient, then?'

'They're clear. I mean – not clear, but clear of cholera, if that's what you mean.' The consultant smiled thinly. 'An intestinal infection – parasite maybe,' the consultant answered. 'They're on the mend, though, so I hear.'

'But...' Garner shook his head.

'We all make mistakes,' Alexander went on insistently. 'It's just a misdiagnosis – there are thousands of them every day.'

'And that's it?'

'That's it. So we move on. Chalk it up to experience,' the consultant continued. 'There's nothing more you can do, is there? As long as a mix-up like this doesn't get into the press, then it's a case of all's well that ends well, really.'

Garner frowned and then nodded slowly. 'I appreciate you taking the time, sir.' He stood up slowly and turned away from the desk.

'You're most welcome,' Alexander nodded. As the locum doctor's fingers reached out for the door handle, he cleared his throat. 'Oh, and Garner – this is a closed case now,' he explained. 'You just need to let the patient recover. And then, you need say no more about it. Let sleeping dogs lie. Understand?'

'Very well, sir,' Garner nodded, exiting the room.

Chapter 9
Texas, USA.

Being the only woman in a room full of powerful men was not an oddity to Stella Cowerman. Though it claimed otherwise, Westminster's card deck was still stacked in favour of the old-school tie. The influence of Eton and Harrow was still writ large on the walls of the corridors of power, and – though female politicians and lobbyists now proliferated – the very fibre of the House of Commons still breathed a white, Anglo-Saxon protestant patriarchy. Any challenges to the status quo felt like they were temporary. Superficial. They rested upon a fragile, frozen ice façade. Though there were claims of openness and accountability, business was still done in backrooms; deals were still confirmed with masonic handshakes, and membership of certain gentlemen's clubs was still a prerequisite for getting ahead. In short, the foundations of male orthodoxy were standing firm. It was a set-up that Cowerman had learned to navigate effectively, but she knew she still had to operate in its confines.

In Westminster, her tabloid fame granted her a certain power. The leverage it offered meant colleagues regarded her with wariness; were she to plant press rumours in the right places, she could undo cabinet ministers. She had notoriety. In Juniper, Texas, though, she wasn't a well-known person at all. In the eyes of those men in the room, she was simply a woman of colour. The Civil Rights Act might have passed in 1965, but Jim Crow cast a long shadow - especially in rural regions. High society in the South-West ran on charity fundraisers; gala dinners, and NRA memberships. People continually claimed equality was the order of the day, but – beneath the surface – old attitudes held fast. It was these that Cowerman felt bearing down on her as she stood before the screen at the front of the room.

Men in dark suits were sitting at half a dozen large, round wooden tables in the room. Their appearances were very similar: they were all old. Most had grey hair; many sported Stetsons and cowboy boots, some with spurs. And all exuded an air of wealth. As Cowerman looked out, they faded into the fug caused by their cigars.

This was Texas.

Smoking was allowed.

***

'Gentlemen...' Cowerman addressed the crowd. During the flight over the Atlantic, she'd prepared copious notes and crafted a presentation which – to her mind – was perfect. Walking into the Texan room, though, she suddenly realised that it was a speech more suited to Westminster; it wouldn't pass muster when delivered to an audience of would-be cowboys, many of whom - thanks to Texas' liberal firearms laws - undoubtedly carried guns.

The speaker screwed up her face in her effort to smile. She passed the laser pointer from hand to hand – its button would allow her to switch between slides. The eyes that stared back seemed empty; they weren't necessarily looks of contempt, nor were they openly hostile. But they were unimpressed – or so it seemed. The disdainful grimace she wore upon her face did little to thaw the hostility. Instead, the room filled with silent expectation as she cleared her throat and took centre stage with a clacking of high heels.

Cowerman was known for her directness. Indeed, the tabloid press had feted her for it. The mantra she repeated to herself in front of the mirror each morning was simple: give simple solutions to complex problems and the people will worship you for it. It was a lesson she'd learned early, and one which had served her extremely well. Once she'd realised that sound bytes held more sway than sentiment, and that tall stories were more effective than the truth, she'd never looked back.

She'd learned that - more often than not –people were happiest being told what they wanted to hear. Anything else was mere white noise that served little purpose.

'...we project growth of over three hundred per cent. And that's in the first year alone,' she began. It wasn't quite her trump card, but she knew she had a limited time to win over the assembly.

The silence percolated with an excited murmur. Ears pricked up. The silent room sat up straight, rubbing its hands together in avaricious glee.

'It's simple,' Cowerman went on, safe in the knowledge she'd secured the crowd's attention. 'The numbers don't lie. They never do.' The politician turned to the screen and centred her laser pointer on a map that had now appeared. 'Once Brynworth is approved by Act of Parliament, we'll have precedent. And, once that's the case, there will be nothing to stop us.' She paused. The room was paying proper attention now. Beneath Stetson hats, ticker-tape thoughts whirled; shrewd features puckered as they calculated potential returns on investment.

'Exploratory drilling at the Brynworth site is proceeding well,' Cowerman continued, indicating its location with the infrared dot of the pointer. 'Its position between Preston and Blackpool means that it's well-served by transport links, but it also has the benefit of being far enough away from any conurbations so as to cause minimum disruption.' She sipped at the iced water that had been placed by the lectern. The air conditioning of the long flight had dried her throat out; the recycled air of the room, the fug of cigar smoke, and the rather frosty welcome given by those in it, had done little to counter the issue. Playing for time a little, she refilled her tumbler from the glass jug provided.

'We've already taken over long-term leases at the following sites: Swanskern Heath; Lochmoor; Mallowkeep; Brightwitch, and Aldness.' As the politician announced each of the names, she indicated their whereabouts on-screen. 'The sites are strategically placed – you'll see from their dispersal that they cover all key regions of the British Isles.' She paused. 'Once one is approved, then approval for the rest will become a formality; drilling practices will be declared safe, and local politicians will have no jurisdiction over what does and doesn't go on within them.' She smiled. 'Once a law is enacted in Britain, it's etched on vellum and placed in the archives. That's how old-fashioned we are... we still write things down on goat skin.'

A round of good-natured laughter rippled through the room.

'And, once a law's passed in Westminster, it's extremely difficult to repeal.' She approximated a grin. 'There are all sorts of ancient statutes people have forgotten about - until a few years ago, it was still legal for an Englishman to shoot a Scotsman on the spot!'

The second example secured more of a laugh. The audience, devoted as they would be to the Second Amendment, was warming to her. A slight thaw – as well she knew – was all that was required.

'Once we're underway, there will be no barriers. Green Fuel Energy will be in place to expand its operation to any and all suitable sites in the United Kingdom.' Cowerman scrunched her face up into a simpering pout once more. 'On behalf of our UK-based shareholders, I extend our most heartfelt thanks for your investment. The drilling funded to date has been exploratory – your contributions are helping us to lobby parliament.' She paused. 'Now that we've shed the shackles of the European Commission and its punitive laws, we are reshaping our legal system to be friendly to commerce; to be enterprising; and to enable us to take back our sovereignty. We're saying no to big government and yes to entrepreneurial spirit!' The temperature of the room warmed perceptibly. 'We're leaving behind woke agendas, and we're moving towards an era of an unchained Britannia; a country that can once again be a true friend to its trading partners overseas, rather than being buried in the bullshit of Brussels bureaucracy.'

Applause broke out. Cowerman stood, beaming. She raised a hand to acknowledge the reception. As the noise of the clapping subsided, she cast her eye around the room. 'Any questions?'

Silence. Those assembled looked at one another, and then the questions began. It was nothing the politician hadn't expected: clarification of profit margins; legal issues; quibbles pertaining to the length of leases; pitches for drilling equipment; planned relationships with brokers and wholesalers. Cowerman answered the questions with clarity and brevity. Most of her responses met with approval. It was only the final question which altered the atmosphere. The man at the back of the room was little more than a hazy shadow in the tobacco smoke. When the microphone was passed to him, he kept his head tilted downwards; his face was obscured by the brim of his hat.

'This is all well and good,' he began in a strongly accented drawl. 'But no new enterprise goes off without a hitch.' The man cleared his throat. 'You've given us all the good stuff. Now tell us about the problems... what's been going on with these protests y'all have been hushing up?'

Stella Cowerman took a sharp breath in and then exhaled slowly. Silence.

'Well?' the drawl pressed. 'Cat got your tongue?'

'The matter is in hand,' she announced.

Chapter 10
Lancashire, UK.

'Who the fuck are you?' The man addressing Rivera was wiry. His dreadlocks were long and matted – it wasn't the kind of coiffure that one might get in a barber's shop. Instead, it seemed like the genuine article – borne of years of road living. The man wore several days of stubble; his bare arms were tanned – his veins stood prominent, disappearing into a maze of home-made tattoos. He looked shifty. Edgy. He bounced from the balls of one foot to another.

'And good fucking morning to you too,' the ex-soldier replied. He smiled broadly, but felt a slight prickling sensation on the back of his neck. He'd been in enough similar situations to know that he was facing a challenge. A test of his mettle.

He wasn't looking for a fight.

Not yet.

'You fucking heard,' the other man pressed, grinding his teeth a little. 'Answer the question.'

Rivera sighed. 'I'm looking for someone called Daltrey.'

The other man bristled slightly, squinting. 'Why?'

'Mark Garner sent me – he's a doctor at Lancaster West.'

'Yeah,' the other man sniffed. 'I know who he is. But what fucking business do you have being here?'

Rivera frowned. 'Look... I'm going to stand here for a minute and admire the view. I'm going to smoke a cigarette, and then I'm going to take a look around this place. Garner told me a few things, and I'd like to check them out.' He paused. 'You can try and stop me if you like. But I doubt you'll manage.' He shrugged. 'I haven't come here looking for trouble. So if we've got a problem, then it's your fucking problem.' He looked hard at the other man, fixing him with his stare. It was a cold, hard stare. A sniper's stare. A killer's stare.

Daltrey stood still, looking back and frowning. He was clearly a fighter – that much was evident from his posture, but it took a proper fighter not to quake under the ex-soldier's gaze. The other man was tough, but not so tough that Rivera's stare didn't give him pause. He took a sharp, involuntary breath and then began muttering. 'Give me a minute,' he began, taking a mobile phone with a cracked screen out of his pocket.

***

'Your story checks out,' Daltrey nodded, stepping back over to where Rivera was grinding his cigarette out. 'Garner vouched for you.'

The ex-soldier nodded. 'Well, who the fuck did you think I was? A tourist? It's not like this is a top secret facility, is it?'

'You'd be surprised,' the other man chuckled drily. 'We've had plenty of spies here from the fracking brigade.' He paused before continuing ruefully. 'Some of them can be right bastards. I wondered if you were one of them, to be honest.' He put his phone back into his pocket and then extended a hand. 'Anyway, no hard feelings. You want to start over? I'm Daltrey. Garner told me you've seen some action before...'

'Yeah, some,' the ex-soldier shrugged. 'But he also told me about the kid from here who's sick.'

'The cholera kid?' Daltrey nodded. 'Yeah – the girl's ill alright. It's a problem that dares not speak its name. Everyone knows what it is, but no one'll say. At least nobody in the medical field.'

'How come?' Rivera frowned.

'It's because the bastards don't want any adverse publicity,' Daltrey replied. 'They've got gagging orders left, right and centre, but that's not the worst bit – their security firm are a right batch of Nazis.'

The ex-soldier nodded. 'So I heard. What's the deal here, anyway? I mean – Garner told me he runs a clinic or something. I thought I might be able to help out a bit. Maybe?'

'Appreciate it,' Daltrey nodded. 'Take a look around. I'll introduce you to a few people if you like? It's always good to have more folk onside. Especially with some of the fucked up things we've had happening here lately.' The protest camp leader spotted a tall man clad in a camouflage jacket who was carrying a couple of crates further down the hill. 'Hold on Rocko!' he bellowed. 'I'll give you a hand.' Daltrey turned to Rivera. 'I'll see you in a bit, yeah?'

Rivera turned away from the camp's entrance and began walking up the hill. Though there were few clues from its current state, Foulmile's history was long and varied. Up until the First World War, it had been part of the Brynworth Estate. The rumour was that in the late Victorian-era, the then Lord of the Manor had drunk away most of the family fortune. A series of bad investments had made him land-rich but cash poor. He'd dealt with his approaching bankruptcy in the only way he knew: crawling into the bottle still further. Most nights, he'd drunk himself into a stupor at a local tavern. At the end of the evening, the landlord would half carry him out to his trap, where he'd slump at the reins. Luckily for him, his pony knew the way back home. Once there, an ageing footman who clung to his position at the coach house at the end of the Manor's driveway would come out and convey his master back to his lodgings. One winter's night, though, the pony had expired of cold in a snowstorm halfway up Black Fell Beacon. The sound asleep Lord of the Manor had never awoken – the frozen tableau had been discovered by a shepherd the next morning.

Between the wars, the estate had shrunk year on year; the dead Lord's descendants were forced to sell off packets of land to keep the wolves from the door. By the 1950s, death duties meant that anyone inheriting the place would have been forced to take on eye-watering levels of debt. The result was that the old manor house fell into disrepair, and nature began to take back the once pristine driveways and gardens.

By the end of the Sixties, Crowe Hall – a property on the estate that had once housed the dowager – had become the centre of a hippie commune. The residents - believing in free love and free living - had taken up squatters' rights in the hall. They'd grown their own vegetables and their own cannabis. The former had been sold in local villages, while the latter fuelled their all-night parties and makeshift music festivals. The last woman of the Brynworth line now lived in Australia, where she worked as an auctioneer. Upon learning of her inheritance, she'd been shown the estate's books; restoring it to its former glory wasn't feasible, and the legal wrangling that would have been required to remove the residents would have been interminable. So, she'd taken the decision to leave things as they were: for a peppercorn rent, she'd allowed the commune to continue its existence.

Ever since, Foulmile had retained its anti-authoritarian air. The commune had ebbed and flowed with the years; at one point in the Eighties and Nineties, it had been home to a community of New Age Travellers. Since then, it had taken on a new breed of environmentalist protestor – it was a situation that quickly escalated once GFP moved in across the road. Hence the arrival of Daltrey and his clan. Crowe

Hall still stood, but it was now a rodent-infested ruin awaiting condemnation or demolition. The protestors weren't housed in it; though it formed the camp's centre point, it was as if it were there solely for decoration. They lived, instead, in a collection of vehicles that were in varying degrees of service.

＊＊

'What the hell's going on over there?' Rivera asked, approaching Daltrey. The protest leader was standing, talking to two women. The first was dressed in tie-dye with hair down below her waist, while the second - who looked to be in her late twenties - had blonde hair tied back and was dressed in combat trousers and a biker jacket. Looking at the fracas taking place on the other side of the perimeter fence, the three of them were turned away from him. A stand-off was seemingly happening between a pair of protestors and five uniformed guards. The guards had their batons drawn and were ordering the protestors to move backwards.

'Happens every fucking day.' Daltrey shook his head sadly, looking at Rivera. 'This here is Tamsin.' He indicated the woman in tie-dye, who smiled sweetly and began walking away. 'And this is Jenna Cronkite - she's a journalist.'

The ex-soldier smiled and shook the woman's hand. His gaze lingered a little too long - her mascara-lined eyes sparkled, and he glanced fleetingly at her chest. She was - he reasoned to himself - probably his type. But then, he pondered, most women were - especially of late. 'Who do you write for?' he asked.

'*The Custodian*. Among other publications.'

'Impressive,' Rivera nodded.

'Yeah – she's got influence,' Daltrey agreed. 'And she's on our side. Fighting the good fight – that right, Jenna?'

'Indeed,' she answered. The journalist then narrowed her eyes and shook her head in disapproval at the scene playing in the distance. One of the fracking facility's guards pushed one of the protestors to the floor.

Rivera frowned. 'Is it worth taking some photographs of what's going on or something?'

'We *could*,' Daltrey shrugged, 'but the gagging order means we can't do anything with them. Jenna here can't print them. We've been down that road before. Stories have been ready to run, and then they've been pulled at the eleventh hour.' He sighed. 'A few weeks ago there was a fucking massive explosion on the road up by Black Fell Beacon. We lost two of our own - good lads they were, too. Nomad and Mohawk.' Daltrey shook his head. 'Their vehicle was obliterated.'

'So, how the hell does something like that stay out of the papers?' the ex-soldier asked.

'This is the way things are round here,' Cronkite explained. 'Any time we try to get the story out, it gets shut down.'

'That's right,' Daltrey nodded. 'An explosion like that... you'd have heard it in Preston, I reckon. But by the time we got there, the area had been sealed off. An official inquiry had started, supposedly. If you believe that, though...' His voice trailed off.

Silence.

'It was an underground pocket of gas,' Daltrey went on. 'That's what we reckon - it must have been to light up the sky like that.' He pursed his lips. 'I mean, it might have been the spark from a cigarette or something that ignited it, but we all know what the root cause was.'

'The fracking,' Cronkite announced.

'How else do you explain that much gas suddenly leaking out onto the moor?'

Rivera nodded. 'So, how can you do it – get the word out, I mean?'

'Jenna's looking for another angle.' Daltrey turned and nodded towards the ex-soldier. 'Rivera here works at the hospital.'

'Is that right?' Cronkite raised her eyebrows. 'As what?'

'I'm in catering,' the ex-soldier replied. 'So don't get excited – no white coat or stethoscope for me! I can flip you a burger or brew you a coffee, but that's about it.'

The journalist looked hard at him.

'Are you thinking what I'm thinking?' Daltrey asked.

'Maybe,' Cronkite nodded.

'What's this?' Rivera frowned.

'Eyes and ears,' the journalist replied. 'Mark Garner's a good guy, but he can't go on the record for us – the Medical Council would boot him off its books. They'd say it was a betrayal of patient confidentiality or some other bullshit.'

Daltrey nodded. 'The girl you mentioned – the cholera case. We think there's a cover-up happening. But Garner's hands are tied. Even though he goes digging, he's limited in terms of what he can do.'

'So you need a source?' the ex-soldier asked.

'We do,' Daltrey nodded.

'Well, count me out.' Rivera shook his head. 'I'm trying to keep my nose clean these days. I can do without losing another job. Know what I mean?'

'You sure?' Cronkite asked. 'You never know, you might do some good...'

'I *might*,' the ex-soldier answered. 'But I've fought all my battles long ago. And it seems to me that most of the times I try to do good, I end up fucking things up instead.'

The journalist nodded, disappointed. She turned her eyes back to look at the dispute beyond the wire. 'Putsch Security,' she explained, looking at the baton-wielding guards. 'They even wear brown shirts.' She paused. 'You couldn't make it up, could you?'

Silence.

'There's a bigger story going on here, Mr Rivera,' the journalist explained, turning to look directly at him while Daltrey wandered off towards the fence. 'So if you change your mind and want to do some digging, then let me know – I can't get anywhere near them these days. They know me now. So my name's mud. It's the same with Daltrey and Garner really, but you're a newbie – you might have a bit more luck.' She shrugged. 'Anyway, this isn't just about Foulmile – it's about the future. This fracking bill is like a *coup d'état*. At least that's the plan when it comes to GFP. If the bastards in government pass the bill, they'll start shale gas drilling bloody everywhere. And it'll be too late to turn back – that's why they're strong-arming those poor guys over there.'

Rivera nodded and grimaced; the stand-off ended as Daltrey crossed the ditch before the road and approached, his open hands held up in pacification. He dragged the two protestors away from the scene.

Chapter 11

Alexander lifted the mobile phone to his ear. It wasn't his usual phone. Nor was it a number he called very often. He'd keyed it in – it was etched upon his memory; on standby for when it was required.

As he waited for the call to connect, he looked out across his property. That he'd risen as far as he had in the world was a matter of continual amazement to him. He knew that many considered him a watchword for success. He had a trophy wife; an incredibly luxurious house that was detached and walled; and several acres of land to his name. Towards the road there was a paddock – his beautiful, much younger wife, spent far more time with the equines he paid for than with him. But, as long as she hung from his arm at the functions he was required to attend and indulged his more amorous intentions from time to time, he was happy. In truth, he was far more interested in his ever-growing collection of classic cars than he was in her. He now had four, but he had his eye on an Aston Martin from the early eighties, and a rare Audi that he was sure would only grow in value.

Looking out across the fountained lake that sat at the end of the huge sun deck beyond the French windows, he could be forgiven for feeling smug. There was, however, rarely enough hot sunshine to make the deck ever seem much more than a folly. It had been his wife's idea. She delighted in hiring catering staff for garden parties throughout the summer months. On such evenings, Alexander would wander from group to group, beaming outwardly; the consummate host. But beneath the surface, he was a man in a state of perpetual anxiety. The consultant knew that – in return for the very obvious riches and luxuries that surrounded him – he'd made a Faustian pact. There were many days when he wished he'd never crossed paths with the benefactors that bankrolled his lifestyle. Splitting his time between two hospitals meant that anyone who ever wondered where his wealth came from assumed that it was the other hospital, which was his cash-cow.

The truth, though, was far from that.

Alexander was a man who found it difficult to view himself in the mirror. Whenever he did, he was consumed with loathing. Once upon a time, he'd been an idealist; a good man – or, at least, a man he thought was good. His first marriage had been happy. He'd had everything he wanted. Until, one day, his head was turned.

Suggestions had been made to him.

Things had changed.

And once they'd changed, they couldn't change back.

The source of his money was simple: he was for sale. He was a physician who was prepared to lend his weight to spurious claims and arguments if the price was right. He would simply turn blind eyes and deaf ears to any voices disputing those claims his backers wished him to make. It was easy; as long as there was doubt, then they were happy enough. Over time, the papers he published in medical journals had veered from attitudes of liberal egalitarian to hard-line views that supported key government policies.

The kind of policies Stella Cowerman voiced support for.

***

Alexander had never called the number before. He'd never had any need to.

But the latest revelation wasn't one which he was prepared for. When the phone number had been issued, there were strict instructions: he had no recourse for it unless it was an emergency. The cholera case – he believed – classed as just that.

'Well?' The female voice on the other end of the line was abrupt.

'This is Zhivago.'

'And?'

'And... we've got a situation.'

The voice addressing the doctor was cold. Hard. Accusatory. 'What kind of situation?'

Alexander sighed. 'Well... I think we might have a cholera outbreak at the Brynworth site. And...'

'Stop!' the voice hissed in response. 'Don't be so fucking ridiculous. The condition you refer to does not exist at the location you mentioned. Full stop. You said you made it go away, right?'

'I have. I mean – I've hushed it up. But I'm not entirely sure that's the same thing.'

'Good. This is why we pay you.'

In the silence that followed, the consultant opened and closed his mouth several times while hoping to receive instruction.

'But what should I do?' Alexander pressed. A sheen of sweat had formed on his fingers as they gripped the phone.

'Do nothing.' The order was toneless. 'If you need to do anything, then we'll instruct you. And in the meantime, do what you can to mitigate any problems. Nip them in the bud.' It was a vague response; a politician's response. Though slightly wrong-footed by Alexander's revelation, the speaker had swiftly righted herself – like a gyroscope.

'But...'

The line went dead.

Chapter 12
Texas, USA.

Five minutes after hanging up the burner call from Brynworth, Stella Cowerman entered Chad Benning's suite of hotel rooms. Though she'd been addressing the assembly, there was no doubt who held the real power – at least not in the politician's mind. When the request for the meeting had come through, she'd dropped everything else. Naturally, the request was couched in the politest possible terms, but there was no mistaking the subtext: it was a demand.

Chad Benning had never known poverty. He'd been born into a world of vast money. His Ivy League education was a formality, as were the places on various boards that he assumed soon after completing it. As he faced Cowerman, he knew there would only be one outcome from the meeting: he wouldn't leave the room until he'd got the answer he wanted – or at least received firm assurances the answer would soon be forthcoming. That was how he operated. It was how he'd *always* operated.

Benning's life experience had shaped him into the figure that sat opposite the British politician. The American took for granted the kind of money most people only ever dream about having. He had four houses in various states, as well as a holiday home near Cancun. Each of his properties had a permanent staff that was bolstered by local caterers whenever he was entertaining. All the properties had been inherited from his father. When the old man had suddenly dropped dead just shy of his seventieth birthday, Benning Junior had assumed Benning Senior's various positions. He'd taken over his properties and his share portfolios. Directorships of a dozen companies had passed seamlessly from father to son, and he'd even had a brief affair with his father's scandalously young wife. She'd drowned off the coast of Baha, California, while swimming from a yacht. Nobody had known that Benning was on board at the time. Save for the recipients of various significant sums, nobody was aware he'd bribed the physicians carrying out the inquest either. Enormous quantities of booze and barbiturates that hadn't been present in her bloodstream made their way into the autopsy report. Along with that, various stories from her college days were dredged up and used to discredit her: when the press got hold of the story, she became a party girl who'd coerced her rich husband into marrying her. And, with her out of the picture, Benning simply settled down into his wealth.

    His daily regime involved meetings, golf, and drinking at his country club. In exchange for her lavish lifestyle, Benning's latest wife was expected to be unquestioningly supportive of her husband. She glittered with smiles beside him at charity dinners and turned a blind eye to his many infidelities. Almost since birth, Benning was a man who'd never been told *no*. He perceived the world as an entity that needed to bend to his will, and not vice versa. The way he saw it, he should be able to do whatever he wanted whenever he wanted; he was a superior being, and anyone poorer than him was inferior by default. The same went for women and people of colour. So, the dark-skinned woman sitting opposite him was making his hackles rise. Benning knew that the British press either decried her or celebrated her as a borderline fascist depending on which side of the political divide they were on. As far as the American was concerned, though, she was far too liberal – that she still tolerated the existence of free public healthcare made her a socialist in his book. His contempt was kept well-hidden; the only reason he desired a private audience with her was because she promised access to something he wanted.

Even though he was president of Insignia TX – the largest fracking company in the USA – he knew that doing business sometimes meant having to compromise. Or, at least, it meant having to show a pretence of compromise. Chad Benning's father had been a good businessman; ruthless. But he was always a great source of disappointment to his son. Benning Junior always felt that the old man tended towards complacency: he enjoyed his money to the detriment of making more of it. That – in the eye of his son – was unacceptable, as was the benevolence he showed to a range of charitable organisations. Benning Junior enjoyed the trappings of his wealth, but he was always on the lookout for more. If he smelled money, he was like a dog pursuing a bone.

And, when it came to taking over Green Fuel Prospects, Benning smelled money.

The plan was straightforward: Britain was ripe for the taking. If the first site was approved, then it would open up the floodgates to more and more sites. And Insignia TX – under the cover of GFP – would be ready to move in. To Benning's mind, there was a sort of poetic justice to it. He'd never listened too much in history class, but he knew the founding fathers had lamented their nation being bled dry by the old country. With the acquisition of its shale gas rights – he told himself – he was turning the tables. It was a Boston Tea Party in reverse.

But he couldn't secure approval for the deal without Cowerman being on board.

Hence the meeting.

Hence the ingratiating, thin-lipped smile.

***

'So, how are things going?' Benning asked. He didn't look at Cowerman as he spoke. His attention, instead, was focused upon the cigar he was clipping. Long ago, he'd learned how to make people feel insignificant; to make them feel worthless. It was a skill he'd honed over the years.

'Good,' the politician nodded. As she did, she couldn't help but be repulsed by the way Benning's jowls flopped over his collar; the two meaty deposits obscured his jaw and his throat, wobbling as he spoke. She didn't wait for an invitation to sit down, but seized the initiative, drawing a quizzical glance from the man across the desk.

With complete disregard for the other person in the room, Benning shifted position on his chair and loudly broke wind. He looked up, grinning a little. 'A legacy of lunch,' he said, before his face clouded. 'I don't know who the hell spiced that shit up – this ain't Louisiana!' He paused. 'I figure they should fire the chef and start over.' He turned his focus back to lighting his cigar, puffing noisily.

As she sat watching him, Cowerman bet herself that the American's flatulence was a result of whichever pills he was taking for weight loss. Though backers from the other side of the pond were her bread and butter, they still – for the most part – disgusted her. With someone like Benning, she couldn't understand the paradox: he wanted to be thin, but he refused to do any exercise. And, as a man who believed his birthright was to act with impunity in all things, he was of the mind that he should be able to eat whatever he wanted, irrespective of calories. The pills were an easy fix. Or at least they would have been had they worked.

'Good, how?' Benning asked, his tone one of boredom. 'I have fucking shareholders to satisfy here,' he went on. 'They need to know that this whole GFP takeover is running smoothly.' He narrowed his eyes at the woman. 'If they get spooked, then they run.' He puffed at his cigar. 'And if that happens, the whole thing's fucked. The money that's on the table right now will disappear like a fart in the wind.' His face grew hard, his jowls becoming almost marble-like for a moment. '*And* if that happens, then I start hunting for a scapegoat. Understand?'

Cowerman nodded. 'The two who were causing the problem,' she began, 'are not a problem any more. They won't be causing any issues now – nor ever again, for that matter.'

Benning nodded, unimpressed. 'How?'

'Drone strike.'

The American laughed, his face cracking into a smile. 'Well, I'll be a sonofabitch!' he grinned. 'You've got some balls, after all!' He shook his head. 'Witnesses?'

'None.'

'Good. But that's only two. From what I heard, there's a whole crowd of pinkos down there protesting in front of their tepees. It's like the Little-Fucking-Big-Horn or some shit.' His eyes lit up. 'Can't you drone strike those motherfuckers too? Wipe them all out in one shot?'

Cowerman shook her head. 'Not without it coming back to bite us,' she explained. 'We'd never get away with something like that on our side of the pond.'

'Typical Limey pussy bullshit.' Benning nodded. He cleared his throat. 'Well, you'd better fucking do something,' he went on.

'Why?'

The American sighed. 'Because I get alerts on my phone every once in a while. Any time GFP and Foulmile are mentioned.'

'And?' the politician frowned.

'And I don't want to hear anything at all,' Benning went on, a hint of anger creeping into his tone. 'I want tumbleweed. I want no-news-is-fucking-good-news. I want jackshit on any social media channels. Crickets. You get me?'

Cowerman grimaced. 'What do you want me to do?'

'I don't give a fuck,' Benning answered, gritting his teeth in annoyance. 'Send in hit men if you have to. Nuke them. Do whatever. Just get rid of those tree-hugging-hippie-bastards quietly and let the pennies roll in.'

Silence.

'Look,' the American continued, his tone ever so slightly warmer. 'It's in both of our interests, right?' He paused. 'I'm giving you a blank cheque here. A blank fucking cheque! And if you need more cash, just holler. And, in return... well, Miss sounds-like-the-House-of-Windsor when she speaks. Your task is really very simple.' He looked hard at the woman. 'Just get the fucking approval. Understand?'

The politician nodded.

Chapter 13
Lancashire, UK.

'So what's the story?' Rivera asked.

'Where do I start?' Jenna Cronkite replied, shaking her head. On her suggestion, the pair had met at the Blackside Café. It was an establishment around three miles away from the Foulmile site. In summer months, it was overrun with road cyclists stopping off for coffee and cakes to punctuate their training rides. Today, though, it was quiet. Both visitors had an americano on the table in front of them. It had been served to them by a young waitress who looked annoyed at being wrenched away from her phone.

'Well – Daltrey said I might be able to assist,' Rivera went on. 'Maybe if I understand the bigger picture, I might have a better idea of how I might be able to help out.' He lowered his voice. 'You know Garner, right?'

'I do.'

'Did he tell you about the...'

'...cholera case?' Cronkite raised her eyebrows.

The ex-soldier nodded. 'Yeah. I don't know much, but I do know that if a kid's lying in intensive care and people are suppressing the explanation for it, then it's going to piss me off.' The ex-soldier's eyes blazed for a moment.

'OK,' Cronkite shrugged. 'So, if you're going to have some skin in the game, then let me give you the lowdown. What we have here first and foremost is an ecological disaster. That should come as no surprise – everyone knows that fracking is ruinous. Not only does it look horrific, but the knock-on effects are dreadful. It's a bloody abomination.' She shook her head before continuing in a rueful tone. 'The trouble is – this has got money behind it. Serious money. And there's enough in the coffers to dispute any stories in the press that try to point out any wrongdoing. Added to that, *The Custodian* seems to have gone cold on my stories of late – glacially so. My suspicion is that someone's putting the frighteners on my sub-editor.' She paused. 'I'm not even sure how long the sub will last to be honest - they might even be going higher up the chain.'

Rivera nodded. 'So, who's behind it?'

'Well, you have Green Fuel Prospects. They're the main instigators. Everything points to them. And it's made worse by Stella Cowerman banging the drum for how shale gas is the greatest thing since sliced bread. That's unsurprising really. It suits her agenda. She can just lambast anyone who opposes it for being a woke leftie who eats tofu. You can imagine a whole load of a certain type of men having to put sofa cushions on their laps as they read about it.'

The ex-soldier chuckled. 'That's an image I'm going to try to erase from my brain.'

'Isn't it?' the journalist nodded. 'But there's got to be more backing for them out there, too. GFP's accounts are public. They're very healthy, but not really fat enough to secure the kind of influence they seem to have. The problem is, we haven't been able to find out where the other donations are coming from.'

'Saudi?' Rivera asked. 'They're dead against wind and wave power and things like that, aren't they? Would support for a fracking company help them out in the long run?'

'I thought so at first,' Cronkite replied. 'But it's not really in their interests. If their money comes from selling oil, then why fund what amounts to an alternative – even if it *is* a fossil fuel?' She paused. 'We're thinking America. At least I am. One of the big fracking companies – there are plenty to choose from, after all.'

The ex-soldier narrowed his eyes. 'You really think they'd be interested in Brynworth?' he asked. 'I mean – haven't they got enough deserts to dig up in the Lone Star State and beyond?'

'You'd have thought so, wouldn't you?' Cronkite nodded. 'But I think they see this as a test case. If Parliament declares Brynworth safe, then it's effectively a green light for fracking elsewhere in the UK too. We already know that GFP have bought up a batch of other sites. They're not publicising it, but the deeds are public domain, so they haven't been able to hide it. I see the other sites as being like sleepers at the moment. Once the law changes, they'll swing into production, of course.' She sipped at her coffee. 'If you have shale gas legitimately available, then you can sell it to the UK market without having to pay transportation costs. You never know – if Europe sees how well it works, then they might even open their doors too – who knows?'

'But you don't know who's behind it?'

'No.' Cronkite shook her head. 'Look. Without wanting to blow my own trumpet, I'd say I'm a bloody good investigative journalist.' She sighed. 'But I've drawn a blank. I've kept coming up against brick walls.' She pursed her lips. 'I suspect there's a network of shell companies – something like that. But, whatever it is, it's been pretty well done. I've been going round and round in circles.'

The ex-soldier chewed his lip for a moment. 'Well, I can't imagine I'd do any better than you.' He paused, narrowing his eyes. 'So, anyway, why me?'

Cronkite smiled a little. 'You mean why ask a burger flipper from Club Med Café?'

'Exactly.'

'Well, I know about some of the investigating you've done in the past.'

Rivera raised his eyebrows. 'You do?'

'I do,' she smiled a little coyly. 'I told you I was good. Although solving some of the cases you've been involved with means you've found your way into newsprint once or twice. No matter how hard you might have tried to stay on the quiet.'

The ex-soldier laughed, a little uncertainly. 'Well, if you're that good, you *definitely* don't need me.'

'They don't know who you are... yet,' Cronkite explained. 'That's the thing. When Daltrey found out you worked at the hospital, he was cock-a-hoop.'

'So, he wants me to go in under the radar, right? *You* want me to as well?'

'Yes - you're untainted,' the journalist said. She smiled slightly. 'In their eyes, at least.'

Chapter 14
Texas, USA.

As Stella Cowerman's plane departed Houston, Chad Benning's final words echoed in her head: 'Let's make sure we remember who our friends are, shall we?' It was a loaded question – a thinly veiled threat. She was under no illusions as to his seriousness; when it came to making money, the US businessman had all the ethics of an Old Testament tyrant. And were anyone to stand in the way of his acquisition of further wealth, it would be tantamount to a declaration of war.

Before leaving their final meeting, the UK politician had endured Benning once more. The American insisted on a timeline for GFP's fracking project being ratified. Cowerman had reluctantly agreed – she knew how Marley Cuthbert-Wayne would react once she got back to London. Her fellow politician had been a mentor to her since her first days in Parliament. His venture capitalism company and hedge fund were the driving forces behind Green Fuel Prospects being bought out by Benning. He was almost as ruthless as his American counterpart – albeit in a manner far more in keeping with the values upheld by the British establishment. Where Benning wore his malevolence on his sleeve, there were daggers in Cuthbert-Wayne's smiles.

But the tips of the daggers were sharpened to fine points.

Barbed like witches' fangs.

Cowerman knew the Member of Parliament for Eastington would doubtless ridicule her for making promises she couldn't keep. For writing cheques she couldn't cash. He'd already been extremely critical of her failure to silence the protestors. When she'd questioned why it was that it had somehow become her responsibility, he sneered at her, reminding her of how much she stood to earn if the deal went through. He'd then given her a lecture about the meaning of responsibility. Cowerman's underlings were only supposed to fire *one* missile; clearing up the evidence from two had necessitated assistance from Cuthbert-Wayne. Though the drone operators had been severely reprimanded and their payout had been reduced, it still felt to Cowerman like it was she who'd borne the brunt of the blame.

As she sipped at a vodka-on-the-rocks, she still couldn't silence the suspicious voice that whispered in her head: what if the scheme failed? What if the American connection was revealed? Who would take the blame? Cowerman had a sneaking suspicion that it wouldn't be Cuthbert-Wayne. Though the MP wasn't necessarily a direct descendent of Henry VII, he had the same lust for power as the first Tudor monarch. If being elected to the House was his Battle of Bosworth, then maintaining his position and silencing all those who opposed him was an ideology that was hard-wired into him. He would never risk relinquishing control of anything. Cowerman knew she would simply become a mannequin thrown beneath the bus of his ambitions if their quest didn't come to fruition. Over time, she'd developed the thick skin of a politician, but the idea of Cuthbert-Wayne's vengeance was something that gave her sleepless nights. Where she was able to shut out other dissenting voices, the demon that whispered in her ear in the wee small hours bore his countenance. Getting into bed with him had been a catalyst for her climb through various committees on a course to the cabinet. But getting out of bed wasn't an option.

She knew too much.

***

As Cowerman's plane flew high above Ohio, cutting through the skies over Cincinnati and Columbus, she scrolled through her online news feeds. She could never quite square the circle between what Chad Benning believed in and what he said to the world. She was well aware that British politicians were wont to tell stories and make outrageous claims, but Benning's shameless 200-character plea for donations in order to help end socialism seemed like the end-point of irony. The Member of the House for Winchcombeshire West rolled her eyes. Before donning an eye mask and noise-reducing headphones, she turned her thoughts momentarily to the next phase of her plan.

Benning had given her unrestricted access to a series of numbered accounts in the Cayman Islands. The money – so he'd informed her – was earmarked for bribes. There were people he could instruct to process the transactions in a manner that was untraceable. Any safety inspectors looking into the Brynworth site would have their palms crossed with silver. The same was true of medical examiners, and – indeed – anyone else who posed a potential obstacle to ratification.

As she'd paused on the threshold of his suite, he'd confided one further fact: where bribes were insufficient, the money could be deployed to fund the facilitation of more permanent results.

Chapter 15

To describe Mark Garner's pop-up clinic as an official set-up would have been wholly false. Rather than being a well-resourced, government-sanctioned initiative, it was simply Garner; his medical bag; a trestle table, and a gazebo lashed to the side of Daltrey's Ford Transit. On any given visit, the doctor would dress wounds; diagnose illnesses; treat rat bites; monitor pregnancies; dispense cough and cold medication; suggest antibiotics; examine ears and eyes, and sometimes suggest in the strongest possible terms that the Foulmile resident before him should make the journey to the Lancaster West hospital. They rarely did; the mistrust those living there had of hospitals was second only to the dubiousness with which they viewed vaccines. Garner, though, for some reason, seemed to be acceptable to them.

'All good?' Daltrey enquired as he handed the locum doctor a fresh mug of tea.

Garner shrugged. 'Good's quite a vague term,' he answered.

'Yeah, right,' the other man laughed. 'Here,' he said, changing the subject, 'I heard you used to live in India. Is that right?'

The doctor narrowed his eyes. 'I heard you used to be a roadie for Ozzy Osbourne.' He looked hard at the other man. 'Is *that* right?'

Daltrey smiled. 'I'll never tell! That's a secret I'll take to the grave with me!'

'The past is a foreign country, right?'

The protest leader laughed.

'How are things here, anyway?' Garner continued, casting his eye around the encampment. 'No more massing of the militia?'

'No.' Daltrey looked at his watch. 'The fascists tend to fuck off for lunch around this time.' He sighed. 'Other than that, half of the residents are sick, and the other half come and go so often that I can't work out who should be here and who shouldn't. The hired muscle could be picking them off like stray antelope for all I know. The only ones we know are gone for good are Mohawk and Nomad. Remember them?'

The doctor nodded.

'Anyway, this doesn't even feel like a protest camp some of the time,' Daltrey went on. 'I mean – think about it. You need a permanent population to achieve things that last. The turnover here's enormous. I suggested having a census, but the committee said it was too authoritarian.' He laughed a little bitterly. 'There were three new vehicles this morning. And none of them were ones I recognised – none of the old crowd, that's for sure.' He paused and sipped at his tea. 'Did you do any more tests on Sapphire Phoenix?'

'Yeah,' Garner nodded. 'She's in intensive care now.'

'And?'

'I still think it's cholera.'

Daltrey pursed his lips. 'Well, that's proof positive that fracking is a fucked up thing.'

'Yeah,' Garner nodded, sipping at his tea. 'But it doesn't matter what I fucking think, does it?'

'So, what did you do?'

'I reported it. Raised concerns. The usual.'

'And?' Daltrey pressed.

'Nothing. Nada. Approximately fuck-all.'

'Bastards!'

'Yeah – can't help but feel like freedom of speech and freedom of expression and all of those other things we hold dear might be taking a battering here,' Garner sighed. 'Someone's intent on suppressing this story, that's for sure.' He shook his head. 'Call me an old cynic, but I think there's a decent chance they've got some big shots in their pockets, too.'

Daltrey nodded as a young child holding his mother's hand was presented at the trestle table. He looked to be around three. His eyes were large and unblinking. A free hand clutched at a teddy bear. His mother had henna tattoos on each arm, and was wearing a headscarf. A sleeping baby was attached to her front in a papoose.

'And what can I do for you, Mister Bear?' Garner asked affably, looking at the youngster. He knelt down to the child's level and smiled, pretending to shake the hand of the soft toy. The child giggled delightedly.

Chapter 16

Trout and Sanderson's belief that they were utmost in the preservation of national security had warped their sense of right and wrong. It was a deliberate ploy on the part of Foxtrot Delta. On his regular visits, the man who purported to be from Military Intelligence updated them. As he did, he provided them with gadgets and news that helped to shape their worldview to one that correlated with his aims. Their isolated location helped, as did the visitor's constant propaganda that there were rogue agents at large in the Brynworth area.

And all the while, they were being remunerated handsomely. The money they were provided with meant they unquestioningly accepted their orders and carried them out to the letter. That they were patsies for someone else's agenda had never even crossed their minds. Where Foxtrot Delta and those above him were using LD Chopper Tours and its drone to thin out the protest population, Trout and Sanderson failed to see the bigger picture. Foxtrot Delta worked hard to keep it that way. After all, they were only a link in the chain.

The first black-op was carefully orchestrated. Their handler had secured footage of dissidents being tortured in a faraway warzone. Using a selection of his contacts, he'd then arranged for the footage to be doctored. What was shown to the helicopter pilots was thoroughly convincing. Neither Trout nor Sanderson were well-versed in photograph manipulation. They simply saw what they were told they were seeing, and the background was irrefutably Brynworth.

Once the first black-op had been completed, the pilots' handler knew he had the men where he wanted them.

There was no undoing the deeds they'd done.

***

Putsch Security – acting on the orders of Foxtrot Delta – kidnapped individuals that his organisation termed dissidents. They were protestors who'd been identified as posing a significant threat to GFP and its future plans. The dissidents were targeted sparingly. But when they were, they simply disappeared. It was an approach taken straight out of the military junta playbook. Putsch delivered kidnapped targets to an anteroom in the basement of LD Chopper Tours. There, they were beaten and gagged; thick hessian sacks were secured over their heads, and their hands were tied behind their backs. After the first couple of times, it became easy for the two pilots to see the prisoners as being nothing more than dehumanised entities kneeling on the floor. They couldn't speak, so there were no voices they could attribute to the bound figures.

And all the while, their handler impressed upon them the terrible crimes the prisoners had committed. He also warned of the lenient treatment lax government officials were intent on giving them if they were ever released. 'You're doing the country a great service here,' Foxtrot Delta had announced the first time they'd been given prisoners to despatch. 'This is a little something we call taking out the trash.' Their captives had been harvested from Foulmile. Drone footage had been used to identify them, and then they were simply snatched. The transient nature of the protest camp residents meant that people arrived and departed at random intervals – though absences were noted, nobody had realised that the long arms of Putsch Security were partly there to reduce the population.

The handler had taught the two pilots how to administer pentothal. The drug was a rapid-onset, short-acting barbiturate general anaesthetic. Once injected, it effectively paralysed its prey, turning their limbs into jelly. That made the next part of the plan easy.

'Straight from MI5 this,' Foxtrot Delta had announced as he flicked the needle and then depressed the plunger slightly, sending a tiny arc of serum shooting from the syringe. 'It's all very hush-hush,' he'd explained conspiratorially. The first captive had groaned a little and moved slightly on the spot before being injected. 'No court would sanction it,' the man had continued, approaching the second prisoner. 'They're all too liberal. So, this is a way of circumventing things.' He paused. 'It's all for the greater good, of course,' he sighed, plunging the needle into the bare arm of the second captive.

Foxtrot Delta had accompanied the two pilots for their first foray.

After that, they'd operated alone.

***

The two prisoners on the first black-op had been delivered to the basement office just before nightfall. The two men had flipped a coin, which landed heads. It meant that – when it came to it - it would be Trout's job to inject the pentothal. The two men loaded the bound captives into the helicopter together. Sanderson had called tails; he had the job of expelling the cargo from the aircraft.

On this occasion – nearly eighteen months after their first operation - few words had passed between the pair. They'd done the job enough times now that it was no longer something with novelty value. Nor was it something that tugged at their consciences. It was simply a task with a definite end point; something which would be quickly forgotten once the first post-flight beer was opened.

Morecambe Bay was the perfect place for Foxtrot Delta's plan. He'd got the idea after reading a book about the tactics employed by the military regime in Argentina and the way they'd disposed of people antagonistic to their regime. The handler had the same aim; rather than a government, though, Green Fuel Prospects was paying him to protect the enactment of its policies. He'd just substituted the Río de la Plata for a body of water off the Lancashire coast. The bay was dynamic: its sands continually shifted, and its channels swerved. Its huge range was bolstered by bores and rips, and its ebbing tides could retreat almost as much as ten miles.

A conscious swimmer would stand no chance.

A sinking victim paralysed by pentothal would stand even less.

***

In the darkness, Sanderson looked down at the treacherous body of water through the open door of the helicopter. He checked that there were no lights visible from fishing boats. The repurposed military aircraft no longer had a gun mounted in the waist position; instead, it had been fitted with seats for tourist sightseers on flights over the Lake District.

The prisoners were laid on the floor in gaps between the seats.

Having administered injections, Sanderson dragged the first captive out. The co-pilot was lashed to a safety cord which was securely attached to a loop in the fuselage. For the prisoner, it was a different story. Trout hovered low over the waves above an area their nautical charts had indicated to be a particularly deep channel. Almost absentmindedly, Sanderson slid the first prisoner out of the open door. They plummeted, falling like a stone into the sea where they sank immediately, dimly visible in the glow of the aircraft's blinking safety lights. The pentothal meant their limbs were useless – they had no way of keeping themselves afloat and would, instead, sink into the dark depths instantly. The tide would propel them out to sea as they sank, and then – settling on the sandy bed – they'd become food for whichever creatures lurked there.

Thirty seconds later, Sanderson repeated the procedure with the second body. It, too, vanished beneath a splash of spray. The man at the rear of the aircraft gave the pilot a thumbs-up.

Trout banked, turning the helicopter around and heading for home. The ditching of the bodies had taken no longer than sixty seconds – not enough time to raise any kind of suspicion were anyone watching their progress on a radar monitor. The co-pilot was confident their action over the waves hadn't been witnessed.

Chapter 17

'The bastards got me pretty good this time,' Daltrey announced, angrily.

'Yeah – you're telling me!' Mark Garner nodded. He was holding a sterilised dressing against the open cut at the edge of the protestor's eyebrow. 'You know... I should really take you to hospital – get you checked out properly.'

'You'd have a fucking job!' Daltrey scoffed. 'You'd have to get me there first. And I'm not going – no bloody way! I need to be here in case they launch another attack.'

'Your choice,' Garner shrugged. 'Anyway, are you going to tell me what happened?'

'They jumped me,' the protestor replied. 'Four of the fuckers. They gave me a right bloody working over too. I wasn't quite left for dead, but I guess it wasn't far off. It was dark, so they probably assumed I was done for and legged it.'

'You sure it was them?'

'Abso-fucking-lutely,' Daltrey replied ruefully. 'Putsch-bloody-Security. I could see their uniforms in the torchlight.' The protestor winced as Garner moved the pad to another position. A fresh line of blood ran down the side of his face. He paused. 'Think it'll need stitches?'

FIVE OF CLUBS

The doctor pursed his lips, grimacing slightly. It was his night off, but he'd made his way to Foulmile after Daltrey called. He wore a head torch and had positioned it so he could see the wound. 'If I was talking to you at the hospital, then I'd say yes. Definitely. But as we're here at Foulmile, I guess my answer is no. Probably not. I think you'll need a clip.' He paused. 'You might get away with some glue, actually. It'll scar, but you're an ugly bastard as it is.'

'None taken, doc!' the protestor grinned.

'Hold this,' the physician instructed, pressing another pad of gauze against the wounded area. Daltrey did as requested.

Silence.

'You know – this whole thing is way more fucking crooked than I thought it was,' Daltrey began.

'That right?'

'Yeah. I was thinking back about some of the things that have happened here.'

'And?' said Garner, looking hard at the wound.

'Well... I love a good conspiracy, but this time I properly believe there is one. Hundred percent – no smoke being blown up anyone's arse this time. Yeah – there's a whole string of strangeness. We ended up sending a few residents over to Lancaster West before. This was a while ago – before your time.' The protestor paused. 'It wasn't that long after I'd arrived here – just after they'd started digging. Anyway, looking back, the ones we sent pretty much had the same symptoms as Sapphire.'

'What happened?' the doctor asked.

'They pumped them full of fluids and sent them back.'

Garner frowned. 'And did they make it?'

'Two did, and two didn't,' Daltrey replied. 'I buried one of them out behind Crowe Hall. We had a service and the like. The other one went to the crematorium on the Preston Road. The two survivors left shortly afterwards; they went to North Wales as far as I know. But I've only heard reports from other people.'

Silence.

'So, what do you make of it, doc?' the protestor pressed. 'You think it's cholera with Sapphire Phoenix? Could it have been the same with those other poor sods?'

'Quite possibly,' the doctor sighed. 'Back in India, we used to see a survival rate of between twenty-five and fifty per cent if it was left untreated.' He paused. 'I know it's a small sample size, but your numbers seem to bear that out, don't they?'

Daltrey nodded. 'So, why the fuck isn't the fracking being shut down?' he pressed.

'You tell me,' Garner shrugged. 'I sometimes think that the government in this country lives in a fantasy land – they seem to think that just because they *say* something, it makes it true.' He sighed. 'It doesn't matter if there's irrefutable evidence to the contrary, they just double down and keep insisting.'

'What's your point?' the protestor frowned.

'Well... things like that rub off on people, don't they? If you've decided fracking's safe, then you're not going to let a few medical worries get in your way, are you? Especially if there are big profits to be made. So you shift the narrative. Propagandise things. You lot cease to be environmental warriors and get painted as terrorists instead. Enemies of progress.'

'Not really.' Daltrey shook his head. Garner finished patching the wound.

'I know. It's not a rational approach. But the last thing they'd want is word getting out about something so serious,' the doctor continued. 'So they'll aim to keep it quiet. Damage limitation – that sort of thing.'

'So, what? You think it's the government's doing?'

'Maybe,' Garner shrugged. 'Or maybe it's just big business. That's probably worse, if anything. They don't even have to pretend to be concerned about the human cost – it's all about profit margins with them. And if your world runs on spreadsheets and column totals, then you're not thinking about some poor hippie kid fighting for their life on a ward in a place most people have never heard of, are you?'

Daltrey nodded, spat, and ground his teeth. 'Bastards!' he hissed.

Chapter 18

Rivera made his way up the steep, scree-covered slope that led toward Black Fell Beacon. The landscape was rugged; rocky. It was more suited to sheep than people – the path was well worn, but the going was difficult. The surface was the kind where it would be easy to turn an ankle – even for someone as adept at climbing as he was. It felt good to get his body moving again; it had served him well in the past, and he felt a pang of guilt at not having taken better care of himself recently, a situation he privately promised to rectify quickly. Earlier that morning, the rain had swept across the moorland in what felt like horizontal swathes. Though it had cleared, clumps of the grass that clung to the edge of the track still glittered with moisture, and the path was puddled with deep, muddy divots.

The ex-soldier removed his sniper scope from the pocket of his rucksack. It was a regimental relic – it had come back from overseas with him and not been inventoried. When he left base, it had simply walked through the checkpoint with him. The sniper scope was no longer used for its intended purpose, though. These days, it wasn't attached to a high-powered rifle. Instead, Rivera used it for bird watching. He knew there were many people from his past who wouldn't have been able to fathom the idea of him as an ornithologist. But it was something he'd consistently involved himself in since leaving the Army. He liked the irony of spotting birds through the scope and then allowing them to flutter away. Its crosshairs gave him accurate readings about range, and its lens was far more powerful than anything he'd have been able to buy in a shop.

Sweeping the scope across the panorama, Rivera was hoping to spot an osprey, or maybe a red kite. His Black Fell Beacon vantage point gave him a commanding view of the surrounding countryside as he moved the crosshairs back and forth. Eventually, it came to rest at a spot further along the road. An osprey was perched; it ruffled its feathers in plumed magnificence. However, its talons were gripping the burned out wreck of a recreational vehicle which seemed entirely at odds with the majesty of the natural surroundings. Rivera reasoned it was from the explosion Daltrey had mentioned. Apparently, the police had ruled it as death by misadventure; the official verdict was that no foul play was suspected. Once the bodies had been recovered, the most pressing issue had become the question of whose responsibility it was to remove the wreckage from the base of the ravine.

The remaining wreckage suggested it was an argument which was still unresolved.

Rivera watched for a while and saw the bird take off. Despite the buffeting force of the wind, it seemed to glide effortlessly across the moor until it was lost to his sight against a carpet of gorse and heather.

Pocketing the scope, he turned his collar up against a fresh band of rain and continued walking.

***

Pausing a turn in the path, Rivera took out his phone and photographed the body of a lapwing. During the four hours he'd been hiking, he'd seen dozens of them – all dead. It was the same with mistle thrushes, too. Jenna Cronkite had encouraged him to venture out on the moor and to see the environmental cost of the fracking for himself. But nothing had prepared him for the extent of its impact.

It was impossible to compute how something that seemed like such an obviously bad idea for anything living in the vicinity – human or animal – could be permitted to exist. That it had support in the highest seats of government made it even more unfathomable.

Jenna Cronkite... Rivera mused to himself. After they'd met in the café the previous day, they'd spoken some more. She'd then suggested they went for a drink in Brynworth. He'd gone along, gamely sharing a bottle of white wine with her. Consuming that much alcohol was contrary to the lifestyle choices he'd tried to live by for the last few years. But she was pretty, and – as they sat across the barroom table from one another – she was giving off all the right signals.

The pair had wound up back in Iris – Rivera's T2 campervan - in the parking lot beneath Lancaster West. It wasn't a glamorous location, but the journalist didn't seem to mind. Indeed, she seemed to be massively enthusiastic in her efforts to please. Rivera was no stranger to wildly lustful women, but he'd been somewhat surprised by just how dirty the ostensibly prim and proper journalist had been. Naturally, he was only too willing to oblige her whims, but – reminiscing during his walk – he was at a loss to work out what she would have gained from the liaison. The way he saw it, unless she was simply an old-fashioned nymphomaniac, he won on all fronts. There was no denying it: he was a deadbeat on the wrong side of forty, and she was out of his league. He only hoped that she wasn't expecting him to go out on a limb to investigate Green Fuel Prospects in return; it wasn't a fight he felt he could win. The ex-soldier had taken on individuals and small groups before, but this was different. He wasn't afraid of going head-to-head with a conglomeration – he just didn't think he'd have any success.

Their parting shot had been her urging him to check out the suffering wildlife. He'd acceded; he felt he owed Cronkite that much.

Chapter 19

Mark Garner caught sight of Mister Alexander a few moments after he arrived for his shift. The ward was busy – certainly busier than usual. Rather than simply having medical staff present in greater numbers than normal, it was the change in the consultant's demeanour that was most noticeable to the locum doctor. He'd always assumed Alexander was unflappable; the consultant bore himself with the aura of one who was utterly convinced by the righteousness of what he was doing.

Now, though, the consultant's countenance was drawn. He looked uneasy. Stressed. His cloak of arrogant certainty had slipped.

'Mister Alexander,' Garner said affably, nodding. 'Is everything alright? You seem, er...'

'Ah, Garner,' the consultant replied, distractedly. 'Yes, yes – quite alright, thank you.'

'And the patient?'

'Which patient?' Alexander's brow furrowed.

'The one from Foulmile – I believe her given name is Sapphire Phoenix.'

Silence.

'We've moved her,' the consultant said bluntly. 'Her condition has deteriorated.' He paused. 'It's nothing to do with what we talked about before – rest assured. I've had a few colleagues take a look – we believe it's an acute case of gastroenteritis. It's our understanding that she might have been abroad recently, and that she's been afflicted with a parasite.'

Garner narrowed his eyes. 'Really?'

'Yes,' Alexander nodded. As the locum doctor regarded him, he saw a sheen of sweat breaking out on his forehead in tiny pinprick dots. Though his expression was unaffected, a blush came to the top part of his neck, and his eyelid twitched a dozen times in quick succession before stilling.

'And the cholera suspicion?'

'Poppycock,' the consultant scoffed. 'And proven to be so.' He looked around, lowering his voice. 'I've told you before – that theory is a load of hokum. It's certainly *not* something you mention in a medical facility such as this.'

The locum doctor nodded in resignation. 'So, can I help?'

'You might wish to take a look at the patient,' Alexander answered. 'She's on the isolation ward now. The diagnosis won't change, nor will the medication we're prescribing – but you might just want to satisfy your curiosity. You certainly seem impertinent enough not to take my word for anything.' He frowned. 'I read your file, by the way.'

'You did?'

'Yes – an impressive resumé all told. *Médecins Sans Frontières*; the World Food Programme; the WHO.' He nodded to himself. 'But your experience is all overseas. Almost *all* of it.' He paused. 'It might be good for you to start understanding how we administer treatment in a civilised country, no?' He raised his eyebrows. 'Ward F.'

Garner nodded and began to walk away down the corridor.

***

When the locum doctor entered the isolation ward, he froze for a moment. It was a world away from the other wards with which he was familiar; the surroundings had more in common with a scene from the aftermath of the Chernobyl explosion than anything he'd seen so far in Brynworth. It had nothing of the bustle of the areas housing regular patients. Instead, specific zones were marked out in tape on the floor. A single nurse calmly checked and rechecked the patient's vital statistics. There was something church-like about the atmosphere.

Lying in the bed, the teenage Sapphire Phoenix suddenly looked very young; extremely small. The patient's bed was sealed off by thick sheets of polythene. Various tubes and machines were attached to her and the beeping of monitoring machines was a constant soundtrack. She was breathing unaided, but – even from the door of the ward – it was clear that her breaths were shallow. Laboured.

Garner regarded the scene through the window of the ward. He didn't have the authorisation to pass through the door. Instead, he looked at the sleeping body of the patient. Her lips were chapped, and her skin looked almost papery in its ivory whiteness. Glancing at the whiteboard with its inked notes, he saw how Alexander's words were reflected entirely: there was no mention of cholera. Nor was there even mention of suspected cholera. But the locum doctor knew that if the affliction *was* what he suspected, the drugs being dispensed were nowhere near appropriate.

For a moment, Garner considered hammering on the glass; he could summon the nurse and overrule what the consultant had said. He wondered if he might be able to insist the patient was given something that might better aid their recovery. Something that might even save their life.

But, deep down, he knew such an action was futile. As he looked up, he saw the visage of Mister Alexander reflected in the glass of the small window cut into the door of the ward. Garner nodded grimly. The consultant stepped into place beside him.

'See?' he said. 'I just thought it was important you should see for yourself.'

'Very well, sir,' the locum doctor nodded.

***

Jenna Cronkite was sitting opposite Garner in the Club Med Café. He'd long ago grown tired of eating the same food from the same menu on a daily basis. For the journalist, though, the establishment was a novelty. She'd taken full advantage of his staff card to order a chicken Cesar salad with a side of fries along with a slice of apple pie.

'So, this is the daily special?' she enquired between mouthfuls.

'It's the daily special every day,' the doctor shrugged. 'Ask Rivera. He gets food for free, but he still doesn't eat it half the time.'

'Oh well – it's not bad.' She paused. 'Beggars can't be choosers. Anyway...' she lowered her voice. 'You still saying it's a cover-up?'

'Yes – I'm more sure now than ever. As far as I can make out, Alexander's deliberately misdiagnosing the kid. She's being given the wrong medication – that's a fact. At this rate, she won't make it.'

'And you still think it's cholera?' the journalist pressed.

'Yes.' Garner nodded earnestly. 'Definitely. Those tests confirmed it.' He paused. 'But I can't do anything – he's a respected consultant. He writes papers for medical journals. And me – well, I'm just a nobody. His word is final. And, if I go against it, I'll be struck off. That's fact number two.'

Cronkite nodded gravely. 'So what are you going to do?'

'What *can* I do?' The locum doctor shrugged. 'I'll help if I can, but right now, I'm stuck between a rock and a hard place, aren't I?'

'She might die...' the journalist implored.

Silence.

'What can I do?' Cronkite went on. 'To be useful, I mean?'

'Dig into Alexander,' Garner replied. 'He's a good consultant. I mean – ask anyone. That's what makes the whole thing even more worrying. He knows what he's doing, so he can't really be believing what he's telling people about this kid.'

'What's your point?'

'My point it this: whoever's pulling the strings here must be pretty bloody scary – if they're putting the frighteners on him enough to make him lie through his teeth, I mean.' He paused. 'Either that or...'

'...they're paying him a hell of a lot,' Cronkite interrupted.

'Exactly.'

Chapter 20
London, UK.

The office in the Houses of Parliament occupied by Marley Cuthbert-Wayne was little different from any of the other offices where members of the House did their business. Its furniture was old and solid, and it had an ingrained smell that hovered somewhere between worn leather and stale cigar smoke – it was an aroma that no amount of modern cleaning products seemed able to shift. In the very corridors in which he operated, monumental deals had been struck. The country had been shifted off the Gold Standard; propelled onto a war footing; states of emergency had been declared; the nation had been locked down. Though he paid lip-service to history, he only really did so when it suited his agenda. Instead, the MP for Eastington had his eyes firmly set on the future.

Cowerman, slightly jetlagged and somewhat unsettled by the torrent of abuse that had been directed at her from the protestors encamped on Parliament Green, had made her way straight to his office. The man's researcher-cum-secretary had half-stood in an effort to keep her out of her boss' office, but she'd breezed through with an air of haughty indifference.

'How was Benning?' Cuthbert-Wayne enquired, looking up from his computer screen. His dark hair was parted in a manner that made him vaguely reminiscent of a moustache-less Hitler. He wore thick, dark-framed spectacles, and seemed to have an unerring ability to stare without blinking. It was a quality that lent his countenance a dour, humourless sternness. His face already bore the beginnings of a five o'clock shadow, which only served to accentuate his grey pallor.

'He's a prick,' Stella Cowerman shrugged.

'Indubitably so. I don't normally approve of expletives,' Cuthbert-Wayne sniffed, condescendingly, 'but I agree that he's far from being a pleasant man.' He paused. 'However, he *is* extremely wealthy, and – for that – we must be prepared to at least tolerate him.'

Cowerman nodded, sighed, and looked around the room. The relationship between her and the politician opposite was akin to a marriage of convenience. They had little in common: he was every inch a man of the establishment. Cuthbert-Wayne was a figure who'd never known anything other than lavish luxury. He was a man whose path into politics, along a well-worn route of boarding schools and Oxbridge colleges, had always seemed preordained. As a director of his Wessex Capital hedge fund, he'd grown even more incredibly wealthy. He'd taken full advantage of the legalised insider trading his parliamentary position offered him and used it to curry favour with those who could bestow further privileges upon him. His latest venture had been smart motorways; as well as being able to secure approval for the redevelopment of the most profitable sections of road, Wessex had also invested heavily in the construction companies that were responsible for the work. It was like a closed-shop. It had been achieved anonymously – nobody was able to definitely establish links between the projects and the venture capitalists; the company's shareholders simply sat back and reaped the rewards. The endeavour had been so successful that he'd vowed to spread his wings further. What had begun as a conservative investment policy had become increasingly aggressive; Cuthbert-Wayne wasn't a gambler, but he wasn't averse to rolling the dice when he thought he was onto a good thing.

Hence the desire to become involved in fracking.

The politician had managed to make a quarter of a billion pounds from smart motorways. He reasoned he could quadruple that if his company could involve itself with the rolling out of fracking in the UK. It was such an ambition that had led him to forge links with Chad Benning. When it came to money, the politician would get into bed with anyone – even someone as irksome as his American counterpart. However, he was a known figure. He'd been ridiculed in satirical newspapers too many times to avoid scrutiny. And, having been in and out of cabinet posts a few times in recent years, he was simply too high-profile to criss-cross the Atlantics for face-to-face meetings.

Hence Stella Cowerman. Though in the ascendency, she was still low-profile enough to escape having too much attention lavished on her. And - as her mentor was well aware - she would make the perfect scapegoat to save Cuthbert-Wayne's skin if the scheme was ever rumbled.

***

'There are still issues, I hear,' Cuthbert-Wayne sighed.

'What do you mean?' Cowerman frowned.

'You know what I mean. Foulmile. Protestors. You said you'd get rid of them.' He paused. 'But – from what I read, their movement seems to be going from strength to strength. It's not good enough – these lawless examples of the underclass...'

'Well, what would you have me do?' Cowerman responded bitterly. 'We've – er – removed some of the key players. But it's not like we can march in there and have a Night of Long Knives, is it?'

Cuthbert-Wayne's look of disapproval was icy. 'Listen, as long as there are stories in the press, then we have a problem.' He paused. 'Surely I don't need to remind you of that. We need the bill to pass – that's it. It's a very simple aim – we just need to eradicate as many potential barriers as we can.'

The woman lowered her voice. 'We had the drone strike. And our helicopter pilots have been – er – disappearing persons of interest. You know that. There's not much more we can do – at least not immediately. And...'

'...but it's not working, is it?' Cuthbert-Wayne huffed, cutting in. 'And as long as they're still active in the press, it's casting doubt.' He paused. 'And doubt is the kind of thing that will derail our plans.' He shook his head. 'I thought they'd be gone now – the protestors. They're living in socialist squalor in a godforsaken place, but they seem to have an uncanny knack of sticking around where they're not wanted. Like nits...'

'So what do you suggest?' Cowerman frowned.

'I'm taking care of it,' the man replied. He lowered his glasses to the bridge of his nose and regarded his opposite number with a look of disappointment.

'You are?'

'Absolutely – you've proven yourself rather incompetent concerning the task I gave you. I dread to think what our American cousins think.' He paused, carrying on distractedly. 'Yes – you've been measured and found wanting, I'm afraid. So, I took it upon myself to root the problem out at its source.'

'Go on,' Cowerman urged, narrowing her eyes.

'Jaggers.'

'What?'

'Not *what*, my dear – *who*,' Cuthbert-Wayne answered. He stood up and stepped to the wood-panelled wall of his office, where he regarded a series of photographs of chess teams that hung there. His younger self was easily recognisable; he wore the same look of contempt – it was as if he was impatiently waiting for the photographer to be shooed away for having the audacity to render his image on film.

'OK, then – who?'

'He's a lawyer. An excellent one.'

'But we've tried all of that!' Cowerman raised her voice in frustration, waving her hand around demonstratively. 'And the camp's still there. No jury wants to be seen as the one that kicked the protestors off the site – not to mention making all those crusties homeless.'

Cuthbert-Wayne chuckled. 'I'm not talking about the site,' he replied.

'You're not?'

'No – I'm talking about the publicity. It's what those lefties thrive on – you cut that out and it's like cutting off their oxygen supply.'

'You think?'

'I know,' the man nodded. 'And so does Jaggers.' He smiled, thinly. 'And it's Jenna Cronkite at *The Custodian* who's the real problem.'

'But she's not at *The Custodian* any more, is she? Not on the staff, I mean.'

'No. But they've still been printing her poisonous rhetoric, haven't they? Until recently, I mean. Jaggers has leaned on a couple of people.'

Cowerman nodded. 'But we can't just warn her off, can we? I mean – we tried the gagging order, and it came to nothing. How will this be any different?'

'We'll sue,' Cuthbert-Wayne announced confidently.

'We will? But what about freedom of the press and...'

'...Jaggers is confident. We can put her in the frame for libel and defamation of character.' He paused. 'He assures me it'll be possible to do things properly this time. If we plant a few stories with our people in the press, then the right-wingers will have a field day. We'll shift public opinion back to our side – and get this thing back on track.'

Silence. The man turned back to look at his framed photographs once more.

'So, how can I help?' Cowerman enquired.

'By keeping your nose out,' Cuthbert-Wayne answered superciliously, not facing her. 'Barring the drone strike – which, I must concede, was very well done - your record to date on all matters pertaining to Foulmile suggests you're something of a liability.' He turned and looked hard at the woman, frowning. 'Was there something else?'

'No, Marley.'

'Well... toddle along then, why don't you?'

As Cowerman left the office, she couldn't help but feel as though she'd been reprimanded by a schoolteacher. Her years in Westminster gave her considerable currency beyond the confines of the House, but such things meant very little to Cuthbert-Wayne. When she went up against the weight of his family history and influence, she invariably felt like she was floundering.

Chapter 21
Lancashire, UK.

Rivera wasn't a mechanic. He made no claims to be. But Iris was an old lady with various foibles. As a result, he'd grown reasonably adept in various areas of automotive engineering; since leaving the Army, necessity had meant he'd become increasingly skilled at maintaining engines. During his time in the military, he'd done various courses in engineering, but it had really been his purchase of the T2 that had kick-started his learning. Ever since, he'd spent almost as much time reading the Haynes manual the vehicle's seller had handed to him as he had reading other books.

That was why – in the staff car park beneath Lancaster West Hospital – his forearms were currently streaked with oil. The T2 had been running, but the running hadn't always been smooth. Consulting his trusty guide, the ex-soldier had resolved to address the various issues. The bright glare of his inspection lamp cast strange, ghoulish shadows on the walls of the subterranean space.

When he'd first started working, Rosie had rubbed herself at his calves. To entice her away, he'd filled a bowl with the contents of a cat food pouch, and placed it upon the interior floor of the Volkswagen. However, the cat had turned up her nose at his offerings; instead, she'd padded away and headed out of the car park. Rivera wasn't sure where she went on her forays – only that she was returning with increasingly larger prizes. Situated right on the edge of town as it was, the hospital bordered the moor. The ex-soldier suspected the tabby was venturing further afield on her hunting expeditions. Mice, rats, and voles were gradually being replaced by stoats and baby rabbits.

***

After a cup of tea, Rivera removed the high tension leads from the centre of the distributor cap and verified that the sparks jumped to earth when the engine was turned on. Reasoning there was a fault, he decided to check the rotor arm; the distributor cap; the plug leads, and the plugs. It was a process of trial and error that involved frequent references to the Haynes manual. He disconnected the lead from the terminal of the coil and checked the current was coming to the end of the lead before checking the wiring from the ignition switch.

He was just about to move on to the next stage of his campervan diagnostics when Rosie returned. At first, the ex-soldier didn't realise it was his cat. Instead, his eye was caught by a strange shuffling movement. Turning to regard her, he thought she almost resembled a damaged porcupine. One of the wings of the dead osprey she was dragging scraped across the floor; the other was sticking out of her mouth and up into the air. In the fluorescent lighting of the underground parking lot, the shadows cast made her look far larger than she really was.

'Is this for me?' Rivera asked, narrowing his eyes. The tone of his voice was pleasant, but what he was seeing caused him consternation.

The cat deposited the bird at his feet, and then stood back, looking at it. She then glanced up at her owner, as if waiting for praise. The ex-soldier knelt down and stroked her for a moment. Then she hopped up into the chassis of Iris and began eating the food he'd left out for her earlier.

Rivera frowned, examining the bird's carcass. It hadn't been killed by the cat – that much was clear. It was far too intact for that; he doubted Rosie would have been able to catch something so large anyway – not if it was healthy.

The bird, though, didn't look healthy.

Its eyes were discoloured, and it has lost several feathers – they didn't look like they'd been removed by the cat. The maggots spilling out of its slashed-open gut were evidence of the fact it had lain dead for a while before Rosie had found it. Frowning, the ex-soldier reasoned the carcass resembled those he'd seen when he'd been hiking up by Black Fell Beacon. Cronkite and Daltrey were insistent it was the fracking and its effects which were killing the wildlife. Seeing the osprey before him, Rivera couldn't help but agree with them.

It also brought to mind the patient Garner had been so concerned about; if fracking pollutants could do such things to wildlife, then it was entirely plausible that they could do similar to humans. He'd explained its effects to the ex-soldier using scientific terms – he hadn't been able to follow everything, but he'd got the general gist.

Rivera had never seen himself as an eco-warrior. He wasn't. He'd only ever taken issue with people. But he knew that it was people and their greed which were causing the problems he was seeing. Sitting down at the edge of Iris' floor, he leaned back against the frame of the door and rolled a cigarette. As he lit it, he began thinking. The ex-soldier had no desire to involve himself in other people's battles. When he'd first left the Army, he'd always vowed he'd never cross anyone unless they crossed him. Lately, though, he'd been drawn into conflicts on moral grounds. It wasn't a thought-out decision. Deep down, he suspected that it was something subconscious. He believed the women he went through were a subliminal attempt to compensate for the violence he'd been forced to mete out when in uniform. He wondered if the inner voice that urged him into more moral situations was some kind of attempt to balance the books for the bad he'd done.

Upon being discharged from the military, he'd vowed to leave society behind; to keep himself to himself.

But it hadn't worked like that.

He was – he felt – forever being drawn to the fray. He ground the butt of his cigarette out on the concrete floor of the parking lot and exhaled a lungful of smoke. Rosie rubbed himself up against his arm. Grabbing the top of the vehicle's door frame, he straightened his arm against it. It was one of a series of exercises the physiotherapist had given him to aid his recovery from the bullet. Without them, he sometimes felt shooting pains in his arm; his fingers would start tingling and turn numb, and his shoulder joint would start to cease up. Recent events had guided him to making renewed efforts to restore full functionality for his injured shoulder and for the rest of his frame.

'What do you reckon then, old girl?' he demanded, looking down at the cat with affection. 'Stick or twist?'

Silence.

The cat nestled herself down on the bench seat in the back of the T2 and purred loudly.

'Yeah,' he sighed. 'That's what I thought. But don't come crying to me if it all goes tits up with Greenpeace!' He carefully set about returning Iris to full working order.

Chapter 22

'Penny for your thoughts, mate,' Rivera said cheerfully. When the locum doctor had entered the eatery, he'd been behind the counter, cooking. It had been busy, so the pair hadn't had the chance to speak. A long line of employees in scrubs had ordered burgers of various varieties. Now, though, the rush had died down; the ex-soldier was carrying a cloth with him and working his way around the room, wiping at tables.

Mark Garner was sitting at a table in the dining section of Club Med Café, staring fixedly ahead. The cup of coffee he'd purchased earlier had grown cold, as had the scrambled eggs on toast. At first, he didn't react to the words spoken to him.

'Hey!' the ex-soldier said, more urgently. He laid a hand on the other man's shoulder, furrowing his brow. 'Are you alright?'

Garner jerked as if he'd been torn from a deep sleep. 'I –er – I'm sorry. I was miles away.'

'Yeah – you're telling me. So what's up?' Rivera enquired. He cast an eye around the room for the figure of his eagle-eyed supervisor before sitting down.

The locum doctor pursed his lips, exhaling slowly. 'Sapphire Phoenix...' he said.

'That's the kid, right?' the ex-soldier nodded. 'The one from Foulmile, yeah?' He paused. 'What about her?'

'She's dead.' Garner's announcement was blunt. The fingers of his right hand drummed absent-mindedly at the clenched fist of his left. He puffed out his cheeks and sighed heavily. 'She died first thing this morning.'

'Shit...'

'Yeah,' the locum doctor nodded. 'They'll do a postmortem, but we all know that's not going to bring her back. And we know what'll happen with the results too, don't we? Approximately nothing.' He grimaced in frustration as tears of rage brimmed in his eyes.

The ex-soldier looked hard at the other man. 'I'm sorry,' he said. 'Truly, I am. I...'

'...I know,' Garner nodded, interrupting. 'We all bloody are.'

The two men sat in silence for a moment. Rivera idly picked at a piece of Formica that was peeling away from the edge of the table while Garner continued to drum his fingers. Across the café, a pair of junior doctors laughed loudly at a joke one of them had just told. Both Rivera and Garner turned, staring at them – for a moment it felt like they should protest, but then they turned their attention back to being morose. There was nothing to be gained by feeling angry; the rest of the world wouldn't know of the hippie girl's demise – the planet would keep on turning, indifferent.

'You *can* help, you know?' Garner began. 'I was thinking about it - you might be the only one that can.'

'How?' Rivera narrowed his eyes.

'You're an investigator, right?' the locum doctor shrugged. 'So I've heard, at least. You're an unknown quantity in the eyes of GFP and Putsch Security. That's what that journalist Jenna's been telling me – she's pinning her hopes on you too...' his voice trailed off. 'You can go where they can't - even Daltrey says the same.'

'He *does*?'

'He does,' Garner nodded.

Silence.

'But I'm a chef these days,' Rivera protested. 'You know that much.'

The locum doctor slowly pushed at his scrambled eggs with a fork. He lifted a morsel and held it out for inspection, raising his eyebrows. 'You are?'

'Well,' the ex-soldier shrugged. 'Currently... I never said it was gourmet.'

'But you know how to investigate. You've got the background; the skills. So, you're the best hope we've got.' He paused. 'You know that if the bill gets passed and Brynworth gets found safe, then it'll be a green light for fracking everywhere.' He paused. 'But it won't be local people who benefit – it'll just be the corporations.'

'I'm a nobody,' Rivera shrugged. 'I'm sorry, but I can't do anything for you. All of this is just wishful thinking.'

Garner sighed. 'You don't need to do anything for me – do it for Sapphire Phoenix instead. How many more kids like her will die if this thing goes through?'

The ex-soldier sighed and grimaced, his conscience stirring in spite of his efforts to quell it. 'You know how to exert fucking pressure on a bloke, doctor!'

'Well, I've got nothing to lose, have I?' Garner shrugged.

'I'll think about it,' Rivera said, standing up and running his cloth over the surface of the table.

Chapter 23
London, UK.

Stella Cowerman glowered. She was no stranger to scandal – the liberal press had delighted in painting her as the pantomime villain of British politics. She wasn't the worst member of the House in that regard – there were plenty of others who were far more hard-line than her – but she seemed to have become the face for a new breed of politician. In the past, there had been various pieces penned about her. Most of them were the kind of thing she could shrug off, or threaten to sue about.

The article on the table in front of her, though, went further than most. In the past, journalists had painted her as a firebrand; she was considered something of a lone wolf – a loud voice that shouted out, decrying things, but not really having any great influence. This time, however, the copy went beyond mere muckraking. Instead, it was an investigative piece that had been published in *The Canberra Morning Herald*. The piece was penned by a writer named Compton Valence. When Cowerman had searched for the author online, the only references she'd found were to a small Dorset village of the same name. Valence was evidently a pseudonym, but the piece was too well written to be the work of a first-time writer. Seething, the politician ground her teeth together. As she read through the article, she swore it bore all the hallmarks of Jenna Cronkite. The journalist had been a pain in the arse ever since she'd started detailing her involvement in extracurricular activities. But, to date, she'd never written anything this brazen. Years before, a story being buried in a lowly Southern Hemisphere daily would have remained buried. But, in the modern world where the internet made things viral, once a story was out, it remained out. There was no way to put the genie back in the bottle.

And the story was out. It had already been picked up and syndicated by a number of other online news feeds.

Cowerman left press relations to Marley Cuthbert-Wayne. Whenever she had to have dealings with journalists, he ensured she was well-briefed in advance. She knew that Cuthbert-Wayne's business interests took in elements of the media. She wasn't entirely sure which papers or news channels he was involved with, nor did she ask. But, she knew he had influence – it was due to this, she suspected, that the piece had been first published in the Antipodean press. It was suitably left-wing to suit Cronkite's stance. And it hadn't been subjected to the kind of controls that abounded in the British press.

The politician sighed. She knew she had to tread carefully; if something else happened where her name was connected, it would only add fuel to the flames.

She pursed her lips and began re-reading the piece:

UK SHALE GAS: US PROFITS

Populist UK politician Stella Cowerman has been a loud, dissenting voice from the back benches of Parliament ever since being elected to the House. The MP for Winchcombeshire West has established herself as one of the leading lights on the far-right of her already right-wing party. Her 'War on Wokery,' calls for a cessation of all immigration to the country. Such demands that all unemployment benefits are cut have made her one of the darlings of the right-wing press. It has been an approach that has gained her considerable traction in recent months.

Cowerman recently went on record to state that all poverty was self-inflicted, and that it was high time the proud institution of the National Health Service was dismantled as 'it encourages idleness.' The ever-accelerating shift towards hard line perspectives in British politics has meant that the kind of utterances that might have had someone ejected from the party twenty years ago are now acceptable discourse. Cowerman has seized the opportunities proffered, becoming more and more outrageous in what she says. Along with half-a-dozen newly elected MPs, she has formed the spine of the 'Make Britain Great Again' agenda about which so much has been written in the international press.

However, recent revelations about her involvement with US business funding will prompt serious questions about conflicts of interest.

It is alleged that an unnamed US corporation is the main source of funding for a newly launched fracking initiative in northern England. Drilling for shale gas has begun at sites around Brynworth, Lancashire, and Green Fuel Prospects (GFP) – of which Cowerman is a director – is overseeing operations. Recent investigations have uncovered plans to expand the operation to a minimum of five further sites if Parliamentary approval is secured.

A standoff between protestors camped at the site and representatives from Green Fuel Prospects' security wing has been ongoing. However, until now, GFP has always claimed it will 'reinvest any profits back into the British economy.' Recent revelations show this to be entirely spurious: while libel laws prevent the naming of the US parties, this reporter can exclusively reveal that a 70% stake in GFP has been purchased by a large energy company based in North America.

When approached, Stella Cowerman was unavailable for interview. Likewise, GFP and Party Headquarters declined to comment. While not a conspiracy in the purest sense, these findings will likely pose difficult questions for the somewhat embattled politician. If nothing else, the US connection is entirely at odds with the supposedly 'Britain First' policy that Cowerman has always claimed underpins fracking in the UK.

Noel Hobbs - a representative for the UK Environmental Commission - stated: 'This is an outrage. GFP clearly has no interest in growing sustainable industry in the country. It is seemingly intent on selling off our natural resources to the highest bidder, ceding control, and exacerbating what is already a dire environmental situation.'

As well as the outrage recent revelations have prompted, there have also been accusations of press manipulation and bribery by fracking groups on both sides of the Atlantic. Opposition groups have called for a series of urgent questions to be asked in the House of Commons. **(Compton Valence)**

*** Full Story on Page 7 ***

Cowerman thumped the heel of her hand against the tabletop in frustration. She gritted her teeth and then massaged the bridge of her nose. As she did, her phone rang. Looking at the screen, she frowned: the number was unknown. Hesitating for a moment, she reached across and accepted the call.

'Yes,' she began.

'You'll have seen the article in *The Canberra Morning Herald* by now, I assume.' The voice was confident; self-assured; plummy.

'Who is this?' the politician demanded.

'Jaggers,' the voice at the end of the line replied. 'I believe our mutual friend has made you aware of what it is I do. Anyway,' he sighed, 'while we're on the subject, there is a considerable amount that we *need* to do.'

Silence.

'Are you still there?' Jaggers asked, brusquely. 'Because I need you listening.'

'Yes – where do I begin?' Cowerman enquired.

'You need to read the lead piece on the website of the *Lancashire Morning Post*,' Jaggers said. 'Litton Chaney is the writer – it's another article damning you - us. Another fake writer taking the name of a Dorset village. It's no coincidence; this is looking more and more like an organised conspiracy. We'll talk more when you're done.'

'But what...?' the politician began.

Jaggers hung up.

***

Cowerman brushed a manicured nail over her eyelashes as she looked in bewilderment at the story Jaggers had directed her to:

*** BREAKING NEWS *** BRYNWORTH: SUSPECTED CHOLERA OUTBREAK ***

Police in the Brynworth area are warning residents to only drink bottled water until advised it is safe to do otherwise. Cholera – a disease associated with unsanitary living conditions – is believed to be present in the water there. Reports have been issued suggesting it has been found in the mains supply. Outbreaks were once common in the area, but that was in the Victorian era in the wake of the Industrial Revolution. The disease has been effectively eradicated across the globe, save for remote, rural areas of some countries in the Developing World. Health workers are greatly concerned about its presence in the UK.

The death of a patient at Lancaster West Hospital has not been confirmed as being the result of cholera, but symptoms strongly suggest it was the cause. The deceased was a resident at the Foulmile Protest Camp – directly opposite the Brynworth fracking site. Protestors have long claimed that drilling for shale gas has the potential to cause a range of health problems. However, to date, the risks were not believed to be as calamitous as recent events suggest.

Health officials stress that – with appropriate medication administered at an early enough stage – cholera can be treated. However, if you live near the Brynworth site and are suffering symptoms such as vomiting, leg cramps, or diarrhoea, you should call your GP at your earliest possible convenience.

Concerned parties are encouraged to call NHS 111 rather than reporting to Accident and Emergency at this stage. Health officials are anxious to contain the outbreak and want to ensure sufficient hospital beds are available for affected people.

*** *THIS STORY WILL BE UPDATED AS INFORMATION BECOMES AVAILABLE* ***

Chapter 24
Lancashire, UK.

'Is this is becoming a regular thing?' Jenna Cronkite asked. She was lying on the fold-out bed in the back of Iris.

'Is that a problem?' Rivera asked. He was sitting on the edge of the bed wearing boxer shorts; a hand-rolled cigarette was clamped in his mouth and it waggled up and down as he spoke.

'Not so much, I guess,' the journalist replied, a coy smile playing across her face. 'I mean – I'm happy for this to be a regular thing, but I just kind of – you know – wondered where we stand.' She brushed a strand of hair from her face and coiled it around her fingers.

The ex-soldier grinned. 'Look – I live in a van in a multi-storey car park that feels like it was designed by someone from Leningrad. It's not like I'm much of a prospect. So don't worry about it – I'm not really much of one for making future plans. Know what I mean?'

'I'm heading over to Foulmile later,' Cronkite announced, ignoring the question. 'Thought I'd see if I can help – you know, after...'

'Yeah,' Rivera nodded. 'Garner told me. Have you spoken?'

'I have,' Cronkite nodded. She looked hard at the ex-soldier. Then she stood up. 'He said you're going to help out, right?'

The ex-soldier rolled his eyes. 'Yeah – that's what I *said*. He seems to think I'm some kind of caped crusader.' He paused. 'But if you ask me, this thing's happening at a government level. They're not going to let someone like me anywhere near – I'm just a retired infantryman with an out-of-control libido.'

The journalist looked back from pulling on her clothes and smiled. 'You never know – you might be able to uncover something. Clean-skin, remember?' She stood with her hands on her hips, and then ran her fingers through her hair, straightening it.

Rivera scoffed. 'I won't manage anything – you need power and influence to beat people like that. It's not like I'm Poirot – I'm just a nosy bloke who likes getting the bit between his teeth sometimes.'

'There you go!' Cronkite smiled. 'You're talking about beating people now – once a soldier...'

'Well, there's a kid lying dead on a mortuary slab,' the ex-soldier shrugged. 'And that's someone's fault.' He paused. 'Talking of which... I saw a couple of quite interesting news stories online this morning.'

'I don't know what you're talking about!' the journalist's eyes twinkled. 'But the pen is mightier than that sword, right?'

'You wield words like a lethal weapon!' Rivera grinned. 'But why the Dorset towns?'

Cronkite shrugged. She drew on her jacket and stepped towards the door. 'Pen names.' She frowned. 'Anyway, you reading them is funny - I thought you were a Luddite. I didn't peg you as the type to be scrolling news feeds. Especially not ones from obscure places on the web.'

'I'm not... I mean, I wasn't,' Rivera shrugged. 'When I first went on the road, I got the oldest, crappiest phone I could. I guess I was spending too much time watching videos.'

The journalist narrowed her eyes. 'OK...'

'Anyway, nice writing.'

'Thanks,' Cronkite smiled as she exited Iris through the sliding door. 'I'll see you later. Maybe?'

The soles of her plimsolls squeaked as she stepped onto the polished concrete floor of the multi-storey parking lot.

***

The four men that intercepted Cronkite did so around a hundred yards away from Rivera's campervan. The parking lot was devoid of people: the headlight eyes of cars simply stared ahead impassively. Each of the men worked for Putsch Security. But none of them wore uniforms. They might as well have though - they were all decked out in blue denims and black jackets. All walked in a Neanderthal fashion, rolling their shoulders.

'Excuse me, miss,' the first man said. 'Does this belong to you?' He held up a purse.

'No,' the journalist shook her head, her pulse quickening. 'Thank you.' She cast her eyes around, looking for an escape route, but knowing there was none. Glancing back, she noticed that Rivera had climbed back into his campervan and wasn't looking in her direction.

'Might I have a word?' the first man went on, moving towards her. He looked to be in his late forties. His salt and pepper-coloured hair was cut short, and he had a scar across his right cheek.

Cronkite frowned. As she turned, a second man stepped out from between two cars. Looking back at the first man, the journalist took a sharp intake of breath, realising she was facing a coordinated approach. In the near distance, she saw a third man standing at the head of the upwards ramp. Turning and looking over her shoulder, she looked beyond the second man. A dark figure stood at the foot of the down ramp. Her pulse quickened further. She turned back, trying to launch herself away from the nearest man. Before she could run, though, the first man was upon her. He reached out and grabbed her forearm, holding it in a vice-like grip.

'What the fuck do you want?' the journalist hissed.

'No noise,' her captor growled. 'Recognise this?' he demanded, thrusting a phone into her face. Its top hit her just above the eye, shocking her into silence. She then focused upon the image on the screen.

Cronkite frowned and then gasped.

'Your parents' house,' the first man announced. '44 Waring Road, Steyning.' He paused. 'Nice place. Commuter belt – near enough. Worth a shit load.' He paused. 'But the problem is that you can't keep your fucking mouth shut. Added to that, you can't stop fucking writing bollocks in the newspaper, either.'

'It's the truth!' Cronkite insisted.

'Pipe fucking down, love,' the man growled. 'I don't give a fuck either way. It's bollocks because my bosses have told me it's bollocks.' He paused. 'So it's bollocks.'

The journalist opened her mouth.

'Listen. Before you think about screaming, know this: there are two blokes in a van parked outside that house right now. Option one: they shoot your folks with a sawn-off. Option two: they've got a shitload of petrol, which they'll use to burn that fucker down. They'll film it so you'll hear their screams.' He shook his head. 'Terrible way to go. Oh yes, and there's an option three: if you stop twatting about, then you and my bosses might be able to come to some kind of arrangement. Understand?'

Cronkite looked hard at the man. He stared back impassively, his nostrils flaring in the anaemic yellow cast by the strip lights.

'Boss!' a shout rang out, echoing from the concrete roof of the car park.

'What?' the first man called. His eyes remained fixed on Cronkite's.

'Boss!' The shout was more insistent this time.

The first man turned and looked towards the source of the sound.

***

The second man stepped stepped into Rivera's path. 'Move on, please, sir,' he began. He was a man used to being obeyed; a figure used to intimidating others by his mere presence. 'This doesn't concern you.'

The ex-soldier ignored him, maintaining his path. Instead of acceding to the demands, he walked calmly towards Cronkite and the first man. 'What the fuck's this, a party?' he demanded. 'How come I didn't get an invite? I live here, don't you know?'

A confused glance passed between the two men in black jackets.

The first man frowned. His hand remained clamped on the journalist's arm. He scoffed. The challenger was a man who looked to be in his mid-forties. He was in bare feet and he wasn't wearing a shirt. His legs were clothed in faded denim jeans with several rips in them. The man's hair was long – a little unkempt; he sported various beads, bracelets and piercings. The first man took it all in: he saw the four bars of the Black Flag band logo tattooed on one of the man's shoulders. On his opposite forearm, he had a messy, home-made inking of what looked to be the crest for Fulham Football Club. The man was of average height. He was trim, but not especially muscular, and he was surrendering almost half a foot in height and somewhere in the region of three or four stone in bulk to each of his would-be assailants.

'Listen, friend,' the first man sighed. 'Do yourself a favour and fuck off, will you?'

'Negative,' Rivera replied, his voice as level as his gaze. 'That's a no can do.'

The first man sighed again. The man before him was a time-waster. His orders were clear: grab the girl and get out without making a scene. The interloper had all the makings of a rock in the road. He'd need to be shifted.

'Bradbury,' the first man ordered. 'Get rid of this fucking clown, will you?'

'On it, boss,' the second man replied. As he spoke, Rivera turned to see the man referred to as Bradbury fitting a brass knuckleduster onto his fist. He grinned a little, his lip curling into a sneer as he regarded his quarry. 'Last fucking chance, dickhead.'

'I wouldn't,' the ex-soldier said. His hands hung loosely by his sides. He breathed slowly: in through the nose and out through the mouth, slowing his heart rate.

'What?' the second man frowned in disbelief. He scoffed, shaking his head.

'That's the kind of thing that could cause a lot of hurt,' Rivera continued, nodding at the man's glittering fist.

The second man grinned, slowly. He was big. Slow. 'I think you've got your cause and consequence messed up, my friend,' he announced. 'The only hurt that's happening is coming your way and your way only.'

'If you say so.' The ex-soldier shrugged and watched as the man's lumbering punch approached. He led with his armoured hand; Rivera had seen buses move faster. As he dodged out of the way, he let the man's bulk pass him by, and then punched him behind the ear. It wasn't a particularly hard punch, but with the man being off balance, it sent him straight to the ground, his head scudding across the concrete. As he landed, Rivera moved quickly over to him and wrenched the man's arm back. Bone and cartilage clicked as he ripped the knuckleduster away.

'You going to stay down?' the ex-soldier demanded as he slid the knuckleduster onto his hand.

The man rose groggily from the floor, saying nothing. This time, Rivera's punch made perfect contact just beneath his opponent's left eye. The impact echoed from the rooftop of the subterranean space as the man fell back against the wheel of a parked car. The other men had been positioned by the ramps to prevent any traffic disturbing them as they put the frighteners on the journalist. Now, though, they both deserted their posts and came sprinting towards Rivera, responding to the threat he posed. Their focus had shifted.

Watching them approach, Rivera stood lithely on the balls of his bare feet. It was clear the man from the up ramp was the speedier of the two. So the ex-soldier turned to face him.

As he approached, the faster man seemed to run out of ideas. He'd sprung into action without question; it was the next phase of the plan that had stumped him. He had no clear objective other than to reach the other man. It seemed, for a moment, as if he'd realised his folly. But instead of changing tack, he simply doubled down and continued to charge. Rivera leaned forward slightly, shifting his weight. Then, carefully calculating the moment, he sprang, executing a reverse roundhouse kick.

The moment the ball of the ex-soldier's bare heel connected with his attacker, the man was unconscious. The impact was enormous – it sent a spurt of blood and a couple of errant teeth spinning out of the man's mouth. Momentum carried his inert body onwards, but it was just physics: the body remained in motion, but it wasn't due to any considered force coming from the man's mind. Whether or not he'd ever be capable of such thought again was debatable. But it wasn't

Rivera's problem. As the man crumpled, it no longer looked as though he was a human form – rather a bundle of disparate limbs grinding into the ground.

Hesitating for a moment, the man who'd arrived from the down ramp lowered his guard and then raised it again, adopting a fighting stance, plainly wary of Rivera's obvious physical competence

'So, you still want to play?' Rivera enquired, barely out of breath.

The third man frowned and looked over at his boss, who still had hold of Cronkite's forearm.

'Fucking do him!' the big man growled. 'Quickly!'

'Your funeral,' Rivera shrugged as the third man accelerated towards him. At the last moment, the ex-soldier dropped to the ground and rolled forwards, clipping the running man's heels. He fell like a stone, smashing into the concrete and landing, immobile.

Rising, Rivera brushed a little at some of the powdery concrete residue that clung to his bare shoulder. 'So...' he began. 'Are you going to tell me what the fuck this is all about?' As he spoke, he looked hard at the other man. 'Only I've put down three of your boyfriends; you're not being respectful of Miss Cronkite's personal space, and nobody's had the decency to tell me what's going on here.'

'Who the fuck are you – her husband?' the man demanded.

'Why?' the ex-soldier enquired.

The man shrugged. 'Well – otherwise why the fuck would you come charging in like a knight in shining armour?'

'Maybe I'm just a concerned citizen.' Rivera shrugged.

'Yeah, and maybe I'm your fairy fucking godmother,' the big man sniffed. He glared angrily at his challenger. Rivera had been in enough altercations to know that the dynamics here were a little off: with three of his men down, the leader should have been unsettled, but it still felt like he believed he was holding all the cards. He released his grip on the journalist and stepped away. 'Kneel down and put your hands behind your back.'

'And if I say no?' the ex-soldier frowned.

At this, the other man drew a Glock 20 out of the inside pocket of his jacket. 'Then I'll shoot you,' he explained calmly. 'And her.' He paused. 'And I won't lose any sleep over it.'

Cronkite gasped.

Rivera frowned. 'Why?'

'Because she's been saying things she shouldn't say,' the big man shrugged. He sighed. 'And if you *are* her husband, then you should learn to keep your bitch on a lead.'

Silence.

'That's pretty disrespectful,' Rivera announced eventually, shaking his head.

'So?' The man shrugged. 'What the fuck are *you* going to do about it?'

The ex-soldier grinned and nodded towards Cronkite. 'What if she's a martial arts expert?'

'Yeah,' the big man chuckled. 'And pigs will fucking fly.'

Rivera moved to his left. It was enough to make the big man move his arm; he levelled the pistol at him. In doing so, he left himself exposed. Cronkite had never been faced with a gun before – it gave her just enough adrenalin to do something she might otherwise have felt was impossible. She turned and kneed her captor in the balls. The impact wasn't sufficient to fell him, but it was enough to make him involuntarily grab at his groin. He gasped, cursing beneath his breath.

The ex-soldier didn't hesitate. Years before, he'd been a decent footballer in the Fulham youth set-up. He hadn't played properly for years, but – during his time in the military – he'd realised that some of the skills he'd picked up on the pitch were transferable to other areas in life.

Like slide tackling an opponent in a way that made all of his body weight smash into the limb bearing all of their weight.

There was a slight moment of quiet directly after the impact, and then the big man screamed as his ruined knee collapsed beneath him. Rivera picked up the Glock that clattered away and then clubbed his opponent with it between the eyes.

The big man's eyes rolled back in his head.

Silence.

'Who the fuck *are* you?' Cronkite demanded as she looked from Rivera to the incapacitated men and then looked back.

'I told you – just a concerned citizen,' the ex-soldier winked. He knelt down and patted at the prone leader's pockets. A second later, he stood, brandishing a key fob. Clicking it, the lights of a large SUV parked opposite blinked, and its horn sounded. Rivera clicked another button on the fob, and the vehicle's trunk opened automatically. The ex-soldier took a deep breath. He then knelt down and slung the big man over his shoulder. Carrying him over to the SUV, he manhandled him into the boot space. 'You did well back there,' he said casually to Cronkite. 'Nice leg action!'

The journalist, who'd been frozen to the spot, suddenly came to her senses. 'Piss off!' She grinned. 'You learn to fight dirty when your big brothers throw their weight around.' She stared at Rivera.

'What?' Rivera shrugged. He half-dragged, half-carried the man from the up ramp over to the trunk and then hauled him upwards, dropping him beside his boss.

'What do you mean *what*?' Cronkite spluttered, still not moving. 'What do we do now?'

'Well...' the ex-soldier paused as he shouldered the man who'd attacked him first. '...I think the first thing we need to do is acknowledge that this is a declaration of war.'

'It is?'

'Yeah,' he nodded, dropping the third fighter into the SUV. He continued talking as he walked over to the final man – the one from the down ramp. 'I may not be what they'd term university material...' He paused as he grabbed hold of the fighter's arm and began dragging. Cronkite couldn't help but notice how unconcerned Rivera was by the abrasions the friction with the floor was causing the unconscious man. Reaching the vehicle, he picked up the final figure and dropped him inside. 'Look - I know how to fight. And I recognise that when people do things to annoy me, they have to be dealt with. Sometimes.'

Cronkite nodded. 'So what now?'

'Now, I'm going to send a message,' he replied. 'You know how I told you I was going to pay a visit to Foulmile?'

'Yes.'

'Well, I reckon I may as well take this great big Chelsea tractor over to GFP en route – get them thinking.' He raised his eyebrows. 'You coming?'

'OK...' the journalist replied, taken aback by Rivera's frankness.

'Cool.' He threw her the keys. 'Take these for a minute, will you?'

'Why?' she asked, catching them. 'Where are you going?'

'To fetch a T-shirt.' He smiled. 'And some shoes.'

Chapter 25

After Cronkite had manoeuvred the black SUV into the parking spot beside the one housing Iris, Rivera climbed in. 'Do you want to drive?' the journalist asked.

'No thanks,' the ex-soldier replied.

Cronkite frowned. 'But I thought all blokes loved driving, no? Isn't it a macho thing?' She paused. 'You might present like a chef, but you're reasonably macho when you need to be. At least on today's evidence.'

'Er – thanks. I guess. But no - I'm not driving. Not unless I absolutely have to.'

'Really?' the journalist raised her eyebrows.

'No. I don't even like driving too much, to be honest.'

'What about Iris?' Cronkite pressed.

'That's different. She's slow and homely.' He smiled. 'Like a well-worn sweater. That's my kind of driving. Slow and steady.' He paused. 'All the new-fangled buttons and screens on something like this give me palpitations.'

The journalist laughed.

***

'What now?' Cronkite asked as she drew up outside the entrance to the Foulmile camp.

'Hop out,' Rivera replied. 'Go on in and see if Daltrey's around. I'll drive down the road a little way and ditch the car.' He paused. 'They might see me walking back and put two and two together... that's fine, but I don't want them seeing you.'

The journalist frowned. 'Won't the guys in the trunk figure things out when they come round... *if* they come round.'

'Yeah. But you weren't the one who dealt with the goons. You just happened to be there, so there's no reason for you to get wrapped up in this.'

'Alright,' Cronkite nodded. 'But when they don't bring me back with them, aren't people going to start asking questions?'

'Yeah, maybe,' Rivera nodded. 'But let's just worry about what we can control for now instead of fretting about things we can't, shall we?'

The journalist shrugged. 'If you say so.' She stepped out of the car and onto the broken ground beside the entrance to the camp. 'In a bit then.'

As the ex-soldier lifted his foot off the brake, the automatic transmission kicked in, moving the heavy vehicle along the road.

***

'I want in.' Rivera's announcement to Daltrey was blunt.

'Yeah – no kidding,' the protest leader grinned. 'I'd say you're pretty much balls-deep involved now as it is.' He cleared his throat, nodding towards Cronkite. 'Jenna here just told me about all the fisticuffs that happened at the car park... nice!' he grinned. 'That's my kind of affirmative fucking action, you know?'

'It wasn't like I went looking for trouble,' the ex-soldier protested.

'No,' the protest leader agreed. 'But I like how you dealt with it.'

Silence.

'There's going to be a fallout, you know?' Rivera announced, chewing his lip. 'Those men were there trying to abduct Jenna. Whoever sent them won't take something like this lying down.'

'No, they'll want a scapegoat,' Daltrey nodded.

'Well, here I am...' Rivera grimaced. 'I won't be much use to you if I'm in the nick, though.'

'Yeah, well,' Daltrey shrugged. 'Putsch Security may be bastards, but they're not above the law.' He paused. 'Them attacking you and Jenna won't wash with anyone – no matter how they slice it or dice it.' He paused. 'We'll keep it in mind, and if they make more trouble, then we'll call it in. Were there cameras in the car park?'

'Not that I saw.' Cronkite shook her head. 'I can't say I was really looking, though.'

'Rivera?' the protest leader asked.

'One or two, but they're for monitoring registration plates – to make sure nobody drives off without paying. I'm not sure they'd have picked up on what happened. The guys GFP sent would have been wise to things like that. Anyway,' he sighed, 'do we know what it was all about?'

'Some genius has embarrassed them in the press!' The protest leader beamed, throwing an arm around Cronkite's shoulders and squeezing tightly. 'Well done, Missus!' he smiled. 'We haven't got them on the ropes, but I reckon they're running scared, at least.' He paused and turned to the woman. 'Using the Aussie press was a bloody masterstroke!'

'Well,' Cronkite shrugged. 'It's not like *The Custodian* is keen on running any of my copy at the moment, is it? My name's pretty much mud with them.'

'True,' Daltrey nodded.

Silence.

Rivera cleared his throat. 'I want to help – really, I do. But you were saying before how I was useful because I wasn't on their radar.' He paused. 'After today, I think I might be very much *on* their radar. So... ideas?'

'Stick around,' Daltrey replied. 'Things are going to hot up around here soon enough, and when they do, I think we'll need someone like you on our side. From what Jenna was saying, you're pretty much a one-man army. You'll have Putsch Security shitting themselves.'

'Yeah?' the ex-soldier raised his eyebrows. 'I thought what you were doing here was all about publicity, though?'

Cronkite chuckled.

'It is,' the protest leader nodded. 'But you can only do so much with propaganda before you need to be pragmatic. After that, you go to war.' He paused. 'Come on – I'll show you.'

Chapter 26

'Whoever was here years ago did a whole load of legwork for me,' Daltrey began, grinning. 'Gawd bless 'em!' He drew out a torch, and switched it on as he and Rivera stepped into what remained of an old Nissen Hut. The structure looked like it dated from the 1940s – it was the kind of thing that was designed to have a thirty-year shelf life. As with so many similar prefabricated buildings, its lifespan had been nearly three times longer than expected. While its walls were falling down, its foundations remained firm.

'I used to go to a scout hut like this!' Daltrey grinned.

'Yeah, me too,' Rivera nodded.

'Anyway,' the protestor continued. 'What's interesting isn't what's above ground – it's what's below.' He looked at the other man. 'You fancy a little trip?'

'What are we doing – going potholing?'

'Something like that.'

'Why not?' the ex-soldier shrugged.

At this, Daltrey opened the door to what looked like it would be a storeroom. In the space beyond, the walls were lined with roughly made shelves. Upon these were pails of paint; tins of varnish and jars filled with rusted screws. The products were dated by their designs – some of them harked back almost to the time of the building's construction. The protestor heaved out an old oil heater with a grilled front. 'Remember these?' he smiled.

'Yeah,' Rivera nodded.

'My granny used to have one,' the protestor explained. 'If you sat too close, and the windows were closed, you'd start to nod off.' He paused. 'Carbon monoxide, I should think.' Once the heater was out of the way, Daltrey stepped further into the space. The rear of the storage cupboard was dominated by a large, rusted immersion heater whose insulated cladding had all but rotted away.

'That looks like a bloody doodlebug!'

'Yeah,' the protestor nodded. 'It'd probably go up like one if someone struck a match too!' He paused. 'Anyway, if you can squeeze yourself around the back here, then things get kind of interesting.'

With Daltrey's torch lighting the scene, the pair picked their way behind the immersion heater. In the space behind, a flight of stone steps led down below the ground.

'Is this safe?' Rivera enquired once the pair reached the bottom. The air was cold, damp, and musty.

'I should say so,' the protestor nodded. 'It's a darn sight safer than a lot of the tunnels I've lived in over the years. I reckon I've got a sixth sense for such things these days – like I've turned half-mole or something.' He played the beam of his torch up and down an underground shaft. The roof was around five feet high. Wooden beams were placed at regular intervals; the shaft looked to widen out thirty or so yards ahead of them into what looked like a larger gallery.

'You sure about that?'

'Yeah – I've spent most of my adult life in bloody tunnels,' Daltrey explained.

'Why?' Rivera frowned.

'Easy,' the protestor shrugged. 'If there are people living under the ground, then construction companies can't send in the diggers.' He paused. 'I've stopped bloody by-passes being built all over the place.' He smiled. 'The thing is, though, most of the time I've had to dig the tunnels myself. They've been shit,' he reflected ruefully. 'These ones, though – they're bloody brilliant. All shored up and lovely.'

'But they're already digging,' Rivera argued. 'GFP, I mean. And they're already fucking up the water supply.' He paused. 'Not to mention there are kids dying and private soldiers going around trying to bust heads. So, what good is you being underground going to do? It just means they can't see you.'

'This is for phase two, brother!' Daltrey grinned triumphantly. 'There's a day of reckoning coming – mark my words. And, when it happens, the bastards are going to come in here like it's a Blitzkrieg. And when they do, I'll be ready for them – *we'll* be ready for them. Jenna will alert her journalist friends, and they'll get lawyers to issue court orders. Stop them in their tracks. Cease and desist.'

'OK...' Rivera nodded, uncertainly. He hadn't spent enough time in the protestor's company to get the measure of the man; he was well aware of the deific terms in which his followers saw him. Nevertheless, the ex-soldier couldn't help but wonder if all the time the other man seemed to have spent underground might have addled his brain somewhat. He sniffed once more at the cold, musty air.

'Feel that?' the protestor enquired suddenly; his ears pricked up, and he was hyper-alert. His straggly hair gave him the look of a prairie dog on sentry duty. He shone the beam of his torch at the roof of the cavern, and Rivera saw how little waterfalls of dust were cascading downwards, dancing in the weak light.

'What is it? Cars?' the ex-soldier asked.

'No – it's the bastards drilling,' Daltrey explained. 'The fracking makes the earth to shift way deeper than where we are now. It causes tremors – over the road at least. What you're feeling now are probably aftershocks from them.'

Rivera nodded, frowning. 'And people know about this?'

'Of course,' the other man nodded. 'They just don't want to have to do anything about it. And Cowerman's lot have money for plenty of seismologists who are paid off to say everything's hunky dory.'

Rivera nodded. 'What did they take out of the ground here, anyway? Coal?'

'Negative.' Daltrey shook his head. 'Sandstone – that's why the fracking is so damaging. It's soft rock – it crumbles. So what they're doing over the way is going to fuck things up terribly.' He paused. 'That's why the water supply's being poisoned – it's not surprising. Any chemicals just seep straight through.'

Silence.

'So what's the long-term plan, then?' Rivera asked eventually. 'I mean... protest; dig tunnels – I get that. But what are they going to do – GFP?'

'Silence us,' Daltrey shrugged. 'In the press, at least.'

'Yeah – they seem to be doing a pretty good job of that already.'

'True,' the protestor nodded. 'After that, they'll want us gone, won't they? We're an embarrassment. A pain in the arse. They want their operation to be slick and smooth and corporate. Nice and shiny and sanitised so that when they tell people fracking is the future, nobody's going to turn around and start asking questions.' He paused. 'It's a whole lot easier if there aren't any grubby little urchins waving banners and shouting through bullhorns. That's what Green Fuel Prospects want. And it's definitely what their Yankee paymasters are hanging out for.' Daltrey cleared his throat and spat violently. 'This'll be a knock-on effect if we're not careful. But you know that already, though. It's like Truman's domino theory, only this time it's not bullshit. Once one area falls to fracking, then the next one will do the same, and so on and so forth. Before you know it, half of Britain will have been dug up; we'll have no wildlife to speak of; no clean water; no edible crops...' His voice trailed off. 'I get it – people want to make money, but this is just about now. Short-term gains and long-term penalties. GFP's shareholders will have a massive pay-out. They'll all piss off and buy islands in the Caribbean. They'll have private yachts and Lear jets full of concubines. But, all the while, they're just selling things off to the highest bidder and fucking everything up for future generations.'

'You should have been a politician.'

'Yeah, but I don't like wearing a tie.'

'Yeah – that's kind of a deal-breaker. Anyway, what then?' Rivera pursed his lips.

'Then the same people who'll own the land that's being dug up will be the very ones who people here will have to buy their imported fruit and vegetables from. They're not precious about any of this stuff – the only thing that interests them is the thing that makes the most bread.'

Silence.

'It's like what the mafia used to do with crooked businesses,' Daltrey went on, his eyes shining in the half-light cast by his torch.

'It is?'

'Yeah – they'd run them into the ground. And then, when there wasn't a drop left that could be squeezed out, they'd torch the fucker. Burn it down like Babylon.'

Rivera nodded grimly.

'It's a ticking fucking time bomb, too. Once the bill passes, we'll be evicted – my guess is that they'll try to do it before. And once that happens, we're pretty much powerless to do anything.' The protestor shook his head. 'What I've shown you down here is a secret – obviously. And it's a fucking last resort.' He shook his head. 'I don't want to end up living down here – I'd far sooner face them down on the surface. But if they evict us... we're fucked. So, if it comes to that, then I'm fighting a rearguard action. It'll mean the war's already lost.'

'So what do you need?' Rivera asked. 'I mean – what can I do?'

'That's easy,' Daltrey shrugged. 'Find a way to win. Figure out how we can beat them.'

'No pressure then?'

'Yeah – that's the spirit.'

Chapter 27

'So what do we do then?' Rivera enquired. He, Garner, Cronkite and Daltrey were standing before the caravan where the locum doctor ran his pop-up clinics. The sky had darkened and low clouds scudded over the emerald hillsides that stretched up behind Crowe Hall. In the other direction, the scarred and broken landscape of the open cast works was pock-marked with bright yellow vehicles and giant rolls of piped tubing.

'I don't know,' Daltrey shrugged. 'My plan's pretty simple – agitate, and then – when the big bad company sends in the bulldozers – go to ground.'

'OK...' the ex-soldier's response did little to hide his disappointment. 'Anything more constructive? Anyone?'

'I think we need more publicity about the cholera,' Garner began. 'You need a groundswell of opinion with something like this. I mean... it was on the front page of the website for the *Lancashire Morning Post,* but now it's been pulled.'

'Really?' Rivera raised his eyebrows.

'Yeah,' Cronkite nodded. 'They have a message up there apologising – something about sources having been unconfirmed. It's a whole load of bullshit.' She paused. 'It tells us something, though: that whoever's behind GFP has got a long bloody reach. I mean the forces that are *really* behind it – it's all happening at a ministerial level, of course. That's what I think.'

'That's right,' Daltrey broke in. 'But we can't prove a fucking thing.'

Silence.

'There's got to be some way of figuring out who's pulling the strings here,' Garner said, eventually. 'I know – they're as rich as Croesus, but they can't hide everything. Surely?'

'That's what I've been trying to do for ages,' Cronkite protested. 'But every time it feels like I've got a lead, it gets buried.'

'It's Cowerman,' Daltrey announced.

'It is?' Garner frowned.

'Yeah,' the protest leader nodded. 'I'm certain of it – she's been the fucking Wicked Witch of the West here right from the get-go. I've read about her – all of that bullshit in the papers; nobody would demonise us as much as she has unless they were responsible. She hides behind the drilling operation, but I think she's running the whole bloody thing.'

'But can you prove it?' Rivera went on.

'It's not that easy, Trent,' Cronkite protested.

'Have you tried following the money?' the ex-soldier enquired. During his time with the Army, he'd been seconded to the Military Police, and had become quite adept at peering into very questionable practices.

The journalist narrowed her eyes. 'What the fuck do you think I've been doing all this time?' Her tone was suddenly bitter.

Silence.

Rivera shrugged. 'Look – I'm just saying that if you follow...'

'...they know what to expect,' Cronkite interrupted. 'They know what to keep hidden. There's nothing they haven't considered. And they've got accountants who are savvy enough to know all the loopholes.' She shrugged. 'Sure, you can chase the money. Be my guest. But sooner or later, you'll come up against the same dead ends everyone else has.'

'I know.' Rivera pursed his lips. 'But what about... seizing the initiative? You could...'

'...fine! Do it your way,' Cronkite huffed. 'Beat people up and bust heads.' She sighed. 'I've spent six months trying to uncover what's going on here – you show up and think you can solve everything overnight.' She glowered at Rivera. 'It doesn't work like that.'

The three men watched as the journalist stomped away over the broken ground.

'Jenna!' Garner called out in a conciliatory tone. 'Wait...' The locum doctor began to hurry after the departing woman.

Daltrey turned to the ex-soldier and gave a low chuckle. 'Doesn't look like you're going to be getting your nuts wet tonight, then?'

'Yeah, thanks for that,' the ex-soldier sighed. 'Very fucking helpful!'

The protestor shrugged. 'So, are we any clearer about anything?' he enquired.

'No,' Rivera shook his head. 'It's as bad as JFK – there was only one thing anyone could agree on with that.'

'That Lee Harvey Oswald didn't do it?'

'Exactly!'

'So... we all agree that Cowerman's the problem, then?'

'We do,' Rivera nodded. 'We've worked out the *what*. Now we just need to figure out the *how* and the *why*.'

Chapter 28

The misunderstanding over how to investigate Cowerman's involvement in the Brynworth fracking operation might have been enough to spark a larger argument between Rivera and Cronkite. His questioning of her methods in front of what amounted to her audience felt massively undermining.

They might have also disagreed after the incident in the parking lot. The nervous tension felt by the journalist hadn't fully dissipated; she would have been within her rights to suspect that it had been his proximity to her that had placed her in harm's way, and not the other way round.

As it was, though, it was neither of those things that led to them rowing.

The altercation went from stationary to full-blown in the space of around five seconds. Having stormed away from the ex-soldier at the Foulmile camp, Cronkite had taken herself off to the Black Fell Beacon Café. Sitting alone at a table, she'd gone through all of her notes on what was happening at the Lancashire site. She was convinced she'd found every slight chink in Cowerman's armour that could be exploited. It was this news she wished to convey to the ex-soldier in person.

Following the Foulmile altercation, Rivera had returned to Lancaster West to complete a shift at Club Med. Towards the end of his shift, he'd started talking to a student nurse named Sadie. The young woman was equal parts stressed, bored, blonde and frustrated. The ex-soldier believed that he'd curbed the worst of his predatory tendencies in recent times, but the seduction of Sadie felt like a step backwards in that regard. She – it transpired – was only too willing to accompany him back to Iris.

Rivera later lamented that if the student nurse had departed two minutes earlier, or that Cronkite had been delayed by traffic lights - or any one of an infinite number of possibilities – then the two women wouldn't have crossed paths. As it was, though, it felt as if the timing of their meeting had conspired against the ex-soldier in the worst possible way. At the exact moment the journalist approached the campervan, a giggling Sadie stepped out. She carried on walking; Cronkite at once began to make her feelings known.

***

Following the argument, Rivera held up his hands and announced he was leaving. He had no idea where Sadie had gone; the student nurse had made herself scarce once Cronkite had begun shouting. From that point, the accusatory vitriol was one-way traffic. He made little attempt to defend himself and only proffered a vague apology. In truth, he couldn't have been caught much more red-handed if he'd tried.

'So, that's it?' she demanded, seething. 'You're just going to leave?'

'I am,' he nodded, sighing.

The journalist stood, frowning. 'Why?'

The ex-soldier shrugged. 'I've had enough conflict in my life,' he explained. 'I don't need any more.'

'But what about the promises you made over at Foulmile? What the fuck will Daltrey say?'

Rivera sighed. 'We've got nothing,' he replied. 'It pains me to say it, but what can we do? We're up against governments here – corporations with limitless funds.' He paused. 'I can beat a few people up; you can write some stories about the information Garner gives you, and Daltrey can piss off underground into his tunnels, but it's not going to do any good. We can't prove anything – even if we know what's going on.' He chewed his lip. 'And you screeching at me is making my head hurt.'

'Well, you shouldn't go around shagging nurses then, should you?'

'I didn't know we were exclusive,' the ex-soldier replied sheepishly.

'Maybe we're not,' Cronkite continued. 'But she looked barely legal – what the fuck's the matter with you?'

Silence.

'I'm a bastard,' Rivera shrugged. 'I'm sorry if you didn't realise. But it's the truth. I'm just a worthless drifter with commitment issues who can't keep his dick down his trousers. Don't take it personally. I...'

'I don't give a shit!' The journalist cut in. 'I'm not talking about sex here. You're right about the commitment issues, though. So, you're just going to run off and leave us fighting the good fight, are you?'

Silence.

'First sign of trouble and you up sticks and leave, is that it?'

Rivera said nothing. Instead, he scooped Rosie up from the floor and deposited her in the cab of the vehicle. He then picked up and dismantled the two folding chairs that had been sitting at the side of the campervan.

'You do know that if you never commit to anything, you'll never be happy, right?' Cronkite went on. 'You should think about that while you're driving off to wherever the hell you end up. You'll just be living life on a loop if you're not careful.'

The ex-soldier nodded at her as he closed the driver's side door. 'Well, thanks for the sermon.' He turned the key in the ignition. On the third attempt, Iris rumbled into life. As he revved at the engine, it seemed extremely loud in the confined space.

Cronkite stood aside, shaking her head as Rivera pulled out of the space.

He was just approaching the down ramp when Mark Garner stepped out of the painted door that led to the piss-soaked stairwell. As Iris approached him, the locum doctor barred the way with his arms outstretched. He waved his hands frantically.

The ex-soldier braked and wound down the window. 'You're lucky this old girl moves so slowly,' he announced, reaching his hand out and adjusting the wing mirror. He narrowed his eyes. 'What do you want?'

'I have news,' Garner answered. 'And you're going to want to hear it.'

Chapter 29

Garner lowered himself into one of the folding chairs Rivera had removed from the cab of the campervan. Iris was parked back in the spot that had housed her previously. Cronkite was seated on the other chair, and the ex-soldier perched himself on the vehicle's threshold, Rosie on his lap.

'What news do you have exactly, then?' the ex-soldier asked.

'There's another cholera case,' the locum doctor announced. He grimaced a little in an attempt to hide the sense of excitement he felt. 'I don't think they're going to be able to hush this one up. Not this time. Too many trained medical people are now involved, and two cases, in the same hospital... way too difficult to keep *that* quiet.'

'They definitely hushed the last one up, then?' Cronkite pressed.

'They did,' Garner nodded. 'There's a consultant – Mister Alexander. I didn't believe it at first, but seeing how he acted today, I'm pretty convinced that he's been suppressing evidence.'

'But isn't that unethical?' Rivera frowned.

'Of course,' the locum doctor nodded. 'About as unethical as it's possible to be.' He paused. 'Which is why I think someone's putting pressure on him. I'm not saying he's a bad man necessarily. But I *am* saying he's done bad things.'

'So why tell us now?' Cronkite asked.

'Because I think he's another angle you can look at,' Garner explained. 'You want to prove a link with Cowerman, right?'

'Yes,' Rivera nodded.

'Well – you're never going to get her to talk. Never in a million years. She won't admit to anything – it's not in her DNA. She sees herself as a superior being. You know, born to rule and all that. So, there will always be someone else she can point the finger at.'

Silence.

'Anyway, as far as going higher up the chain,' Garner went on, 'forget about it. If you've got people who're prepared to sink their money into fracking and bribe people to keep quiet about the health risks, then you're looking at a certain type.'

'True,' Rivera nodded. 'Wealthy and unscrupulous.'

'Exactly,' the locum doctor nodded. 'And if they're suitably wealthy *and* suitably unscrupulous, then they'll likely be pretty well-versed in covering their tracks.' He paused, turning to look directly at Rivera. 'You used to do military investigation, right?'

'That's right,' the ex-soldier nodded.

'So, you'd have followed the money, yes?' Garner went on.

'I...'

'You may as well admit it,' Cronkite protested. 'That's what you were telling me to do yesterday.'

Rivera nodded. 'Yes – but I think Jenna's already exhausted that particular pathway.'

'Oh, what - is that an apology?' the journalist questioned archly.

'I guess,' the ex-soldier looked at the floor. 'I don't know enough about it, but what Mark says is correct. If these are big fish, then a freelance journalist might have trouble making money links. I'm not saying I'd be able to do any better. You'd need a forensic accountant to do that. And, even if you had one, they'd have to have access to the kind of accounts that people who don't want to be uncovered will keep pretty well hidden.'

'So, other than you being slightly admonished, we're not much further to achieving anything, are we?' Cronkite began, relishing the opportunity to make sure Rivera felt her displeasure.

'Not really,' Rivera replied. 'And I still think that chasing financial proof will be like banging our heads against a wall. Accounts like that will be off-grid. Either that, or they'll be in Zurich or the Caymans – places where only the moneymen have any jurisdiction. Places where heavy investment buys silence.'

'So what do we do?' Garner enquired.

'I think we go old-school,' the ex-soldier answered.

'Old-school?' Cronkite frowned.

'Yeah,' Rivera nodded. 'Word of mouth. The word's out about the cholera.' He shrugged. 'If enough local people get pissed off, then they'll want to join in with the protests.' He paused. 'With any luck, that'll force GFP's hand. They won't want to risk the media coverage, especially as things seem to be snowballing now. So, hopefully, they'll panic. And if they do, they'll fuck up. There'll be a mistake – there always is.'

'And then?' Garner asked.

'And then we move,' the ex-soldier replied. 'So far, whenever we've looked at the fracking operation, it's looked like a solid wall. But I don't think it's like that – things rarely are. Usually, when you get set-ups like they have, they're too big. Too unwieldy. There are too many plates to keep spinning at the same time.' He paused, looking at his audience. 'And then, you tend to find that you're really just looking at houses of cards; they look solid from the front, but when you look at them from other angles, they're weak; fragile.'

'And you really think that's what we're looking at here?' the journalist frowned.

'Well, here's hoping,' the ex-soldier nodded. 'The cholera cases might be enough to shake the foundations. Then we just need a big, bad wolf to blow the whole thing down. They can't keep their eyes on everything. Not if the public gets involved. And, if they drop the ball, then let's see if we can look at Alexander. Cowerman and GFP are going to be guarded by firewall after firewall. But a consultant...'

'I'm on it,' Cronkite nodded. She turned to the locum doctor. 'Good stuff Garner – you're a dark horse, you know that?'

'Agreed,' Rivera nodded, looking at the other man. Secretly, he was pleased to re-enter the fray - walking away from a problem really wasn't his style. But he vowed to curb his baser instincts - he really didn't need any more drama.

Chapter 30

Prior to Cowerman's visit to LD Chopper Tours, Trout and Sanderson had either received orders remotely or they'd come via their handler. As the woman they'd only known before as Sierra Bravo strode into the room flanked by Foxtrot Delta and one other man, the two pilots did a double take. They were equal parts amazed at finally putting a face to the code name, and fearful. Brynworth was well off the beaten track, but the men still watched the news, and – in doing so – couldn't avoid the almost ubiquitous presence of Stella Cowerman. She was either in the press for all the right reasons or for all the wrong reasons. But she was always being talked about, nonetheless. Hers was a toxic brand of celebrity, but it was something that felt impossibly glamorous for Brynworth.

An hour earlier, the men had landed Big Bird. The drone flight had been a routine one, and they'd stowed the drone in its hangar as usual. After a night flight, both men usually sat up for a while unwinding with a bottle of beer and a few games of pool before they went to sleep. It was during their downtime that Cowerman had walked in. The fear came both from the unexpectedness of her appearance, and also from the knowledge of what she and her companions were capable of. Though neither of them mentioned it, rarely a day went by without them thinking of Granger's violent demise.

'Gentlemen,' she said breezily, her high heels clacking on the floor. 'Good morning.'

Trout and Sanderson mumbled a greeting in reply and watched as she formed her approximation of a smile for them. The politician was dressed for business in a black trouser suit. Over her shoulders, a dark, woollen knee-length coat hung open. She wore black leather gloves on her hands and stared at the two men with a piercing intensity emphasised by copious amounts of eyeliner. In the silence, the clear contempt she felt towards all such underlings was only thinly veiled.

'What can we do – er – Miss Cowerman?' Sanderson began – always the more confident of the pair. 'It's nice to put a face to the name of Sierra Bravo. And...'

'...we need somewhere to sit down,' the politician cut in impatiently.

'Of course,' Trout nodded.

***

'So, it's like this,' Cowerman started. Sanderson noted how Foxtrot Delta – who usually loved the sound of his own voice – was almost mute in her presence. He simply nodded in agreement with everything his superior said. 'You two have been doing decent work.' She paused. 'Or at least you have been since the other chancer was – er- dealt with.'

A heavy silence hung over the room, full of malice. Trout noticed the bulges of concealed weapons beneath the coats of both Foxtrot Delta and the other man.

'Anyway,' Cowerman continued. 'The data the drone has been gathering is extremely useful. *Extremely*. We're talking useful on a national security level here that we can share with our allies.' She paused.

'I'm sure my colleague has impressed upon you how vital secrecy is in this kind of an endeavour? It's not the kind of thing that can be taken lightly. We are fighting a war here – even if the rest of the country doesn't know it. And it's a war where gathering intelligence is key.'

The two pilots nodded eagerly, falling once more for the rhetoric that had hooked them in the first place.

'But it's not enough,' the politician went on, her grimace tightening further into a pained expression.

'It's not?' Trout's brow creased.

'No,' Foxtrot Delta insisted, interrupting his superior for the first time.

Cowerman turned to her associate and nodded. 'I'm just going to step outside. For a cigarette,' the politician announced, standing up abruptly.

'I never had you down as a smoker!' Trout raised his eyebrows quizzically, attempting an almost flirtatious tone.

'I'm not,' the politician smiled in reply.

As she walked away, accompanied by her other assistant, the pilots turned to Foxtrot Delta, frowning.

'Plausible deniability,' the handler announced in his mild London accent.

'What?' Sanderson's brow furrowed.

'Nothing incriminating,' Foxtrot Delta replied. 'You notice – she never says anything to give anyone the chance to pin things on her.' He grinned. 'Slippery shoulders! It must be bloody exhausting!'

Silence.

'If you're going to get done for something, then you have to have been in the room where it happened. Do you get me?'

The pilots nodded.

'But, even if you know what's going to be being said in the room, you can't be in there when it's said. Understand? Not if you're a woman in her position.'

Trout and Sanderson nodded once more as they processed the other man's words. The handler's accomplice, meanwhile, simply stared at them.

'Anyway... there are a couple of things her ladyship needs doing.' Foxtrot Delta paused. 'And that's where you come in. It's all to get this fracking bill passed.'

'Why's it such a big fucking deal?' Sanderson pressed brusquely.

Silence.

'I'm going to overlook that moment of familiarity,' the Londoner announced. His tone was thin-lipped; his face was stony. 'You are paid to follow orders,' he continued. 'Nothing more. Nothing less.' He sighed. 'I could get Sierra – er – Stella – to explain all this to you, but she's busy enough.' He paused. 'You know how much fuel we have to import in this country?'

The pilots stared back blankly.

'Too fucking much,' Foxtrot Delta went on. 'And that makes us weak. It puts us at the mercy of all sorts of rogue states and bad, bad people who have oil and know they can bend us over a barrel as long as we're reliant on it.' He paused. 'Hence fracking – if we can get this thing off the ground, then we loosen those shackles. This isn't just a matter of national security. It's a matter of national pride. This is the kind of thing that can make us regain our place in the world. Understand?'

Trout and Sanderson nodded back, uncertainly. Though neither of them were avid readers of newspapers, the other man's diatribe sounded almost exactly as though it had been peeled from the printed headlines that had pride of place on the racks of tabloids that bordered garage forecourts up and down the country.

'And that's why the bill needs to be ratified.' He paused. 'You've been flying sorties every night to gather information. We've given you the coordinates, and you've done a good job. A really bloody good job.' He grinned. 'If it was down to me, you'd have chests full of medals already. You've been combing the fracking site, and the Foulmile camp – it's full of terrorists, you know. Enemies of the people.' He grimaced. 'Just ask Cowerman – they're dressing up what they're doing as being about the environment, but it's got nothing to do with any of that.' He shook his head. 'They're in league with our enemies – them putting the kibosh on fracking is all because they're acting as agents for those who would threaten us.' Foxtrot Delta gritted his teeth; his voice grew steely. 'They *want* us to be dependent on foreign oil. They *want* us to be beholden to the whims of foreign dictators.' He slammed his hand down on the table. 'They may dress like tree-hugging hippies and present themselves like left-wing crusties, but they're terrorists. They're sponsored by Gulf states. They're bloody raking it in. And all the while, they make us look like a bunch of pussies.' He lowered his voice, speaking sadly. 'It's only brave people like Cowerman who have the strength and courage to stand up to them; to speak the truth. This is all part of a much wider conspiracy – to undermine our institutions and to enslave us under a modern version of communism.' He smiled suddenly. 'But Big Bird has been tracking their movements. We know where their supply lines are now. It's almost time for the endgame.'

The pilots nodded, their resolve clear.

'What do you need us to do?' asked Sanderson, seriously.

***

'And you think this guy – this Mister Alexander – is the problem?' Trout asked. Their handler had displayed a series of glossy prints. They were laid across the baize surface of the pool table and had clearly been taken with a long range lens. None of his behaviour was untoward – at least none of that depicted on the prints: he was entering the hospital; exiting the hospital; climbing into his car; talking with a colleague; standing on the enormous lawn in front of his house.

'Unfortunately, yes. I'm certain of it,' Foxtrot Delta replied. '*We're* certain of it. The problem is – he's delusional. He's fallen for the crusties' propaganda. And, as a result, he's got it into his head that there's a cholera outbreak.' He paused, uttering an exclamatory laugh at the ridiculousness of the idea. 'There isn't, of course. And, even if there had been, it would have nothing to do with the fracking.' He shook his head. 'But there's none so deaf as those who won't listen...'

'You want him – er – taken care of?' Sanderson asked.

'No,' Foxtrot Delta shook his head. 'Not yet, anyway. I just need you to put the frighteners on him. He's a very influential man. As Chief Medical Officer, what he says goes. He's been with us so far for the most part – we've given him a hymn sheet and he's sung straight from it - but he's starting to waver. And we can't have that.' He indicated the print of Alexander in the grounds of his house. 'He's got too much to lose to want to go against us – it should be easy to remind him about which side he's on.'

Sanderson nodded. 'And the other thing?'

'What?' Trout asked, frowning at his colleague.

'He said there were two tasks,' Sanderson replied, turning back to the handler.

'Three,' Foxtrot Delta announced. 'You're going to put those weapons on Big Bird to good use again.'

'Cool!' Trout chuckled gleefully. 'When?'

'When instructed,' the visitor replied. 'You see, there are old mine shafts beneath the Foulmile site. You're going to hit them. Well... hit the buildings above them on the surface, at least. We have scientists and geologists onside who will swear blind that the explosions are due to the protestors messing with the workings of the mines and uncovering pockets of gas. They'll also insist that it has nothing to do with the fracking.'

'And you think people will go for that?' Sanderson frowned. 'I mean...'

'...yes,' Foxtrot Delta nodded urgently. 'Especially when you get the third thing done. And that's getting rid of Jenna Cronkite – the journalist. She's been a pain in the arse of this whole operation from the beginning.' He paused. 'A thorn in our fucking side. We put the frighteners on some of her papers and magazines. They've played ball now – they won't touch her; they've realised that her left-wing rants are merely a veil for her communist, anti-British sentiments. But we can only really do that in this country. And even now, she still won't shut the fuck up. We'd hoped that cutting off her outlets might silence her, but it hasn't. We even thought about cutting out her tongue, but she'll still be able to fucking type. So... we're going to need to do something more drastic.'

The handler let the comment hang in the air for a moment.

'With the Foulmile camp gone, the movement won't have anywhere to coalesce around,' Foxtrot Delta continued. 'And with Cronkite out of the way, they won't have a voice.' He paused. 'They'll lose momentum. And if that happens, the bill will pass.' The man grinned. '*When* that happens, there'll be no turning back.'

Chapter 31

'She's not bloody held back this time, has she?' Mark Garner announced as he strode towards Daltrey brandishing the front page of *The Daily Despatch*. It was the day that he ran his weekly clinic at the Foulmile site. He'd picked up the paper at a newsagent near the hospital.

'Yeah – you've got that right!' the protestor nodded. 'What amazes me is how it's suddenly become OK to print bullshit like that.' He paused. 'Back in the day, I reckon even Enoch Powell would have baulked at using that kind of language. And yet there she is – bold as brass.'

Garner nodded. 'Have you read it?'

'No mate – I just saw the headline on the garage forecourt when I was filling up this morning.'

Daltrey was finishing putting out the awning for Garner's clinic. He attached it to the edge of a recreational vehicle's roof and then looped the other end around a stake that was driven into the ground. Garner looked back down the hill. Thirty yards away, a group of crows was pecking aggressively at the carcass of something unidentifiable. Further on, a pair of primary school-age children were throwing a ball back and forth. And, towards the perimeter fence, a group of men were gathered around the open bonnet of a truck engine. They were loudly pointing and gesticulating with wrenches and screwdrivers.

Still further away, by the wire itself, a couple of protestors looked to be standing sentinel. They'd tied their banners to the chain link as if in challenge to the members of Putsch Security, who would doubtless confront them later in the day.

'Want some selected highlights?' the locum doctor enquired, his tone a little playful as he scanned the newspaper.

'Go on then, doc,' Daltrey shrugged. 'Let's get my blood pressure skyrocketing, shall we?'

Garner cleared his throat. '*Cowerman's Cockroaches...*' he began. 'In media res.' He shook his head.

'What?'

'It's a Latin term meaning that something jumps straight into the action.'

'Fancy!'

'Yeah – pretentious, more like! Anyway... blah-blah-blah *The protestors at the camp are vermin.*' The locum doctor paused. 'It's all a bit 1930s Germany, isn't it? Language like that, I mean?'

'Too fucking right,' Daltrey nodded. 'They'll be painting yellow stars on our organic food stall down on the main road soon and having Putsch Security stand around saying *kauft nicht bei crustie.*'

Garner shook his head. 'Here we go, though – this is where it gets *really* good. *Cowerman announced in the House yesterday that she would be pushing for emergency amendments to the Public Order Act of 1986 and the Criminal Justice Act of 1994...*'

'... Jesus!' the protest leader spat.

'*... granting the Army emergency powers that will allow them to forcibly evict those resident on the Foulmile site.*' Garner paused. 'She then goes on to describe us all as *terrorists.*'

'Well, she's a fucking charmer – isn't she just!' Daltrey shook his head. 'This is as good as a declaration of war, isn't it?'

'Yeah, I reckon,' the locum doctor nodded. 'And it's as good as proof that she's definitely behind all the shit that's happening around here,' he went on. 'Even if we can't actually *prove* it. And even if we knew it already.'

Daltrey lit a cigarette. 'Clever though, isn't it?'

'What?' Garner's tone was incredulous.

'The way they've done it,' Daltrey went on. 'The way money goes to money.' He paused. 'I reckon for a while back there, the establishment started shitting bricks about how the commoners were going to rise up. They were worried it was going to be Wat Tyler all over again. The aristocrats lost their land and their influence, and then they went and gave the great unwashed forty years of free education! They must have been mad!' He drew hard on his cigarette. 'But the establishment's clever – people don't give them enough credit sometimes. They're patient and cunning. And they just double down on things.' He paused. 'That's what this whole shift to the right has been about. It's like chipping away at a coal seam. When you start out, you get powder and a few little scraps of the good stuff. But – if you keep going – you end up with nothing left.' Daltrey shook his head. 'That's what they've tried to do with our resistance, isn't it?'

'How do you figure that?' the locum doctor enquired.

'Well, they've shrunk school curriculums for starters, haven't they?' he explained. 'They want everyone doing maths and science.' He shrugged. 'I've got nothing against those subjects, but they're not the kinds of things that make people question the world very much, are they? From what my union friends tell me, they've done the same with English. Quantified it. Made it binary. That's how you suppress dissent.'

'All very Chomsky,' Garner grinned.

'Yeah, manufacturing consent,' Daltrey nodded. He paused. 'I got up early this morning.'

'That right?' the locum doctor replied, unsure of where the other man was going with his comment.

'Yeah,' the protestor nodded. 'There's a mission – a café out behind one of the churches in Brynworth that caters for us crusties. Pretty much anyone who's down on their luck – homeless. Drunks. You know the kind of place.' He paused. 'I guess I fit right in.'

Silence.

'They do scrambled eggs and toast for like a quid fifty.' Daltrey paused. 'The coffee's good too.' He yawned for a moment, scratching at his stubble. 'It's a good place to go and think every once in a while – everyone keeps themselves to themselves in a joint like that. It's not the kind of place you go to if you don't have problems. Anyway,' he went on, 'I cast my eyes around in there and got a decent look at most of the people: crap clothes; unwashed; bearded; hopeless; helpless.' He scratched at his stubble once more. 'It kind of felt like people just waiting around to die.'

Garner nodded. He opened his mouth to speak and then closed it again.

'All of those people Cowerman criticises in the papers – they're all in there. All of lowlife's rich tapestry.' The protestor shook his head. 'And that constant drip-feeding of hatred towards them – the unemployed; the homeless; the crusties – it's taken root. It doesn't shock anybody any more.' He paused. 'It's like what the Nazis did way back when – if you spend long enough dehumanising a section of society, then people start to view them as different – almost like they're not the same species.' Daltrey shook his head. 'And that makes it far easier to accept it when those same people are treated badly.'

'You think that's what Cowerman's doing, then?' the locum doctor said.

'Yeah, I'm sure of it – so when the bulldozers eventually roll over Foulmile, your average Joe will probably think they're doing everyone a favour. That's what they've been trying to do from the start – make us seem like the enemy.'

Garner nodded. 'Sad but true.'

'It's right out of Goebbels' playbook mate,' Daltrey continued. He frowned. 'Have you ever heard of a country called Muzayaf?'

'No,' the locum doctor shook his head. 'Why?'

'It was mentioned in an article I read while I was at the mission the other day.'

'Yeah?'

'Yeah – Cowerman claimed that we're entirely reliant on oil from there, and that it's causing massive increases in immigration.' Daltrey shook his head. 'But both of those things are absolute bullshit. It turns out Muzayaf is a tiny emirate in the Persian Gulf. It's so small, it'd give the Vatican City State a run for its money. There's a little oil there, but nothing like the amount she's talking about.'

'So she's lying?' Garner said.

'You could say that,' Daltrey nodded. 'If you wanted a medal for understatement. And linking it to immigration is absolute nonsense – in the article she claimed that fracking will solve everything; it'll mean British jobs for British workers and…' he rolled his eyes, 'it'll magically mean no more immigration.'

The locum doctor shook his head in disbelief.

'I know, right?' the protestor went on. 'That's what she's shitting herself about more than anything – she's been making promises about cutting numbers and stopping the small boats. I reckon she's going to claim that - through things like this – she's the only one doing anything about it.' Daltrey shook his head. 'But the more of this stuff they print, the more people start to believe it.' He paused. 'And immigration is a hot topic anyway – it was, even before her. You just use invasion rhetoric and people will swallow lies left, right and centre. It's like at Nuremberg – Goering said that all you have to do is tell people they're being attacked, and denounce the pacifists for lack of patriotism. It forces people to choose sides – as if they have a binary choice.' He shook his head once more. 'So in Cowerman's eyes, you're either a good-honest-pro-fracking-patriot, or you're the enemy.' Daltrey paused. 'And you and me, my friend – well, certainly me... are very much in the latter camp.'

Chapter 32
London, UK.

Marley Cuthbert-Wayne practically collapsed into the large plush chair behind his office desk. When Cowerman had arrived that morning, he'd excused himself immediately. Five minutes later, he'd returned. His eyes were bloodshot, he was sniffing loudly; he periodically rubbed his finger across the end of his nose in an absent-minded fashion.

His visitor frowned. The Managing Director of Wessex Capital had always presented as flawless in the past. His wardrobe was immaculate, albeit more suited to the Edwardian era than the modern world, but the figure before her seemed dishevelled; unhinged. Previously, the man had always carried himself with the calm assurance of one who was utterly convinced by the righteousness of his actions. He'd always borne himself with the bearing of one who considered himself born to rule, and he'd always moved in a manner that suggested he regarded all those who crossed his path to be several fathoms beneath him in importance. This morning, though, it felt like the man's mask had slipped. Cowerman saw something she'd never seen upon his face before.

Doubt.

***

The night before, Cuthbert-Wayne had been at The Ivory Club. Bankrolled by the trade in elephant tusks during the Victorian era, it remained one of London's oldest and most exclusive gentlemen's clubs. Indeed, it was so exclusive that it didn't even have a website; there was no need – if you were not a known figure, then there was no way you'd be permitted to cross the threshold. It didn't matter how much money one possessed – access to the institution was determined by reputation and privilege alone. Once upon a time, it was rumoured that prospective members had to be able to prove their lineage going back through three centuries of aristocratic breeding. These days, things had changed, though. Even a place like The Ivory Club realised that it was money that made the world go round. Commerce trumped cultural capital every time. But there was still a hangover from the old days. Beneath its vaulted ceilings and behind his stained glass windows, new money was still considered crass and uncouth. Everyone that availed themselves of its mahogany-furnished reception rooms was enormously wealthy, but they were also in possession of the other, more difficult-to-define quality the club's overseers considered a pre-requisite: class.

Cowerman had no clear idea about what Cuthbert-Wayne had been up to. It wasn't just that women weren't permitted to join The Ivory Club; women weren't even permitted to enter the establishment. Members were sworn to secrecy – it was rumoured that representatives of the royal family and even ex-prime ministers had spent time on the Mayfair premises, but there was no public record of this. It was understood that new members had to be vouched for by a minimum of forty signatories to maintain exclusivity. Fees were undisclosed, but annual payments were thought to be in the region of thirty thousand pounds. There would – almost certainly – be a hefty joining fee, too. The Masonic secrecy of The Ivory Club was such that the exploits of its members had become the stuff of legend; they were wrapped in rumour. It was widely believed that a pharmacist was in situ who could dispense pure versions of whichever pills, powders and serums members wished to procure. In response to steep bribes and heavy tips, willing women and men were smuggled into members' rooms. There were also unsubstantiated whisperings of further, more depraved actions, too. Cowerman had no desire to know about such things. Nor did she have much interest in what Cuthbert-Wayne had been doing. She was simply shocked at how rough he looked.

'Well?' he began, clearing his throat and spitting into a silk handkerchief.

The visitor opened her mouth to speak. As she did, she shook her head slightly, as if in an effort to banish the vision before her. Three years previously, Marley Cuthbert-Wayne had been the third most mentioned name in British politics as surveyed by the UK Press Commission. His ascendency had been on a steep curve; through continually banging the drum about the need for dismantling the National Health Service, he'd become a right-wing totem. His self-assurance and calmness under pressure were all but legendary.

But, the man in front of Cowerman was a mess. Against the dark wooden panelling of his office, his visage appeared to be pale; ghost-like. He lifted a paper from his desk, but then put it down as it accentuated the uncontrolled shaking of his hands.

'Well, what?' the visitor frowned. 'You called the meeting.'

Cuthbert-Wayne narrowed his eyes. The red rings around them spoke of sleeplessness. As Cowerman watched, the man opposite scratched vigorously at the skin of his forearms. He gritted his teeth, as if – by force of willpower alone – he could rid himself of the chemical residue that was clearly racking his thoughts. 'I did?'

'You did,' Cowerman nodded.

'I mean – I *did*. Of course I did,' the man nodded. He placed his hands flat on the desk. Usually, his nails were filed and manicured. Now, though, a couple of them were rimed with black dirt. Where he'd picked subconsciously at the flesh on his thumbs, the broken skin had formed itself into the scabs of stepmothers' blessings. He lifted a hand to scratch at his neck. Where it had lain on the desk, a handprint of clammy perspiration remained.

'So... what did you want to discuss?' the visitor pressed.

'I had a call from our American cousins yesterday,' Cuthbert-Wayne said, lowering his voice. 'The deal with Insignia TX is hanging by a thread.' He raised his voice in an angry timbre. 'A fucking thread! Do you hear me?'

'I... what the fuck do you want me to do about it?' Cowerman frowned, annoyed. 'I thought you were dealing with that side of things now? You and Jaggers?'

'Update me,' the man replied, regarding his opposite number with searing contempt. 'Now.'

The visitor nodded. As she prepared to make her report, she caught a slight glimmer of something in Cuthbert-Wayne's eyes. It was only a flicker, and it died as swiftly as it had arisen. But it was definitely not something she'd seen written on his face before.

She gave a small start as it dawned on her: it was fear.

Chapter 33
Lancashire, UK.

'You've done a number here, then!' Rivera looked around at Daltrey's handiwork with a mixture of approval and astonishment. The pair were in one of the tunnels that he'd dug. It led away from the mine shaft the ex-soldier had been shown previously. It was smaller and narrower; its supports weren't as strong and they were more spread out. But it was illuminated by strings of fairy lights, and the protestor had built in ventilation holes at regular intervals. Where the mine tunnels had been dry and dusty, this one was damp, and boggy underfoot.

'Yeah,' the protestor nodded. 'Years ago, I worked with an old American guy called Herb.' He paused. 'He'd been a tunnel rat. You know what I mean?'

'Vietnam, right?'

'Correct,' Daltrey nodded. 'He was one of the poor fuckers who had to go in and clear the underground passages the Viet Cong had dug. It was an impossible task.'

'So you thought you'd do the same here?' the ex-soldier asked.

'Exactly! I was almost done and then I struck the mine shaft – that opened up a whole different set of possibilities, of course.'

Rivera nodded. 'You didn't do this all on your own, though, did you?'

'No,' Daltrey laughed, tracing a rivulet of water as it ran down the tunnel wall. 'I had a few of the lads helping me – it would have taken years otherwise.'

'So, why are showing me this?'

'The hour is nigh, my friend. I think we've spooked them. I wouldn't be too surprised if they come rolling over us any day now.'

The two men carried on, picking their way into another shallow tunnel that ran nearer the road. Both of them switched on the head torches that Daltrey had provided.

'This was all built using Herb's instructions,' Daltrey said. 'All my tunnels were.' He paused and looked at the ex-soldier, blinding him for a moment with the glare of his torch. 'The Yanks used to flush tunnel entrances with gas or water. Sometimes, they'd just drop a few grenades down and hope for the best, but it never worked. They carpet-bombed Củ Chi with B-52s, but it did fuck-all. The tunnels are still there today.' The protestor shook his head in admiration, and – as he did – the beam cast wild shadows on the rough tunnel walls. 'Uncle Sam was shipping over a thousand refrigerators a week, and Charlie could survive underground for a month just on the rice they were carrying in their pockets.' He paused. 'Of course, they all had malaria and terrible parasites, but you can't have everything, can you?'

Silence.

'It's easy for us, anyway. Herb used to talk about the unfriendly wildlife that anyone underground had to contend with out there.'

'Snakes?' Rivera began. 'Scorpions?'

'Yeah,' Daltrey nodded. 'And spiders; ants; centipedes – horrible bastards, he said.' He paused. 'Anyway, when you build them zig-zagged, any infiltration only affects one section. They're pretty much blast-proof as a result. We haven't had time here, but – if we were *really* serious – we could put in blind alleys and extra storage areas – stuff like that.'

The protestor nodded to himself. 'We don't really need to now, though – not with the mine and all.' He smiled for a moment, lost in reverie. 'Crazy as a fucking wedge Herb was – he grew up in Brooklyn. They have their own version of a Chelsea Smile over there, you know?'

'That so?'

'Yeah,' the protestor went on. 'He was smart, though – Herb. I mean, smart enough to see how the VC designed everything. They were very careful with air flow, so we've used the same tactics here. And we've done the same as they did with having multiple exits.' He paused. 'Right now we're down by the road, but there are seven other places you can hop in and hop out at. I'm going to give you a map.'

'You really think that's necessary?' the ex-soldier frowned.

'What? The map?'

'No – all the exits.'

Daltrey sighed. 'I love all the guys we have here. And I love the way they've all come to join me.' He grinned. 'Their hearts are in the right place, but none of them will have a fucking clue what to do once the shit hits the fan. Present company excepted, of course – I reckon you'll be just fine.'

'Speaking from experience, are you?' the ex-soldier enquired.

'I am – and that's why I know what bastards the police can be.' He coughed, the dusty subterranean air catching in his throat for an instant. 'I'm an old git now, but when I was a youngster, I left home and fell in with *The Peace Convoy*. They used to call us New Age Travellers back then in the mid-Eighties. Anyway, we were heading for Stonehenge for a free festival, but the coppers had other ideas.' Daltrey shook his head. 'It was wild, man! They went ballistic. Full riot gear. They were clubbing anyone that moved. I swear to you that I saw kids being hit with truncheons, and pregnant women too. It was a fucking outrage!'

Silence fell in the tunnel. The flow of air from a distant ventilation shaft made a strange, black echo.

'It was the biggest round of civilian arrests since the Second World War,' the protest leader went on. 'They call it the Battle of the Beanfield now – The Levellers even wrote a song about it, so it's all romanticised and nicey nicey. They pass it off like a piece of folklore, but it was no fucking picnic being there at the time. We had nowhere to retreat to.'

'Hence the tunnels,' the ex-soldier said.

'Too fucking right,' Daltrey nodded. 'The thing is, they had no motive for doing what they did. Some of them were done for GBH and ABH, but not many. There was a full-on press cover-up.' He paused. 'But that was *then*. These days, when the right-wing press can print anything they want, they'll just demonise any victims. It's not like there'll be any benevolent old Earl of Cardigans to bang the drum for democracy and the rule of law, either. The bad guys have stuffed the House with peers who're sympathetic to them.' The protestor cleared his throat once again and spat on the mulched floor. 'What freaks me out is that these guys have a motive now. They're not just pissed off about us protesting, or gathering. Someone stands to make a whole lot of money; that's always going to make things worse. And then there's Putsch Security – it's like their own private army.'

Rivera nodded. 'Yeah. I'd far sooner face the boys in blue.'

'Damn right!' the protestor agreed. 'But it's a line in the dirt we're drawing here. If we lose this, then we can kiss goodbye to any kind of liberal equality ... that's the way I see it.'

'So you're making a stand?'

'We've all got to have a hill to die on,' Daltrey said ruefully.

'Or a tunnel to dig in ...' Rivera shrugged.

'Yeah – fucking comedian, you are!' the protestor scoffed. 'But there's nothing funny about innocent skulls being busted with billy clubs.'

'No,' the ex-soldier nodded. 'You're right about that.'

Chapter 34

'I can't do it, Ms Cowerman.' Nola Scruggs had a tone that was polite but insistent. As Head of the Brynworth Town Council, she didn't wield enormous power. Nevertheless, when it came to political issues, she was able to exert a significant amount of influence. It helped that she'd been in post for nearly twenty years - there was nobody from any side of the political spectrum that she didn't know. She was a canny negotiator; when it came to passing motions, the chamber very rarely voted against her. But that was largely because Scruggs was a rarity. She was utterly altruistic and had Brynworth's best interests at heart in all that she did.

'What do you mean can't?' the politician seethed at the other end of the phone line.

'You heard me, ma'am,' Scruggs replied, her voice unwaveringly calm. 'Were I to agree with what you're proposing – which, incidentally, I do *not* - I wouldn't be able to pass it myself.' She paused, and doodled on a pad of paper she kept beside her landline for jotting down memos. Beside it was a framed photograph of her late husband. It had been five years since he'd passed away from a sudden heart attack – he'd been twelve months off retirement, but his memory still burned brightly within her at all times. When he was alive, they'd joked about how they were a civic power couple: she, head of the council, and he – head of Brynworth Comprehensive. The high school – one of the largest in the country had an enormous catchment area which made Eli Scruggs a very well-known man. He worked tirelessly for the benefit of his charges, doing battle with inspectors and advocating tirelessly with external agencies to improve the life chances of his students. At a dinner party, a friend of theirs had described Mr and Mrs Scruggs as being entirely incorruptible.

It was a fair assessment.

And it was this that Cowerman was finding so difficult to process. 'How much?' she demanded.

'Excuse me?' Scruggs frowned.

'You heard,' the politician sighed. 'How much will it take for you to change your mind?'

'Ma'am,' the Councillor began in a matronly tone. 'I'm going to pretend I didn't hear that.' She paused. 'Now... if there's nothing else I can help you with.'

'I...' Cowerman began.

But the line had gone dead.

***

Cowerman and Scruggs knew each other reasonably well – in return for the funding of a new public library, the Councillor had secured the chamber's vote to modify the existing zoning laws surrounding the fracking site. It had seemed like an innocuous enough proposal; Green Fuel Prospects had sold itself as doing exploratory work for thermal energy. The pitch its representatives had delivered to the council had made much of its eco-friendly credentials. Various graphs had been displayed, outlining aims of becoming carbon neutral, and jobs had been promised to the local community. The company had secured its zoning application; the council considered it a victory shortly afterwards when they'd made GFP commit to building a new service road. And the deeds for the site had been rewritten as a result in order to change the route of the existing two-lane. Its reclassification meant it was now considered an area that was removed from local council adoption. Corporate representatives had justified this by promising the company would now take over the cost of maintaining both the land and the new road. Seeing a possibility to save money, the council had acceded.

It had been a mistake.

Once the fracking machinery moved in, the council realised it had been sold a dummy. It wasn't something they reacted to kindly. They were – by and large – well-meaning, civically minded souls, and Scruggs, in particular, was desperate to bring the public back onside. Hence the obstacles they'd thrown up to delay GFP's initiatives.

Put simply, anything Stella Cowerman or the GFP proposed was flatly refused. The council had been horrified at the way their vote had been interpreted. They'd been shocked, too, at how the terms of their local bill had allowed the group they now saw as their number one foe to have so much latitude. Putsch Security had been an additional surprise. A sting in the tail. With the area no longer under adoption, the police had no jurisdiction.

As a result, the army of private security guards held sway.

GFP believed the new zoning law would be enough. What they hadn't reckoned on were the legions of protestors that descended on the Foulmile camp. What had been even more irritating was that – owing to the terms of the peppercorn rent agreement in place for the former commune – the protestors were free to remain in place. It was a conundrum that Marley-Cuthbert-Wayne's Wessex Capital had engaged several different firms of lawyers to contest. They wanted the protestors gone, but they could find no legal statute to support their aims.

To date, all its litigiousness had been to no avail.

Following her strange meeting with the still-half-drunk Cuthbert-Wayne, Cowerman had made another call to Scruggs. With the blank cheque Wessex Capital had given her, she'd proposed a compulsory purchase order being placed on the Foulmile site. But, no matter how many promises of either cash or construction she'd made, the Councillor hadn't been interested.

Nola Scruggs was holding firm.

***

'Yes?' Scruggs said, picking up the handset.

'You would dare to hang up on me!' Cowerman's tone was thin-lipped with hatred.

'I would,' the Councillor replied, unimpressed. 'I think the *real* question, ma'am, surrounds the fact that you would dare to attempt bribery upon me – an elected public official.'

'You forget that I'm an elected public official too,' the Westminster politician huffed.

'My dear,' Scruggs said, tonelessly. 'I believe you forgot that fact long ago. We must be mindful that elected officials don't just have privileges; they have responsibilities too.'

Silence.

'Watch yourself, Scruggs,' Cowerman spat.

'I beg your pardon?'

'You heard,' the politician answered.

Silence.

'Is that a threat, ma'am?' Scruggs said, eventually.

Cowerman sighed. 'You think you're so fucking smug, don't you? Living there in your rural backwater.' She paused. 'Be warned – it might not be quiet for too long... ma'am.'

This time, it was the politician who hung up.

Chapter 35

'I've got a problem,' Mister Alexander announced as Stella Cowerman answered the phone. He was sitting in his Mercedes in the hospital car park, calling on an app that encrypted any calls or messages. He didn't even know such a thing existed until his dealings with her.

'You're telling me,' the politician replied. 'I gave you a very simple task – to keep a lid on things. But you don't even seem to have managed that, do you?'

'It's not that simple,' the consultant protested as he watched the driving rain cloud his windscreen.

'So find a solution,' Cowerman said icily. The line was delivered with a vitriol caused by desperation. Bullies bully: she was simply lashing out at the consultant in reaction to the mistreatment she'd received at Cuthbert-Wayne's hands.

Silence.

'I believe I might need some assistance with doing that,' Alexander sighed.

'Go on...'

***

'Mark Garner? Who the hell's he?'

'A locum – I mentioned him before.'

'But I thought you'd taken care of him?' the politician said, frowning.

'I *had*. At least I tried,' Alexander answered. 'But he's more committed than I thought he'd be. Certainly for someone in his lowly position. I've headed him off and shut him up – I've even given him false test results, but he's like a dog with a bloody bone. He's just not letting these cases go.'

'Cases plural? I thought you said there was only one.'

Silence. The consultant was suddenly aware of the drumming of rain on the car's rooftop.

'We're talking about cholera, right?' Cowerman continued, cautiously.

'We are,' Alexander nodded. 'Yes. I told him there was only one case, that it was gastroenteritis - but he didn't fall for it. And that was with only *one* case - we've got something of an outbreak now.' He paused. 'This has gone beyond being just the kid who was on the isolation ward at Lancaster West.'

'So?'

'So, now we've got cases at Brynworth Health – the private place.'

'And?' Cowerman pressed impatiently.

'It's a private hospital. It's clean and shiny. I would imagine you have constituents that are on the board, and cholera is borne of poverty. It won't look good.'

Silence.

'Brynworth Health looks the part for glossy magazines and brochures,' Alexander went on. 'But when it comes to actually dealing with things like this, it's the NHS place that has the expertise. We've had to move the private cases over there.' He paused. 'We're not going to be able to keep a lid on things for long. People will start asking questions.'

'So, what the hell do you want me to do about it?' the politician asked; her tone was one of exasperation.

Alexander sighed. 'You said that your ways were always simple, right? Identify the problem and then find a solution.'

The call was not a video one, so the consultant didn't see Cowerman roll her eyes. 'Haven't you figured it out yet?'

'What?'

'What the hell's the matter with you? Just because politicians say things, it doesn't mean they mean them literally. What are you – stupid?' She sighed. 'Go on then – tell me. Who's the problem?'

'Well, you know *what* the problem is,' Alexander answered in annoyance. 'Cholera – and we can be pretty certain that it's being caused by the waste water from the Brynworth fracking site.'

'Dammit, doctor!' Cowerman's tone was terse. Angry. 'I didn't ask you *what* the problem was – the drilling will continue whether the crusties like it or not. The site will be declared safe, and fracking will be rolled out across the country. Bullshit accusations of cholera outbreaks or no bullshit accusations.' She paused. 'We *all* know that – that's why you're remunerated so handsomely for your troubles.' The politician cleared her throat. 'You'll have hidden that money, no doubt – but sums like that can always be located. And, when they are, people will wonder where it all came from.' She tapped at the desk. 'Anyway, I didn't ask you *what* the problem was. I asked you *who* the problem was...'

'Take your pick,' the consultant shrugged. 'There's that journalist, for starters.'

'Don't worry about her – things are in-hand as far as she's concerned. If I'm going to help you, then you're going to need to be specific. Now, you mentioned the locum?'

'Yeah. Garner - Mark Garner. He splits his time between Lancaster West and Brynworth Health.'

'And he's the one that's been sticking his nose in where it's not wanted?'

'He has.'

The politician sighed. 'Leave it with me. We obviously haven't talked...'

'Understood.'

Cowerman made a clicking noise as she ran her tongue against the back of her teeth. 'Any updates, you let me know. I'm your first call every time.'

The politician hung up.

Chapter 36

'Are you sure you want to go ahead with this?' Jenna Cronkite enquired. She and Daltrey were sitting beneath the awning where Garner ran his pop-up clinic. She had a thick coat zipped up against the wind. He, meanwhile, seemed all but impervious to the cold. Two chipped mugs of strong tea sat steaming on the trestle table between them.

'Yeah,' the protestor nodded. 'We need to roll the dice one last time. I'll go fully on the record.' He paused. 'Where did you say you'll get it published?'

'Everywhere and anywhere,' the journalist replied. 'Anywhere that'll stick it up online. We'll just have to hope your notoriety will be enough to make places run with the story.'

'So, we're not using fake names?'

'No – I think we'll have to break cover for this one,' Cronkite answered. 'You said yourself that there are storm clouds brewing, right?'

'Yeah.'

'So, I reckon we just put the pedal to the metal this time. If people aren't going to go for this, then they're not going to go for anything. We have nothing to lose.'

Daltrey nodded, grimacing. 'And you're going to write about Sapphire Phoenix and the cholera cases?'

'I will – if you put your name to it.'

Silence. He ground his teeth for a moment, looking hard at her.

'Yeah – you've got it. A man needs a cause to fight for. I guess this has been my one long enough.' He paused. 'I don't know if we'll succeed here – there's a part of me that doesn't really see how we can when we're up against the kind of resources they've got. But I may as well go down fighting. They're going to do me for libel and defamation and all sorts of things anyway, so why not go the whole hog and publicly link Cowerman to this whole fucking fiasco?' He grinned. 'That should ruffle a few feathers...'

***

'So,' Cronkite enquired, having gone through her list of questions. 'Other than the cholera, are there other health issues?'

'Yes,' Daltrey nodded, speaking into her Dictaphone. 'But they're not very easy to prove: respiration problems; the kids living onsite continually have the shits; coughs; sickness bugs.' His voice trailed off. 'The problem is that the powers that be would put all of those things down to living in caravans and the like. Them demonising and dehumanising us in the ways they have means that people will be pretty accepting of ideas like that too. They just painted us as deadbeats – members of the underclass. Know what I mean?'

The journalist nodded.

'Then there's the pollution, of course,' Daltrey went on. 'Petroleum hydrocarbons like benzene and xylene – neither of them are going to do anyone any good. And they're only the ones we've been able to test for with our limited equipment.' He shrugged. 'Plenty of scientists have written about how fracking raises ground-level ozone levels too, so you get issues with asthma and other things.' The protestor scratched at his stubble. 'You've only got to look at the amount of dead fish in the streams and rivers around here to see how much fluid contamination there is in the water.' He paused. 'You might want to quote a recognised scientist on some of this stuff if you can. Then you have toxic air pollutants like methane.' He grinned. 'GFP stands for Green Fuel Prospects. The biggest misnomer there is the word *green*. They're claiming their operation is good for the environment, but the amount of greenhouse gases they're producing is off the scale. It'd turn Dubai green with envy.'

Cronkite smiled thinly. 'Then there's the noise too, right?'

'Yeah,' the protestor nodded. 'But they get around that pretty easily. They have inspectors wandering around with SLMs from time to time.'

'SLMs?'

'Sound Level Meters – they're pretty much within accepted limits.' Daltrey paused. 'At least they always are when the emissions are being measured. The fact we're so remote here stands in their favour too – they can always claim that nobody is really impacted.'

The journalist nodded.

'And last but not least,' the protestor went on, 'are the earthquakes.' He sighed. 'They call it micro-seismicity. Any drilling is going to cause disturbances – it always does. But they've had geologists and seismologists come here who've sworn blind the magnitudes are always less than 2.0 on the Richter Scale. That means they can't be felt by humans.' Daltrey laughed, bitterly. 'I'm here to tell you that's absolute bullshit.' He paused once more. 'That's the only thing that freaks me out about going underground – if it comes to it, I mean. I've spent a great deal of my adult life in tunnels. Too much of it, really. It's what I'm known for if you search for me online. But I've been down in those tunnels when they're drilling and blasting and flushing over the road. And I can tell you that what they're doing is definitely detectable by humans. *Very* fucking detectable.' He looked hard at the journalist. 'I'm brave enough – I guess. Either that, or I'm pretty stupid – and there are plenty who'd tell you that's the case.' He sighed. 'I'll go underground if they send in the troops, but I'm not overly keen on the idea of being buried alive. And those shafts and supports aren't as strong as I'd like. The fracking has weakened them. Compromised them. There's no doubt in my mind. The scientists who say there's no tectonic movement have been paid off. Fact.'

Silence.

'So, what now?' Daltrey asked as Cronkite pressed a button on the Dictaphone to cease recording. She took the device off the trestle table and slid it into the inside pocket of her jacket.

'I write it up, and we see who'll carry it,' the journalist shrugged. 'Just like we said. And if people like it and want more, then I come back here for round two and we give them something else to chew on. You've pretty much bared your soul – you'll just have to bare it some more. You OK with that?'

'I am,' the protestor smiled. 'I've got nothing to lose. Good on you, Jenna!'

Chapter 37
London, UK.

For a law to be passed by Parliament, first a bill has to be proposed. Though it was Amanda Dodderington – the MP for Chikfield - who'd first proposed the Environmental Standards Bill, it was common knowledge that Stella Cowerman and Marley Cuthbert-Wayne were the forces behind it. They'd distanced themselves in the first instance, lest they became too closely linked with it in the mind of the public. But it had gained a presence seldom afforded to other bills.

The press had seized upon its introduction, and common parlance now referred to it as The Fracking Bill. It was a topic interesting enough to dominate the front pages of many tabloid newspapers; it divided opinion. Plenty believed the rhetoric spouted about fracking being the solution to the nation's economic ills. Indeed, there were many who supported the idea of it being rapidly expanded. On the other side of the fence, though, there were those who were vehemently opposed to shale gas drilling.

Calling in favours, Cuthbert-Wayne had managed to sneak the bill's first reading into a session of Parliament that was sparsely attended. All those involved knew the road to approval by the House and the securing of the Royal Assent that would turn the bill into an Act would be a long and difficult one. In a couple of weeks, it was scheduled to have its second reading, where it would be debated in the House. Though contentious, with the majority their party had, the proposers of the bill were reasonably confident they could get it over the line. The issue was the number of irksome amendments that would doubtless be proposed.

Had the drilling at Brynworth simply taken place quietly, and out of the public eye, it was highly unlikely there would have been much furore.

But that was not the case.

The more column inches the issue was given, the more amendments would doubtless be proposed. More amendments meant the essence of the bill being diluted. This was something GFP was anxious to avoid; Insignia TX had come on board with a set of very clear demands. Benning's company had a clear priority: its responsibility to its shareholders. They'd invested considerable sums of money and expected to see significant returns. As a result, the American company had no time for amendments.

***

The charm offensive behind the proposed bill faltered from the start. Neither Cowerman nor Cuthbert-Wayne were likeable enough to convince people to side with them.

And that included members of their own party.

Politicians are pragmatic. Many are Machiavellian. But, even then, many of them failed to be seduced by the promises GFP made. At their core, many members of the House are governed by self-interest. Feathering their own nests is only possible if they remain in post. No matter how positive the proposals being proffered, the issue of fracking had become toxic. Members of the party were well aware their voting stances on the issue would be scrutinised. Drilling for shale gas was not popular, and most voters had a not-in-my-back-yard mind-set. Even engaging a top-drawer PR company had done little to thaw attitudes.

Support had waned, so Cowerman and Cuthbert-Wayne had shifted away from attempting charm. Instead, they adopted a willingness to secure votes by any means necessary. When in Westminster, their days were largely consumed by cajoling, bribing, and threatening colleagues to do as they desired.

Their current focus was on planting amendments. The plan was straightforward; if a wealth of amendments was proposed, it would appear to the general public that the bill had received proper scrutiny. In truth, the amendments were irrelevant – they were purely minor adjustments to bolster pre-existing ideas. It was designed as a sleight of hand, but – in order to have the bill pass in a way that suited their aims – the pair needed to enlist the help of supporters who were prepared to go on record as being in favour of it.

Despite their best efforts, it still wasn't going well. Cowerman's face was perpetually screwed up with her scowling smile and puckered nose. Cuthbert-Wayne, meanwhile, wore an unmoving mask of automated indifference. His fixed smile was unconvincing; his contempt was continually clear. Had either of them ever possessed any charisma, it had seemingly been transplanted long ago.

And the MP for Eastington was drinking more and more heavily. The public persona he wished to portray and the reality of his nocturnal behaviour was becoming blurred; he was a Twenty-First Century version of the Victorian Compromise. As a married man who'd sired several children, he portrayed himself as a staunch family man. But for the last couple of weeks, he'd slept at the Ivory Club. The excesses he'd indulged in on a nightly basis there had started to show; it was taking him longer each day to loosen himself from the claws of whichever hangover or comedown was clutching at him. With every obstruction the bill faced, he seemed to crawl further into the bottle, and to bury his nose deeper in the mounds of white powder his club provided.

His second most pressing issue – he was convinced - remained the newspapers.

And, in particular, Jenna Cronkite.

Cuthbert-Wayne despised the freedom of the press. Along with his other missions, he'd been working to remove articles relating to freedom of expression in the Human Rights Act – he felt they weren't applicable. But, with every gagging order he and Wessex Capital tried to impose, there was wiggle room; there was always somewhere on the internet that would publish stories counter to what he wanted. The web was too porous and too liberal for his liking. His preference would have been for a new style of democracy; one where the country would be governed by a kind of altruistic totalitarianism. One where he could control the narrative.

But that was a long-term plan.

For now, he just wanted to get the bill through Parliament. Deep down, the politician was worried about the lack of progress he was making. He was concerned by the veiled threats his American allies had made. Cuthbert-Wayne was only too aware that a slip-up on something like this could have massively negative consequences for the other projects he involved himself with.

The politician stared at his glazed, vampire expression in the glass of the wall mirror above the sink of the bathroom. His eyes were bloodshot, and his skin had the grey, unhealthy sheen of not having been troubled by sunlight. Pressing issue number one – Cuthbert-Wayne sighed to himself – was that the law was too nice. He spat into the sink and vowed it was time for real action.

If any obstacles existed, he would simply remove them.

Chapter 38

That Jenna Cronkite's article caused a reaction was unsurprising. It was posted online on a number of sites. Some of them were reputable, while others were the type given to pushing sensationalist stories. The GFP's lawyers were swift to act, but they weren't so quick that the story wasn't shared through innumerable channels before it was taken down.

In writing the piece, the journalist pulled no punches. Fracking at the Brynworth site was blamed for poisoning the water supply; damaging crops through its release of contaminated wastewater; destroying plants; causing earthquakes; putting dangerous chemicals into the food chain, and also for ruining bird habitats. The blame for anything bad that had happened in the area – it seemed – was laid at the door of the company, overseeing it. She ended with news of the cholera and the sad demise of Sapphire Phoenix.

Naturally, Cowerman's first call had been to Cuthbert-Mayne. The MD of Wessex Capital had called Jaggers, and the man's massively expensive law firm had put into motion the start of a legal chain reaction. It was exactly what Cronkite expected. The journalist had confided to Daltrey that publishing the story would be like a Los Alamos moment. She knew that her position at *The Custodian* had all but evaporated. And she was aware that publication of her latest piece would make her being there ever again an impossibility. She knew the paper would never run something so incendiary.

So, it had been a huge surprise when they did.

Cronkite had circumvented her old sub-editor – a pompous man by the name of Griffin. Instead, she'd sent the story to an old acquaintance who'd then passed it through a series of channels until it had – for a sum total of twenty-three minutes – been the top story for *The Custodian* online. Looking back, the journalist couldn't believe her luck. She assumed – bizarrely – that those overseeing the news desk at that moment were either on their lunch break or asleep. But the traction the story gained from the broadsheet's huge online presence was enormous. Countless screenshots were taken and shared among the multitudes.

It was Daltrey who'd first alerted Cronkite to the story's sudden infamy. The protestor was naturally delighted at what had been achieved. He called at about the same time that the piece was taken down. What happened next, though, was even more unexpected: the publication of the story became a story in its own right. That an article of questionable authenticity and discredited authorship had gained such prominence was suddenly a matter of great interest. It was due to this that it became the lead story on national television. As Cronkite sat back and watched, she pinched herself, gazing at the screen in disbelief. That her actions had suddenly become a cause célèbre was a source of astonishment.

'This is our moment, Jenna,' Daltrey grinned. 'You spend enough time in the shadows and you'll catch a little sun once in a while. This is our lucky break!'

If the Foulmile residents were feeling the world was turning their way, Jaggers' legal firm was thinking of the polar opposite. The veteran lawyer was fielding calls so frequently it felt as though his phone was set to catch fire. It felt like he'd been fighting a war of attrition: no sooner had a story been removed, then another one sprung up. He'd started with the online sources, issuing cease and desist demands like they were going out of fashion. But then, just as he thought he'd doused their flames, the story broke on TV. And – as the lawyer knew – the reach of TV's coverage was so vast that it would all but negate anything he was able to do.

Eventually, he was able to shut things down. But the damage was done.

In Cuthbert-Wayne's Westminster office, he and Cowerman seethed. Over an aged malt whiskey, they drank to the imminent death of Cronkite.

Chapter 39

Neither Cowerman nor Cuthbert-Wayne moved from the latter's office for the rest of the day. Instead, in a détente of defeat, they worked their way into an alcoholic alliance. They consumed several glasses of the amber liquid he poured from one of the crystal decanters residing inside a decorative wooden globe. As she'd sat disbelievingly watching the TV screen on his office wall, Cowerman had tucked her feet up on the leather sofa that lined one side of the room. Cuthbert-Mayne, meanwhile, paced the room, swearing beneath his breath, and quoting lines in Latin.

'It's gone,' Cowerman announced eventually.

'What?' muttered Cuthbert-Wayne, looking up distractedly.

'The story. It's gone – it's no longer running.' She paused, pointing at the screen. 'Look – it's not even being mentioned on the ticker tape at the bottom. Jaggers must have sorted it.'

'About fucking time!' The man peered at the screen from above the rims of his glasses. When he turned to face the woman, his bloodshot eyes looked hooded beneath his drooping eyebrows. His cheeks were hollow. Sunken. As his spectacles slipped down, they caught on the bridge of his nose. The expression he wore was halfway between complete hatred and a simple disdain. For a moment, Cowerman wondered how the hell she – once upon a time Head Girl at a posh private school with an unconditional offer to read law at one of the oldest colleges in Oxford – had ended up in such a position.

'I blame you for this, you useless fucking witch...' Cuthbert-Wayne began.

'I thought you didn't approve of swearing,' she sneered.

'Fuck you. I...'

His utterance was disrupted by the ringing of a phone.

***

It wasn't the receiver on the office desk. That had rung so much that it had been left off the hook. Neither was it the endless buzzing of the politicians' mobile phones – they'd grown immune to the constant barrage of messages and calls each one had been subject to since the story had broken. Instead, this was a shrill, old-fashioned ringtone. Cuthbert-Wayne froze, a look of horror on his face.

Reaching into the pocket of his suit, he drew out a Maraphone X1.

'Where the hell did you get *that*?' Cowerman scowled, looking at the phone in puzzlement.

'Africa,' the man replied quietly. 'By way of... never mind. It's untraceable. I've got one for you too.'

He pressed the button to accept the video call and beckoned her over.

For an instant, the picture buffered, and then the shot stabilised. Chad Benning, replete with Stetson, stared out. 'I thought you'd be there,' he sniffed, when he saw Cowerman. 'The witch and the wizard.' He paused, shaking his head. 'You're a fucking useless pair of assholes. You know that?'

'Chad...' Cuthbert-Wayne began.

'...don't fucking interrupt me, you limey faggot.' The venom in the American's voice was too much for the politician. He sank back in his chair, chastened and admonished. 'Take a fucking good look at this – both of you.'

Benning held the phone up so its camera took in the full scene. The call was coming from an arid, red-brown landscape – the asphalt surface of what looked like an airstrip lay a few feet away. On the other side of the strip, the ground was desert-like: sand; rocks; cacti, and – miles away – the saw teeth of purple-tinged mountains that rose from the horizon.

The view shifted to an ageing Dodge Ram parked on the airstrip. Behind it was a man. He was clearly screaming, but his screams were being drowned out by the sound of the truck's revving engine. At least he'd been a man once upon a time. He was beaten and bloodied, and his face was disfigured by bruising. His hands were tied behind his back. And, from his wrists, another, much longer rope snaked across the floor to where it was tied onto the towbar of the truck.

Both politicians looked at the screen in horror.

'This prick planted stories in the press,' Benning began, a grin now crossing his face. His tone took on a rasping, growling timbre. 'This is how we deal with things in Texas: when someone fucks us over, we fuck them right back.'

The American raised a hand, and the truck sprang forward in a tight, doughnut curve. The man rolled, skidded, and then rose momentarily to his feet. But, as he did, the curve of the turn made the rope go taut. He was wrenched off his feet, flung onto his back and dragged around. The off-white colour of his shirt turned instantly crimson where asphalt flayed the skin of the man's back. He managed to rise almost half-heartedly to his feet once more before being floored again. The driver made one more turn, and the man half rolled, half knelt before landing headfirst on the ground. From then on, the vehicle kept on in an established rhythm. The driver of the Dodge simply locked his hand in position and kept whirling around in ragged circles.

'Fun, huh?' Benning leered as he turned the phone to frame his face. He sneered. 'You said you would take care of things... you didn't.' He shook his head. 'Don't make me fucking come over there, because I can do this shit anywhere. Understand?' The American paused. 'Someone puts stories in the press that you don't want to hear – you take care of them.'

As the footage played on, neither politician could wrench their eyes away. As the figure on the end of the rope was reduced to something one might expect to see slung from a hook in a slaughterhouse, they looked on. Cowerman sobbed silently, while her colleague continually swore beneath his breath, spluttering occasionally.

'Peace out, bitches!' Benning said eventually, framing his face on the screen and then hanging up.

Silence.

'We can't...' Cowerman began.

'Take this,' Cuthbert-Wayne said, handing her the phone.

'But... why?'

'I have an idea.' As Cowerman's hand closed on the phone, she wondered whether the faith she had in the older politician was misplaced. To date, he'd always managed to manoeuvre successfully; he'd always second-guessed the opposition. But, suddenly, she wondered whether he was simply a faint-of-heart coward trying to absolve himself of blame.

Chapter 40
Lancashire, UK.

'Here she is!' Daltrey beamed. 'My fucking hero! Or should that be heroine?' He grinned. 'Never mind. Come here!' Stepping over to Cronkite, he embraced her in a giant bear hug – he'd been hugging her repeatedly ever since the story had broken. 'I'm proud of you, love. Really – we all are.'

The journalist blushed. 'I was just doing my job. I told you that before.'

'No mate,' the protestor shook his head. 'Doing your job would just be writing down the bare bones. You went above and beyond. That was Pulitzer Prize stuff. George fucking Cross stuff!' He chuckled. 'Besides, I bet you didn't even get paid for any of it anyway, did you?'

The journalist shrugged and caught Rivera's eye. 'So, you decided to stick around then?' She raised her eyebrows and then turned to Daltrey.

'He's doing a few jobs for me,' the protestor explained. He paused, frowning. 'Trouble in paradise with you two lovebirds, is it?' He grinned. 'What light through yonder window breaks and all that immortal bard stuff, no?'

'Fuck off, Daltrey,' Rivera muttered.

'Yeah, fuck off Daltrey!' Cronkite glowered.

'There you go,' the protestor laughed. 'You can agree on something – I should charge fees as a fucking counsellor.' He turned to the journalist. 'Anyway, I'm not being funny, but you're back in the tiger's mouth here. Don't you want to head down to London or somewhere to make yourself scarce?'

'No.' The journalist shrugged. 'I reckoned I'd see this thing through. Besides, I found some things out.'

'Yeah?' Daltrey pressed. 'Like what? What kind of things?'

'Well, I've been doing some more digging. I ran down a couple of sources I'd half-forgotten about.' She paused. 'I guess their attention wavered a little when the story broke – Cowerman and company, that is. I reckon they might've let their guard down a bit. They certainly didn't put up barricades around the consultant.'

'No?' Rivera pressed.

'Don't get too excited,' the journalist replied, looking coldly at the ex-soldier. 'It's not enough, I don't think – it's certainly not irrefutable proof.'

'Come on, Jenna!' Daltrey implored. 'Don't leave me hanging in suspense over here. What have you got for us?'

Cronkite shrugged. She looked at the floor for a moment, digging in the mud with the toe of her boot. 'Well, much as it pains me to say this, Rivera was right. It *did* make sense to follow the money.' She paused. 'And when I followed Alexander's money, I found a link. I managed to trace down three transactions in the Cayman Islands.'

The ex-soldier gave a low whistle.

'What?' Cronkite frowned.

'You did well to get anywhere close to things in the Caymans,' Rivera said. 'The security at Fort Knox is more lax.'

The journalist smiled a little bashfully.

'Will you stop fucking interrupting, soldier!' Daltrey growled. He turned back to Cronkite. 'What's the link?'

'Stella Cowerman and Marley Cuthbert-Wayne.'

'I knew it!' the protestor said triumphantly. 'I fucking told you, didn't I?'

'No great surprise, is it?' Rivera said, softly.

'No,' the journalist replied, looking directly at the ex-soldier. 'But there's another name that cropped up: Chad Benning. Insignia TX.'

Silence.

'Who's he?' the ex-soldier asked.

'A big shot political donor,' Cronkite replied. 'He's MD of the largest fracking operation in North America. How's that?'

'Sonofabitch!' Daltrey grinned. 'So all my tree-hugging-hippie-mad-left-wing-conspiracy theories were right after all!'

'It looks that way, doesn't it?' the journalist grinned.

'So what do we do now, Napoleon?' the protestor asked, turning to face Rivera.

'We stop the bill,' the ex-soldier shrugged. 'Or at least we try to. We do that, and this is worth something. If not...' his voice trailed off.

'Roger that,' Daltrey nodded.

Chapter 41

'I remember you – Rivers, right?' Sergeant Hoode looked almost as beleaguered as he had at the pair's previous meeting. The two men were standing on the service road a short distance away from the protest camp.

'Rivera,' the ex-soldier replied. 'How goes?'

The policeman shrugged. 'How do you think? Any time I look around, it feels like someone else has peeled away another piece of police authority on my patch. I've spent thirty years building up trust in the boys in blue around these parts. And it feels like it's taken GFP about five minutes to destroy it.'

Rivera nodded, grimacing. 'More trouble, then?'

'Just a little.' He paused. 'It mainly comes down to Putsch Security.' He looked hard at the other man. 'You'll have heard of them, no doubt – I know you've been hanging around on the fringes of that protest group over there.' The officer nodded in the direction of the Foulmile site. 'Nothing much passes me by. I just can't do anything about it. Putsch in particular.'

'Yeah?' the ex-soldier answered. 'So what – they have all the clout now, right?'

'They do,' the policeman agreed. 'Although GFP – their lords and masters - were trying to do a compulsory purchase of the site the other day.' He sighed. 'Thankfully, it didn't go through. But, if it had, it would have cut my precinct entirely.' Hoode shook his head. 'It would seem like a joke if it wasn't so bloody serious – anything east of Foulmile would have felt like it was east Berlin back in the day. I wouldn't have been allowed access through the fracking site, so I'd have had to go the long way round if the whole thing had gone through.' He paused. 'Imagine that – the area would have been like one of those mad, old Caribbean islands ruled by pirates!'

'Dodged a bullet, then?' Rivera asked.

'Yeah – but I don't know for how long. It kind of feels like we're living on a knife edge in these parts. And what's so infuriating is that I can't do a damn thing about it.' He shook his head. 'This stinks of government involvement... and it's the government – indirectly – that pays my wages. So...'

'...so you have to button down your lip?'

'Something like that,' Hoode answered sadly.

'You know what this is all about, though, don't you?' Rivera asked.

'I have a few ideas,' Hoode nodded. 'But enlighten me.'

***

'Unbelievable!' Hoode shook his head. Rivera had provided a brief synopsis of most of what he knew. He'd left out the Viet Cong-like tunnels Daltrey had dug, but he'd explained the Cowerman and Cuthbert-Wayne link Cronkite had uncovered in the Caymans. He'd also told the police officer about the suspected involvement of Insignia, TX. And about the cholera outbreak.

'Yeah,' the officer nodded. 'I knew those kids had something worse than the flu.' He paused. 'Bastards! So, this is a full-on cover-up then, isn't it?'

'Yeah,' Rivera nodded. 'And, I guess if the bill passes, then Cowerman gets her way. And *if* that happens, it'll be a green light for everything she wants to do. It'll be curtains for Brynworth.'

The policeman pursed his lips. 'I'm a pretty simple man, Rivera,' he explained. 'I try to do good by people. There are rogues here just like there are everywhere else in the world, but this... this is just about bloody greed. This is selling off Brynworth by the pound, isn't it?' He shook his head. 'The likes of Cowerman don't give a shit about the folks around here. They're not even people to her – they're just barriers in the way of her making more money. The same goes for all those others who are helping to bankroll her. They don't care about anyone. And they certainly don't care about the future – it's just profit now and damn the consequences.'

'Yeah, you're right enough about that,' Rivera nodded.

Silence.

'So, what can I do then?' the policeman asked.

'What do you mean?'

Hoode narrowed his eyes. 'You haven't invited me into your confidence and told me all of that just to have me walk away, have you? Surely not!'

Rivera sighed. 'Look, Sergeant - I don't really know what you *can* do. And you've sworn an oath, so you're going to have to uphold the peace, aren't you? However immoral that may be. To be honest, I'm not really sure what *any* of us can do. All I know is that things are going to hit breaking point pretty soon.'

'How so?'

'Well, Daltrey is the main man over in Foulmile.'

'Mmm. I'm pretty familiar with Mr Daltrey.'

'Yeah? Well, he was telling me that the fracking bill has its second reading in Parliament coming up.'

'And?'

'And there will be all sorts of horse trading and wrangling, I should think. But it'll all be corrupt as hell.' He paused. 'The bottom line is that – if that bill gets passed – they win.'

'And will it? Pass, I mean?' Hoode pressed.

'I'm not sure,' Rivera answered. 'A few weeks ago, it looked like a certainty, but all the negative press coverage has muddied the waters a bit. Even people who were behind it before are beginning to have their doubts.' He cleared his throat. 'Not about the fracking or the environment – the money outweighs that, of course. The issue seems to be that the idea of drilling for shale gas is pretty unpopular with all the NIMBY voters. So, the tide's turned a little.'

'And you want to make it turn some more? Am I right?' The hint of a smile passed across the policeman's face.

'It would be useful,' Rivera nodded.

'How?'

'Search me,' the ex-soldier shrugged. 'After the last round of press coverage went viral, the belief is that GFP's lawyers will pretty much silence everything.' He paused. 'They were caught napping a little bit – taken by surprise. It won't happen again.'

'So... you want an incident?'

Rivera laughed. 'How very ethical of you, officer!' He shook his head. 'No – I appreciate the thought – it would be great to keep this thing in the public eye, but you wouldn't be able to organise anything like that.'

Hoode smiled. 'No – I can't organise it. But I can smell trouble. So, tell your journalist to stick around. You should invite any photographers you know along as well.'

'Why?'

'Because, when I was driving past the fracking site this morning, Putsch Security were getting tooled up. They looked like they were getting ready for war. You want a public incident – this might be just the thing.'

'You think they're going to try to clear Foulmile?'

'I believe so,' the officer nodded. 'I can't imagine what else they'd be up to.' He paused. 'There'll be a stand-off at the very least. And it's not going to make GFP look any better. It'll be like the Democratic Convention in 1968 – especially if you can get some kids to put flowers in the barrels of the flare guns!'

Rivera nodded, smiling briefly. 'I appreciate the heads-up, Sergeant. But excuse me - I need to make a couple of calls.' He looked hard at the other man. 'I guess we know which side you're on then?'

Hoode smiled meekly.

'You sticking around?'

The other man shrugged. 'Maybe.'

Chapter 42
London, UK.

Neal Griffin – editor of *The Custodian* – was not having a good day. It wasn't the *worst* day of his professional career, but it was certainly down in the bottom five. It had started well enough; he'd only been six months in post. His seismic rise through the paper's hierarchy had been a surprise even to him. Though the organisation prided itself on being the nation's leading liberal voice, Griffin was anything but. He'd started writing during his university holidays; he'd seen the posting he was offered after graduation as a mere stepping stone before he moved on to writing for different publications. But every time he'd been about to hand in his notice, he was offered a promotion. More money. More influence. But, most of all – more power. The only time he'd genuinely come close to leaving was during the two-year period he'd worked as a sub-editor. Though that was the period which had truly made his name, he'd despised the journalists he'd had to deal with.

The Bethnal Green Set – as they'd termed themselves – were the leftist core of the paper. It was they who called the shots. They who fixed the agenda. For a while, anyone who wanted to get anywhere in the organisation had to toe their line. It was the Bethnal Green Set which had launched the career of Jenna Cronkite. Prior to receiving their patronage, she'd been a jobbing writer on the staff desk, but –

once they'd taken her under their wing – she'd risen to prominence. Her views had correlated with theirs: it had been a perfect match.

Griffin hadn't been so lucky. Their values and his values were at odds. And, as a sub-editor, he lacked the clout to do anything about them. He'd edited the articles and commissions but agreed with virtually none of the copy produced.

Since then, times had changed. Towards the end of the Bethnal Green Set's period of dominance, *The Custodian* had fallen on hard times. For years, print circulation had been falling. But it had suddenly hit desperate levels; even the Home Counties left-of-centre commuter crowd had moved into the digital realm. The shareholders, fearing a collapse, made the decision to move to a subscription model.

It was a disaster.

Where other papers had introduced membership fees and managed to weather the financial storm, *The Custodian*'s approach was met with outrage. Its readers believed that the subscription model went against everything the paper stood for. They decried its owners for putting profit before principle and deserted in their droves.

It was the vacuum which followed that provided the opportunity for Griffin's meteoric rise. If nothing else, he was a pragmatist; he sold himself to the shareholders as being liberal-lite. They appointed him on a fixed-term contract, but this was soon made permanent owing to the way he steadied the ship.

Griffin's success wasn't all down to the quality of his management: there were a few other forces at play. Firstly, the abolition of paid subscriptions attracted a number of big money advertisers. Meanwhile, in the background, the newspaper – though ostensibly remaining independent – affiliated itself with a much wider media group. It was a deal done behind closed doors, but it was one that shifted its publishing policy significantly. As its chief backer, Wessex Capital – by way of a shell company - was insistent on a change in stance. *The Custodian* remained a liberal voice, but it was a voice that had been tempered; its wings were clipped. The Bethnal Green Set was a thing of the past, and Griffin – now firmly ensconced as editor – continued to make profits grow.

The previous six months had been his finest yet. The only issue was the re-emergence of Jenna Cronkite. Marley Cuthbert-Wayne had counselled that it was better to have a firebrand like her in a place she could be seen rather than operating off piste. Griffin hadn't agreed, but he'd reluctantly acceded. In truth, he didn't really have a choice – the MP held most of the cards. The main challenge – as the editor had repeatedly pointed out – was how to square the newspaper's stance on the environment with the pro-fracking stories Cuthbert-Wayne wished to plant. In the end, the MP had given Griffin a free hand, but he'd let his displeasure be strongly known about some of the stories the paper had carried. It was he who'd eventually instructed Griffin to fire Cronkite; she'd taken to openly criticising the politician – it was a bridge too far. The editor had done as instructed, but he'd also watched the fallout of the rogue stories the journalist had gone on to publish elsewhere.

Cuthbert-Wayne hadn't called him since Cronkite's stories had gone viral.

But he knew it was only a matter of time.

***

In the end, it wasn't a phone call. It was a car with blacked-out windows that collected him from outside the office. The receptionist had simply conveyed a message that a limousine was waiting to take him to his next appointment. Griffin hadn't quibbled. He'd known who it was.

'Well?' Cuthbert-Wayne asked as Griffin slid across the luxurious leather of the rear seat.

'Well, what?' Griffin shrugged. Deep down he knew that, no matter how high in the ranks he rose, the MP for Eastington would always have the ability to make him feel insignificant.

'Nothing to say about yesterday's farce, then?'

'What should I tell you...?' the editor's voice trailed off. 'Look,' he continued. 'Yesterday's news is tomorrow's fish and chip papers – everyone knows that. It was a storm in a teacup. It's done with now.' He hoped his voice sounded confident; if so, it was a tone completely at odds with how he felt.

'Pretty damn sizeable storm!' Cuthbert-Wayne glowered. His breath smelt of strong alcohol and stale tobacco. Griffin thought he saw his hand was shaking – whether in rage or drunkenness was unclear.

Silence.

'Where are we going?' Griffin enquired. The car's driver was fidgeting with a sat nav in the front seat; he was making no effort to move the stationary vehicle.

'Just a little drive.'

'Really?'

'Correct. And you're going to get on the phone to that office of yours and pull the lead story.'

'But...' the editor began to protest. 'You said...'

'Forget what I *said*,' the MP interrupted. 'The gloves are off now. Forget keeping up with the paper's old-fashioned stance. We're doing things my way now.' He looked hard at the other passenger. 'So, get on the phone.'

The story in question concerned plans for gerrymandering. Altering the electoral boundaries in Brynworth was the latest in a long line of schemes to force the council into accepting the fracking operation. If it went through, it would give GFP just enough sympathetic politicians to make those who opposed them ineffective. *The Custodian* had run several such stories in recent times – it was something that resonated with their readers: the notion of big business buying into the politics of nations they stood to profit from always caused a stir. And Brynworth was already big enough news to guarantee clicks aplenty if the story was run online.

'Are you sure about this, sir?' Griffin began.

His utterance was met with stony silence.

'Driver,' Cuthbert-Mayne called out, tapping at the dividing screen between front and rear cabins with the handle of his ivory-topped cane.

The window was lowered with a faint buzzing sound. It was a new addition to a very old car whose plush interior had been fitted long before such electrical accoutrements were on offer.

'Sir?' the driver enquired.

'Westminster. My office.'

'Very good, sir,' came the reply from the front. The car gently pulled away from the pavement's edge to join the flow of traffic.

Chapter 43

'The way I see it,' Cuthbert-Wayne announced calmly, 'your choice is very simple.' He and Neal Griffin were sitting in the MP's office in the Houses of Parliament. It was a place the editor of *The Custodian* had only been to on a handful of occasions. The editor cared little for the fawning sycophants with which the other man seemed to surround himself. He cared even less for the way they regarded him with such distaste.

'But what's my purpose then, Marley?' Griffin pressed. 'I'm supposed to be the editor, aren't I?'

'That tone's a little familiar for my liking,' the politician frowned. 'It's simple,' he continued. 'Like I said. You were installed at the newspaper as a sleeper. The left is forever on about how it likes to put people in place to bring down the system from within. This time, we did the same – *I* rather fancied the idea.' He smiled, thinly. 'Most readers aren't so bright – they won't notice tiny shifts in tone. At least not most of the time. And that meant we could reframe things; normalise more extreme behaviour. And then – when we were safe in the knowledge that views had hardened, we'd pull the pin. That's all you were – a loss leader. The kind of pawn we put in place to take the buffering and battering until we put in someone we *really* trust.'

Griffin looked crestfallen.

'Don't look so shocked!' Cuthbert-Wayne chuckled. 'Did you really think any normal sub-editor would have had your kind of career trajectory?' He smiled. 'We had some of our people look at your social media – that's all. We identified a kindred spirit. It had nothing to do with talent.' He sighed. 'It had vanishingly little to do with you at all, really.'

Silence.

'You're probably wondering why I'm telling you this now?' the politician went on.

The editor nodded, his jaw set firm.

'Well, the truth is – you were a long-term project. Let's just say that recent events, and an increased urgency in the minds of some of our backers, have shifted the goalposts somewhat. Things have become more pressing.' The politician had recovered his sense of focus. The hazy, blurred outlines caused by too many nights of chemical ingestions at The Ivory Club had vanished. Instead, Chad Benning's threat had sharpened the MP. He was once again taut. Ruthless. 'There are two things I need you to do...' his voice trailed off, and he sipped at a glass of sparkling water.

***

'The first thing – as I said - is to get rid of the gerrymandering story. No ifs. No buts. It just needs to vanish. It's of no interest to the kind of people we want to influence.' Cuthbert-Wayne ran his fingers around the rim of his crystal glass until it made a high-pitched squeak.

Griffin nodded, slowly. 'But won't people ask questions...?' he began. 'I mean – a story like that doesn't just vanish, does it? That gerrymandering is still going on – whether it's written about in the paper or not.'

Cuthbert-Wayne laughed. 'You know what the best thing was that Thatcher ever did? Apart from crushing the unions and privatising industry, that is?'

'Enlighten me,' Griffin said, a hint of boredom creeping into his tone. Long ago, the man seated before him had been his idol. He now wondered if some of the attitudes in *The Custodian* office had rubbed off on him, turning him against such people.

'The Falklands,' the politician announced triumphantly. 'Las Malvinas. She was down in the polls and everyone hated her, so what did the old girl do?' Cuthbert-Wayne's eyes glistened. 'She started a war.' His eyes glazed over for a misty moment. 'And that, young man, is exactly what we're going to do.'

'We are?' Griffin was incredulous.

'Oh yes! I mean – not in quite the same way.' The politician paused. 'What was so clever was that it was nothing more than a diversionary tactic. I mean – she claimed otherwise. But all the flags and fandango and sending out the task force was the best thing that ever happened to her. It was a distraction. It captured people's attention – made them look the other way.' He grinned. 'And that's what we're going to do at Foulmile.'

'How?' The editor shook his head, uncomprehending.

'You're going to be glad you've cleared the front pages,' Cuthbert-Wayne smiled. 'Because I'm going to give you one of the biggest news stories of the year.'

'What?'

'We're sending in Putsch Security. The site's going to be all but levelled.' He chuckled. 'We've planted people beyond the wire – they're going to set smoke bombs off at the allotted time. And then the security firm are going in. The local police can't stop them – it's beyond their jurisdiction. It's all going to be filmed, of course. And you and your people are going to write up what they do as being an act of self-defence. Protection of property. Preservation of public safety - that kind of thing.' He paused. 'It'll be *The Custodian* that people look to for this one, so you can shape people's thoughts. Some of the other plants we have in the camp are going to start throwing bottles and rocks – things like that. With any luck, the photographs will look like the miners' strike. And people aren't so keen on public disorder any more... we've gradually dragged them around to our way of thinking, haven't we?' The politician smiled. 'We're not in the mid-eighties any more.'

Griffin nodded slowly. 'It's pretty audacious, isn't it?'

'Guilty as charged, dear,' Cuthbert-Wayne shrugged. He smiled, but there was no warmth in the icy glint of his eyes. 'Anyway, it's a done-deal.'

'Really?'

'Yes. You either do as you're told, or I have you hauled up in front of a Parliamentary commission.'

'On what grounds?' Griffin blazed.

'On the grounds that you've deliberately misled the public; taken bribes from third parties; deliberately contravened the press code of conduct; undermined journalistic integrity; and breached impartiality rules.' He grinned smugly. 'I could go on, but I don't think there's any need.' The MP paused. 'Needless to say – at the very least, you'd be out of a job. Possibly even in prison.'

The editor sat back in his chair and sighed. 'One of these days you're going to...'

'...my ancestors have been doing deals like this since the Normans invaded,' Cuthbert-Wayne cut in. 'This is how the status quo is maintained. We may not be able to hang miscreants these days – more's the pity. But we can use the tools we have at our disposal to ensure that our way of life goes on unaffected.' He looked directly at the other man, an almost impossible-to-distinguish smile playing across his features. 'Now... are you going to accept my terms and conditions, or do you wish to take umbrage with them?'

'I'll accept,' Griffin grumbled.

'Oh – and one other thing. It's only a small one.'

'What?' the editor looked up.

'In your Foulmile piece, you're going to name Jenna Cronkite, Mark Garner, and that fucking idiot Daltrey as terrorists. I mean explicitly. I want anyone who reads your writing to think the only logical place for them is somewhere like Guantanamo Bay, dressed in orange scrubs. You're going to suggest their behaviour is traitorous. That a firing squad would be too good for them.'

Griffin sank back further into his chair, defeated.

Chapter 44
Lancashire, UK.

What became known as the Foulmile Rout began suddenly. Mark Garner had given Rivera a lift to the site from the hospital. Jenna Cronkite was already there. The three were standing around talking; animosity between the ex-soldier and the journalist had thawed somewhat – they were being cordial to one another, at least. Storm clouds were clinging to the peaks of distant hills, and the sky was painted battleship grey. Wind whipped up in gusts that pulled at the pegged down tarpaulins which were clinging to various vehicles.

As sometimes happens when there are large gatherings of people, a tinderbox spark can ignite. It's as if the energy of an electrical pulse sweeps through a crowd; an excitement takes hold. Rivera had been in enough threatening situations to recognise it – it was as though an old acquaintance was whispering in his ear. The last time he'd felt such a surge had been in a marketplace in Kandahar. Thirty seconds later, a car bomb had been triggered. Back then, people had sensed something. There'd been a clue; they'd began fleeing.

Turning, he watched as a gathering of people drifted over towards the site's entrance. They moved as one. It was a subconscious movement – as if they were anaesthetised.

'What's going on?' Cronkite enquired, sniffing the air, her journalistic senses all of a quiver.

'It doesn't look good,' Garner announced. He turned to look directly at the ex-soldier. 'Trent?'

'No - it's not good,' he replied, casting his eye down the hill. 'Look.'

As his companions shifted their gazes towards the bottom of the hill, they saw a scene developing. The dark figures of Putsch Security were massed on the road that divided the Foulmile site from Green Fuel Prospects' fracking operation. The security guards looked less like what they were advertised as being, and more like a malevolent military force. Them having a stand-off on the road was nothing new, but there was a vehemence about them this time that had been absent previously. The threat of violence hung over the valley.

'There's something not right here!' Daltrey's tone was urgent as he ran across the field to Rivera. His eyes darted wildly – it was difficult to tell whether he was talking to the other man or to himself.

'Yeah, you're fucking telling me!' the ex-soldier nodded. 'Why? What's happened?'

'No clue,' the protestor answered. 'One minute it was all quiet on the western front, and now it looks like we're *on* the bloody western front!'

'Are you sure there's been nothing? No trigger?' Cronkite pressed.

'Yeah – why now?' Garner added.

Daltrey shrugged.

'This is planned,' Rivera said. He looked hard at the protest leader. 'I was talking to Hoode – the Sergeant. He said he had a bad feeling – maybe it's this.' He paused, looking at Daltrey. 'You said this day was coming, and it looks like they've got organised. They're coordinated.' He shook his head. 'Just bloody look at them.' The black-clad figures were now moving in organised ranks.

Garner looked pained. 'I'd better get down there. We'll have casualties if we're not careful.'

Rivera nodded, and the doctor departed. Putsch Security were in full riot gear. Their jet-coloured helmets had dark, dehumanising visors that made them look like clones of one another. Each of them was armed with an extended baton. They remained still, but their presence had drawn a gaggle of younger protestors – they approached them with taunts and curses, throwing the occasional stone that bounced from the riot shields they held before them.

'You'd better get down there and stop those kids,' the ex-soldier continued.

'Why?' Daltrey replied, combative.

'Because those bastards have got itchy trigger fingers,' Rivera replied. 'Look at them. They can't wait to get stuck in. All they need's an excuse.'

'You think?' Daltrey pressed.

'I'm sure of it,' the ex-soldier answered. He turned to Cronkite. 'Do you have a camera?'

The journalist nodded. 'Of course. And I have my phone.'

'Then get snapping,' Rivera instructed. 'This has all the makings of a battle.' He paused. 'Someone's set this up – there's an agenda here.'

'What, though?' Daltrey pressed. 'This is our land. They know that.'

'Yeah,' Rivera nodded. 'So they need a reason to cross the boundary. Whoever's behind this won't want it to look like an act of aggression; they'll need to make it look like self-defence. Otherwise you can throw the book at them.'

'And you think calling the kids off will be enough?' the protestor asked, his tone a little panicked.

'Do you know who those kids are?' the ex-soldier asked.

'Yeah, most of them,' Daltrey nodded.

'Then, no,' Rivera shook his head. 'If you're going to have a bloody Charge of the Light Brigade, then you need a big enough reason.' He paused. 'They look like they're waiting for a signal.' He turned to Cronkite. 'How would you do it, Jenna?'

'Me?'

'Yeah,' the ex-soldier nodded.

'Well,' the journalist shrugged. 'If I was *really* serious, then I'd probably plant a couple of people over this side. You know – get them to start a ruckus. Something like that. I've seen that sort of thing before.'

'My thoughts exactly,' Rivera said. He smiled. 'Not bad for a pen-pusher!'

'Piss off!' Cronkite grinned.

'So, what the fuck do I do?' Daltrey asked imploringly.

The ex-soldier cleared his throat. 'Can you say, hand on heart, that you know everyone on this site?'

'No,' the protestor shook his head. 'Nobody could – you've seen them bloody come and go, haven't you? Why do you keep bloody asking me that?'

Rivera pursed his lips. 'Alright then – do you recognise them all? Even if you don't know them fully?'

'Probably. Near enough. Maybe.' Daltrey frowned. 'Why?'

'Well, if there's anyone that doesn't fit, then they'll likely be your mark.' He paused. 'Come on. Let's take a look around. We might be able to scoop them up and get rid of them before they do anything.'

'What is it they're going to do?' Cronkite asked.

'Not sure. But if it's going to be enough to bring those guys into battle, then it's going to be something pretty significant.' Rivera cast his eyes down towards the road. The field was suddenly filled with people from the protest camp. Banners had appeared, and many held sticks and stones as armaments. The fractiousness of the atmosphere was clear – even from a distance. 'It looks pretty bloody busy down there,' he went on. 'Make sure Garner sticks around – if this turns nasty, he might end up doing a pretty brisk trade.'

The journalist nodded, grimacing. 'If you – er – neutralise the threat, then be careful – you're not going to be much good if you're locked up as a perpetrator, are you?'

'Negative,' the ex-soldier replied. 'Anyway, I'm off to find Sergeant Hoode. He was around earlier. I reckon he's got his nose to the ground - I'll see if he can help quell things.' He looked at Daltrey. 'You have my number, right?'

The protestor nodded.

'Good – go and find the mark.'

***

The moment that sparked what became known as The Foulmile Rout took place when Rivera was a little way down the road talking to Sergeant Hoode. The police officer had greeted the ex-soldier with an anxious expression. As Rivera implored him to order the Putsch Security guards back, Hoode held up his hands as if in surrender.

'What can I do?' the other man had asked, defeated. 'I have no jurisdiction on the fracking site. You know that!'

'So, why not head onto Foulmile?'

'There's an old injunction – I only found out about it yesterday. Bizarrely, the documents were couriered to me from a legal practice in London.' He paused. 'Convenient, no?' In the distance, the noise of the ensuing argument grew; both men looked over. 'It dates back to the hippie era – I guess some of the people living on the commune were getting fed up with what they saw as police interference. Lord knows how they managed to get it passed, but they did.'

'And what does it mean for you?' Rivera asked.

'Basically, I can't set foot on the protest camp unless I have reason to believe there's either serious criminal activity taking place, or the threat of imminent loss of life.' He paused. 'Or both.'

The ex-soldier nodded, grimly. 'And you don't think this counts?'

'Not yet,' Hoode shook his head. 'This is handbags at twenty paces right now. And, until the point anything worse happens, I'm restricted to being on the bloody road. It's like being fucking hamstrung.'

'What about back-up?' Rivera asked.

'You're joking, aren't you? The nearest squad car's fifteen minutes away. The force's numbers have been cut and then cut some more.'

'Ambulances?'

'Yeah. I've radioed a couple as a precautionary measure. But – as the law stands – neither side is doing anything other than shouting. It wouldn't even class as a breach of the peace. And...'

Rivera thought the first explosion that rang out sounded like a smoke bomb. When the second one exploded a few seconds later, he was sure of it. Thick white clouds rose almost immediately from the Foulmile field, and suddenly the Putsch Security line which had held firm, disintegrated. The black-clad battalion raced across the road and bridged the gap between them and the protest camp, screaming and shouting in bloodcurdling howls. At the foot of the hill, the youths who'd been swearing and spitting at those dressed in riot gear turned tail and ran. As they did, they encountered a mass of humanity moving in the other direction. Some of the protestors were armed; some of them wished to meet the enemy hand-to-hand. Many others were there in peaceful dissent; at that point, they simply wanted to flee the scene. The ensuing melée saw people moving chaotically in a mass of different directions.

Though the incline was steep, it only took the attacking force around fifteen seconds to reach the protestors. Once there, they waded in with truncheons flailing. The sounds reaching the roadway resembled those of a medieval battle.

And then a shot rang out. The din almost obscured it. It was little more than a high-pitched crack. But the ex-soldier had heard enough such noises to know exactly what it was.

'Get on that fucking radio!' Rivera shouted at Hoode as he sprinted towards the action.

***

Rivera thought more in terms of right and wrong than anything else. When he'd first arrived in Brynworth and met the protestors, he hadn't thought they were perfect. He hadn't even been completely convinced that what they were doing was right. But it was clearly a lot less wrong than what the representatives of Putsch Security were doing.

The first black-clad figure he encountered spied him running towards him and raised his truncheon. It was a mistake; before he had a chance to bring it to bear, the ex-soldier had slammed his shoulder into the other man's chest. As he fell to the ground, winded, he lost his helmet and dropped the truncheon. Rivera rolled away, picked up the weapon, and – as his foe attempted to right himself – flicked it across his head. It wasn't a devastating impact, but it was hard enough to send the other man headlong into the ground, unconscious.

Looking up, Rivera watched as one of the security guards smashed his truncheon across the calves of a fleeing woman. As she fell screaming in the mud, her child grabbed at the man's arm. The guard turned and elbowed the child full in the face. As he turned, leeringly looking for his next victim, the ex-soldier broke his jaw. The man crumpled to the ground.

Up until that point, Putsch Security had faced little effective opposition. Rivera's arrival drew the attention of four or five of the guards. They began to move across the broken ground to engage with him.

It wasn't a predicament that troubled the ex-soldier much. His foes were large and lumbering. Their charge up the hill had already tired them; they weren't built for speed, nor were they in possession of much stamina. The first attacker lunged at him; the ex-soldier swept his legs from beneath him, and he landed awkwardly, skidding away down the hill. After that, the next two foes swung their truncheons at the same time. Dodging out of the way, the ex-soldier shoved one of them in the back and into the path of the other man's weapon. As he fell, the handle of his truncheon tangled in the uniform of his fallen friend. He looked up, helpless, as the ex-soldier hit him beneath the visor with the weighted end of his stolen weapon.

The man crumpled. Rivera stamped on the exposed face of the other fallen security guard for good measure and then turned to face his final foe. As he did, the other man slipped on the boggy ground. He was even larger than the others had been, and his weight meant that he hit the floor hard, his chest landing on the handle of his truncheon. As he bellowed in pain, the ex-soldier smashed his boot into the man's face, rendering him insensible.

Then, he saw the gun. A SIG-Sauer P-225.

The man wielding it looked to be calmer than his colleagues. Rather than flailing about and attacking people at random, he simply stood his ground, assured. A few of the other members of Putsch Security had formed a protective cordon around him; they had their visors raised to give them a better field of vision. The leader had evidently been given clear targets; in the sights of his pistol, he covered Jenna Cronkite. She was kneeling on the ground – whether her leg was broken was uncertain, but the bone looked to be protruding at an unnatural angle. Above her, Daltrey stood. His hand was placed reassuringly on the journalist's shoulder. He regarded the gunman with a sullen look of hatred. The group's postures made it clear - this was going to be a moment of execution.

Rivera smashed the handle of his baton into the mouth of the nearest guard in the cordon. The blow connected ferociously; he felt the toughness of teeth give way to the slackness of sinew. Before him, the man stood for an instant, as if waiting for his body to register the impact. Then, the ex-soldier watched as the light went out in his eyes. He dropped stiffly, crashing to the ground like a felled tree.

Without pausing, Rivera sprinted towards the gunman. Though he had his back to him, the armed figure perceived the light of hope in Cronkite's eyes as she recognised her potential rescuer. As the man whirled around, he raised his gun, aiming it at the newcomer. But, at the same moment, the much smaller Daltrey thumped the gunman's shoulder. It wasn't a great punch; the impact was minimal, and his fist glanced off the other man's limb. But it was enough to destabilise the shooter momentarily. Though he swiftly shook off the protestor and brought the pistol to bear, he did so with Rivera almost upon him.

As the gunman pulled the trigger, the ex-soldier dropped like a stone. He slid across the muddy ground towards the other man, connecting with his knee in the kind of thuggish challenge beloved of footballers from a bygone era. As he did, he noted with satisfaction how the gunman's limb folded back on itself with a loud crack. Tendons, gristle and bones crunched as Rivera's boot continued its passage. It was a move much like he'd used in the multi-storey, but the slippery ground gave him an increased momentum.

For a moment, the gunman stared in disbelief at the impossible angle of his shattered knee. He didn't give a howl of pain; instead, he simply began to whimper on the ground. Rivera retrieved the man's gun and then slammed the sole of his boot into his ribs. Taking aim, he then fired off two quick shots, hitting the last two remaining members of the guards' cordon in the leg and incapacitating them.

Being faced with an active shooter changed the dynamic instantly. As Putsch Security became aware of its depleted numbers, members of its ranks began to doubt themselves. Their talisman had postured before; he'd waved the SIG around theatrically and had fired it into the air to create panic. Having the tables turned and seeing colleagues felled by a trained combatant had never been part of the plan.

It wasn't a retreat at first. Uncertain, the security guards simply regarded Rivera. He then held the pistol aloft, gambling on it being the only firearm the attackers had.

He was correct.

Moments later, the trickle of black-clad troops heading back towards the road became a tide. A few of the Foulmile protestors cheered half-heartedly, but most were too traumatised to do anything other than remain where they were.

'Fucking hell, mate!' Daltrey chuckled. 'That was brilliant! You were like bloody Rambo or something!'

Rivera bent down and grabbed Cronkite's shoulder. She winced as he raised her up. 'Think you can walk?' he enquired.

She nodded.

'Let's get you to Garner, shall we?' He paused and looked at Daltrey. 'Any ideas?'

'No, mate. Sorry. I haven't seen him.'

Rivera nodded. 'Are you going to give me a hand, then?'

'Negative,' the protestor replied, distractedly.

'What?' the ex-soldier's tone was indignant. 'What do you mean?'

'I've got to get down the mines,' Daltrey replied. 'Get ready for round two. I'll see you on the other side.' He wandered away, dazed, his mind already elsewhere.

Cronkite frowned, and then looked hopefully to Rivera.

'Come on,' the ex-soldier said. 'Sergeant Hoode will have called in his ambulances.'

The journalist nodded. 'This will get spun, you know – this whole thing,' she began.

'Yeah, don't worry about that now.'

'It will, though,' she insisted. 'Everything will be recorded as our fucking fault. You watch.'

Rivera chewed his lip. 'You know... I was all set to leave here the other day. Now, I'm beginning to think it wouldn't have been such a bad idea. I'm ready to vanish for a while, I reckon.'

'Really?' she frowned. 'After all this?'

'Yeah,' he shrugged. 'I've been spat at; shot at; kicked and punched. *And* I've seen a full-scale battle. And that's only today.' He paused. 'Afghanistan felt safer!' He shook his head in disbelief. 'Right,' he continued, hoisting her slightly. 'Hold on tight.'

Chapter 45

Mark Garner's abduction was swift. Putsch Security had been given a very clear briefing about who their targets were. His persistence with the cholera questions had elevated his status. Where previously he'd classed as an irritant, now his photograph was one of those tacked to the pin board with a red border around it. Once the charge began, the Foulmile residents were sent into disarray. The marauders attacking them weren't much more disciplined, but their uniforms gave them the appearance of being a cohesive unit. They'd nominated operatives to snatch their various targets while people's eyes were drawn elsewhere.

Only one of the attackers had a firearm – it was a consideration Putsch Security had struggled with. In the end, they reasoned that a bullet fired into the air would be sufficient to create pandemonium, and that once any of those individuals they were trying to seize saw the gun, they would surrender immediately. The black-clad men who grabbed Garner were not pointing pistols, therefore. Instead, when he headed down the hill to see what was happening, they simply grabbed him; he was intercepted when stuck between the first and second waves of the charge. He was threatened with truncheons, and then strong-armed behind some of the parked vehicles. From there, two men marched him through a small wooded area and down to one of the liveried vans waiting on the road. With all the noise, nobody heard his cries for help. And, once they hit him in the stomach and cut off his wind, he no longer cried for help, anyway.

The Foulmile Rout was still going on when the van was driven away. The orders were clear: once a target was secured, they should be removed from the area immediately. If any of the attackers hit the jackpot and managed to abduct two or more of their quarries, then all well and good. But, in the meantime, it was easier to transport them straight away before there was any chance of them being rescued. Neither Cuthbert-Wayne nor Cowerman wished to risk any accusations of leniency from Benning if things didn't go according to plan.

***

By the time the captive Garner reached the premises of LD Chopper Tours, he was bruised and battered. He wasn't sure how long the ride had taken – prior to departure, one of his captors had hit him on the side of the head with a wrench. He'd then been flung into the wood-panelled rear of the vehicle. When he'd come to, he was aware of dried blood on the side of his face. The locum doctor had his hands securely tied, and so was unable to prevent himself from careering into the van's sides as the driver swerved along the country lanes. He'd just managed to stand when a particularly sharp incline had thrown him to the floor so violently he'd lost a tooth.

The uneven ground at the end of the journey meant he was still on the floor when the doors opened. His captors remained faceless behind their mirrored visors.

'What are you doing?' Garner protested as they dragged him out of the vehicle.

'Shut up,' came the reply. It was accompanied by a punch to the stomach that made the captive retch. He cried out in both pain and frustration.

From there, he was dragged into a building roofed with corrugated iron and manhandled down a flight of stone steps.

'Greetings,' Sanderson laughed as the captive was conveyed into the basement.

'Who the fuck are you?' The locum doctor's voice rose in anger.

'Ooh, he's a wily one, isn't he?' Trout chuckled, turning to his colleague.

Sanderson checked his watch and then addressed the members of Putsch Security. 'Ninety minutes until nightfall,' he announced. 'If we've got no more by then, we'll take this one solo.'

***

'How's it all going back there?' Trout laughed above the sound of the rotors. He cast a glance back at the aircraft's loading bay.

Garner's hands remained bound, but he'd also been lashed to a hook by an additional restraint. A brown hessian sack was tied over his head. The helicopter was flying low and fast across Morecambe Bay. As instructed, the two pilots had waited for the sun to set before they'd departed. The orders from Foxtrot Delta had been clear: once darkness came, they departed, irrespective of how many prisoners were or weren't with them.

'I expected more,' Sanderson announced over the intercom. Both of the men in the front cabin wore headphones.

'Yeah – well, it's not our fucking problem,' Trout replied, his voice grating and metallic over the headsets. 'Are we ready?'

'Three minutes,' Sanderson nodded.

Trout unbuckled his safety harness, stepped out of the cabin, and clipped onto another safety hook located at the rear of the helicopter's fuselage. The captive was huddled, shaking. Whether he was shivering with cold or with fright was unclear. Trout didn't know. Or care. During the previous day's call, Foxtrot Delta had outlined the crimes committed by each of the organisation's terrorists. The men piloting the helicopter were resolute; they were doing the right thing.

The London-based operative had told them it was very important they didn't aim to converse with any captives. They would probably attempt to spin sob stories. The likelihood was that they – as literary types – would probably try to pull the wool over the eyes of patriots. It was those words that echoed in the co-pilot's head as he stepped over to Garner. In the darkness of the aircraft and above the noise of the rotor blades, he doubted the captive would even be aware of his presence.

Bracing himself against the fuselage, the pilot withdrew a hypodermic syringe. Holding it aloft, he pressed the plunger slightly in the way he'd been taught. A thin stream of fluid shimmied like a strand of cobweb in the light from up front. Kneeling down, Trout held his other arm hard against the man's neck and then plunged the needle through the fabric of Garner's shirt and into his arm. The man tried to buck against his restraints, but the pilot's arm held firm. Ten seconds later, the pentothal took hold; he began slumping to the floor.

'Sixty seconds,' Sanderson announced through the headset.

Checking his safety line, Trout stepped over to the side door and slid it open. It was stubborn, requiring several wrenches to move. He was at once buffeted by the force of the incoming draft. He gripped onto the frame of the door and steadied himself against the frigid wind.

'Thirty seconds,' the voice came.

At this, Trout stepped back and undid the restraints holding the captive. He dragged the inert form of Garner over from the far edge of the helicopter towards its open door. Below him, in the moonless night, the sea was a black mass flecked by occasional, barely visible streaks of white horses.

'Ten seconds.'

Trout hauled the captive up to a sitting position and waited. Up front, Sanderson suddenly slowed the aircraft. The onrush of wind from outside receded, and the helicopter's nose dipped slightly. They were in the area they'd nicknamed the LZ. The pilot steadied the aircraft, hovering fifty feet or so above the surface. He looked to the front and saw Sanderson, silhouetted by the lights of the controls. His colleague gave him the thumbs up.

The vicious kick in the small of the back from Trout was unnecessary. He gripped tightly to the handle on the side of the fuselage as the captive spiralled downwards out of the open door. For an instant, Trout glimpsed the spray of sea splash, and then there was nothing.

'Bomb gone,' he announced on the intercom as he wrestled the door shut.

Chapter 46

The chances of Mark Garner surviving were minuscule.

In the face of the drop and the impact of the water, the odds of being conscious were long. When the monstrous tides of Morecambe Bay were added into the equation, any possibility of remaining afloat was negligible. And then, of course, there was the pentothal. The paralysis the drug rendered meant the only thing that could save the locum doctor was a miracle.

But he survived, nonetheless.

When he looked back at the event, Garner – a confirmed atheist – couldn't help but wonder whether some kind of guardian angel had been looking down upon him. The factors contributing to him staying afloat were a once-in-a-lifetime chain of events that happened just at the right time. Firstly, Trout – having dropped so many other soon-to-be-dead-bodies into Morecambe Bay previously – was complacent. He felt no need to look too closely at the dark water beneath the helicopter.

He knew the body would disappear.

They always did.

Had the co-pilot have bothered to look downwards, he may have noticed a disturbance in the channel. A navigation buoy was floating, anchored to the seabed. That its warning light had stopped working was an added stroke of luck.

But those things alone would not have been sufficient to save the falling figure.

Paralysed by pentothal, he dropped from the helicopter and plunged far beneath the surface of the frigid water, dimly aware he would never be likely to surface again. The air remaining in his lungs was sufficient to draw him up to the surface one last time. And, as it did, he hit a confluence of currents; the enormous power of the ebbing tide picked up his nearly lifeless form and dragged him with great speed out to sea.

It was at the exact moment his head broke the surface that the sack placed around his head by Trout and Sanderson snagged onto one of the buoy's metal prongs. The outgoing tide rolled him like a rag doll, twisting and turning until it had the effect of fixing him in position. Lying on his back, wedged against the buoy, his mouth was just above the water. He was held fast.

He later realised that the pentothal had at least one positive side effect: it inured him to the bitter cold. As the tide raced out around him, he could see little. The hessian sack around his head acted as an anchor between life and death, but blocked his vision entirely. It was only much later, when the current had steadied and the effects of the drug had partially worn off, that he began thinking about escape. The rusted, jagged prong of an old service ladder occasionally brushed against him. Eventually, he recovered enough mobility to drag his wrist restraints against it until they gave way.

Wearily, Garner pulled his frozen form out of the water and managed to half-sit, half-lie on the frame of the navigation buoy as it slowly rose and fell on the waves. He had the crushing realisation that the miracle of surviving the fall would swiftly be undone if he wasn't rescued quickly. Left clinging to the structure, he would quickly perish from exposure otherwise.

***

As the swell picked up further, Garner crawled towards the centre of the buoy, where he hoped it would be more stable. The white water was beginning to slosh over the frame of the structure, freezing him as each wave broke. He was not a man given to praying – his life was usually one governed by logic, but he reasoned that his situation remained utterly hopeless. The miracle of survival would be undone by the mundane fate of drowning. The locum doctor knew that his only chance of rescue would come by daylight, but he also knew that it was extremely unlikely he'd last that long. Almost resigning himself to simply slipping off the structure and being cast into the tide, he examined the bulb at the top of the buoy. A sliver of light had emerged from the cloud and glinted softly on the water. It didn't provide much illumination, but it was just enough to allow him to locate the beacon atop the mast. Shakily, he clambered up and peered at it. There were no obvious faults. He ran his hands down the sides of the mast but could see no damage.

In desperation, he thumped at the bulb.

It flickered.

Garner thumped at it again. This time, it flickered and took hold – like a fire, tentatively chewing its way through kindling. The light was a bright red colour that cast lurid crimson pathways across the heaving surface of the water. The locum doctor wasn't au fait with Morse code, but he remembered the SOS signal. Using the sack that had previously been placed over his head, he covered and uncovered the light.

Dot-dot-dot. Dash-dash-dash. Dot-dot-dot.

FIVE OF CLUBS

***

Repeatedly flashing the emergency signal, Garner lost track of time. Sometimes the bulb died, and he had to thump it again. On occasion, several minutes passed before it flickered into life; sometimes the sea stilled, and other times the wind howled and the waves seemed to attack him with a renewed fury. Several times, he was thrown down from the structure. And once, he was thrown clear of it entirely. Mercifully, this coincided with a moment of calm, and he was able to clamber back aboard. After that, he removed the belt from the waistband of his trousers and used it to lash one of his arms to the buoy's mast.

He was still secured in that fashion when, in the early hours of the morning, a fishing boat drew alongside. The crew didn't say much at first. Strong arms dragged him over the gunwale and, draped in thick blankets, he was led down below the deck and into a kitchen where a wall heater was turned up full to blast the cabin with hot air. The man who Garner took as being the captain regarded him with a worried expression. He then helped him drink an inordinately strong, sickeningly sweet cup of tea, pouring it gently into his mouth. By that stage, the locum doctor's hands were shaking so much with cold and shock that he would have been unable to hold the cup himself. Following another cup of tea and a stack of energy bars, Garner's colour began to return. Throughout, the other man fired questions at him, trying to ascertain why he'd been found clinging to the buoy. The locum doctor had simply shaken his head and claimed he didn't remember. The captain had shrugged – the only thing he'd readily gone along with was the castaway's insistence that the coastguard wasn't summoned.

'You feeling a bit better?' the skipper enquired, eventually.

Garner nodded weakly.

'Someone up there must be smiling down on you,' the man said gruffly. 'When you see a navigation buoy with a faulty light, you're supposed to call it in. And, if you do, you have to stick around and light up your vessel like a beacon, so other boats don't run aground. That puts you behind schedule; then there's all the paperwork the coastguard makes you do. It's a pain in the arse.'

'So what are you saying?'

The captain shrugged. 'Any time you see a navigation buoy with a faulty bulb, you give it a wide fucking berth.'

'So, why didn't you, then?' Garner frowned.

'Because the bloke I've got on lookout is a bleeding heart liberal - that's why.' The man sighed, shaking his head. 'Listen, I'm glad we got to you. You seem alright - and it's always better pulling a bloke who's alive out of the water than dredging the drink for a stiff.'

Silence.

'You didn't stick around by the buoy when you picked me up, though, did you?' Garner frowned.

'Yeah, well - the bulb was working when I saw it. I'm sure it still is now.' The response was terse. 'You ask any of my crew and they'll tell you the same thing.'

Garner opened his mouth to speak and then closed it again.

'Right,' the skipper announced. 'I'm going to leave you to it for a couple of hours.' He cast a hand around. 'Help yourself to anything you want.' He paused. 'Promise me you'll keep eating and drinking. There's a stack of dry clothes on the side, so get changed out of what you're in.'

'Thanks,' the locum doctor replied.

'I'd have a kip if I were you,' the skipper continued. 'You look bloody awful.' As the man stood by the door ready to leave, he turned once again – a look of awkwardness on his face. 'Listen – you can relax.

I'm not going to call out the coastguard; it would carry a charge for us if nothing else.' He narrowed his eyes. 'You look to me like you'll make it, though.' He cleared his throat. 'You must have some kind of fucking luck, mate – you're like Jason bloody Bourne.' The captain moved towards the door. 'Anyway - if you worry you're starting to feel like dying, just holler, and someone'll come down and sort you out.'

Garner nodded.

'We'll be in Fleetwood shortly after dawn.' He frowned. 'You sure there's nobody else I can radio that we've got you?'

The locum doctor shook his head.

'And you say you don't remember your name?'

'I don't remember anything.' Garner shook his head, knowing the bloodied purple bruise on his temple which the skipper had patched up would make his claim plausible.

'OK...' the other man said, uncertainly. He turned and walked out of the door.

Chapter 47

The fishing boat reached the dock at Fleetwood shortly after dawn. Its progress was closely followed by a swarm of seagulls that squawked in eager anticipation of a feast of fish guts and discarded entrails. Garner stood on deck and watched as the outline of the town came into view.

'You feeling better then?' the skipper asked him as he stepped over to Garner's side of the deck. He handed the locum doctor a steaming mug of tea, which he took; the cigarette he proffered was declined.

The locum doctor nodded his thanks.

'Look,' the other man began, uncomfortably. 'It's not my business... but I've never plucked a bloke out of the drink before like this.' He scratched at his neck a little. 'I mean – I have, but none of them have been alive.' The skipper looked hard at the other man. 'You sure you don't want to tell me what the story is?'

'I don't know.' Garner shrugged. 'I'm sorry.'

The other man pursed his lips and nodded slowly. 'Alright then, but if I hear they're searching for a missing boat, then I'm going to be telling them about you. I don't have a choice. Understand?'

'How do you know I got there by boat?' Garner asked.

The skipper smiled. Then he broke into a laugh. 'That's a fucking good one, that is!' He started coughing, cleared his throat, and hacked a ball of phlegm over the side of the vessel. 'Well, you might not remember how you got there, or who you were with, but we can be damn sure of one thing,' the captain announced.

'What's that?' the locum asked.

'That you didn't bloody swim there, son. Even Michael Phelps wouldn't stand a chance – the current's too fucking strong. So you either sailed here, or you fell out of the sky.'

Silence.

'Here, Mickey,' the skipper said, addressing his crewman. 'Take a look, will you?' He reached over and turned Garner slowly around on the spot where he was standing. 'You see any wings on this lad?' The skipper laughed heartily. Both Garner and the crewman joined in. 'I think we can safely say you're too fucking ugly to be an angel...'

***

Garner parted company with the fishermen on the dock. The skipper handed him over a banknote and a scrap of paper with an address on it. 'For returning the clothes,' he explained. 'They're mine. I'm not a bloody charity organisation.' He paused. 'Anyway, I hope your memory comes back well enough that you remember to pay me my money back, too.' The skipper left the last comment hanging.

'I still feel like I should report you,' he went on. 'Either that or someone should write a story about you.' He paused. 'You might not be an angel, but you've sure as hell got somebody upstairs watching over you right now. I wasn't even supposed to be sailing last night.' He shrugged. 'Anyway, that cash should be enough to get you to the hospital,' he continued. 'After that, you're on your own, son.'

The locum doctor nodded and proffered a hand. 'Thanks,' he said.

'Good luck,' the skipper nodded.

Garner walked away. Along the dock, the fishing fleet was putting in. Marauding seagulls angrily announced their presence and squabbled with one another for scraps. The boats' crews were busy unloading their catch. Occasionally, tired-looking mariners with red-ringed eyes looked at the passing figure with idle curiosity. But most of them paid him no mind – he was dressed like they were; his hands were thrust deep into his pockets, and he walked with purpose.

On reaching the dock, the locum doctor's main fear was that the skipper would accompany him to the hospital; that he'd be forced to admit himself as a patient. Garner had no time for such an action. He wanted to head back to Foulmile - to see what had happened. As the events of the previous day came back to him, his attitude hardened even further. Putsch Security and those working alongside them had tried to kill him. He'd spent time in foreign countries working in savage conditions, often contending with disinterested, even corrupt authorities; he wasn't the sort of man who gave up easily. Nor was he as soft as these men had seemed to believe.

In leaving him for dead, they'd assumed he was no more.

He wondered, therefore, if he might be of some use to the protestors. After all, why would GFP's enforcers be looking for a man who was several fathoms beneath the waves?

The dark forces surrounding the fracking organisation were ruthless; hateful; suspicious. But even they weren't so suspicious that they'd spend time searching for ghosts.

***

As he made his way through the faded seaside glamour that surrounded him, Garner saw all the usual telltale signs of deprivation.

FIVE OF CLUBS

The locum doctor had grown up in a similar place; a once thriving port that was designed to cater for tourists who no longer visited - a yesterday's beachtown. Picking his way down long terraced streets, he saw houses with boarded-up windows; discarded shopping trolleys in front gardens; crowds of angry-looking youths hanging around on street corners; cars whose wing mirrors had been kicked off. It was a scene he'd witnessed in plenty of other places – forgotten locations that nobody wrote about in the newspapers; scenes that nobody ever saw portrayed on television. Instead, they just became broiling cauldrons of hatred and resentment. Those who'd once passed their time at union halls and working men's clubs now sat at home, unemployed and resentful – their fears forever being stoked by politicians like Stella Cowerman. The part of town the locum doctor found himself in was a district of despair; it was the kind of postcode where desperate people swallow stories about spurious scapegoats that get screamed about in tabloid headlines.

Garner caught a bus. The journey to Brynworth lasted just over an hour. He worried the vehicle's rattling heater would send him to sleep, but he found himself to be too wired. En route, he ate a bacon sandwich procured from the side window of a greasy spoon café. It was swimming in mustard and ketchup and tasted like one of the finest meals he'd ever been served. He'd washed it down with a monstrously sweet can of energy drink. It sent his mind into overdrive.

The locum realised he had enough of the pieces now to solve the puzzle. He just needed someone to act on his findings.

He decided to head straight for wherever Trent Rivera was.

Chapter 48

'Well, you look bloody dreadful!' Rivera leaned back against Iris and regarded the dishevelled figure that approached. Upon reaching Brynworth, he'd headed to the underground parking lot where the ex-soldier had previously been resident. Finding nobody there, he'd gone to the Club Med Café and begged the number of the former chef. A disgruntled supervisor had handed it over.

Iris was now parked near the café on Black Fell Beacon – it was suitably removed from the Foulmile site to make it somewhere that Putsch Security wouldn't be monitoring. Garner had hitch-hiked there. It wasn't a mode of transport he'd previously employed. Indeed, looking as he did, he was surprised that anyone stopped for him at all. But they did. A kindly elderly couple gave him a lift out towards the protest camp, and then a truck driver pulled over and drove him the rest of the way up the long drag leading to the Beacon. Leaning back in the luxurious warmth of the Scania cab, the locum doctor imagined himself as a Kerouac-like figure. The romance of the situation swiftly dissipated, though, when the driver began talking about football.

As he stepped down from the cab of the truck, Garner saw that Iris was one of only three vehicles in the parking lot. He crunched across the gravelly ground in the ill-fitting steel toe-capped boots he'd been provided with; a woollen beanie hat was pulled down low over his forehead, and a thick, lined lumberjack shirt was fully buttoned. At first, the ex-soldier had barely recognised the other man.

Garner nodded at Rivera.

'What the hell happened to you?' the ex-soldier asked, frowning. 'You look like you're decked out for a fancy dress party!'

***

The ex-soldier whistled softly as the locum doctor finished recounting his tale. 'You should write a bloody book, mate. That's insane!' He paused. 'So what does it tell us?'

'A few things. They were pretty good at filling me in.' Garner smiled. 'Mainly because they didn't think they'd ever see me again. Anyway, we now know how Cowerman's been getting rid of dissenters. She's not fucking about – Daltrey said he was always a bit confused about how the numbers at Foulmile seemed to fluctuate.'

'Yeah,' Rivera nodded, scratching at his stubble. 'But even he wouldn't have predicted she was doing that. He just thought it was because they were a bit New Age and free-spirited – I guess we all did. I certainly didn't think people were being bumped off.' He shook his head. 'And they injected you?'

'Yeah,' Garner nodded. 'I guess I was still conscious – kind of.'

'It's like Argentina back in the day.'

'You think?'

'Yeah. They disappeared,' the ex-soldier explained. 'The junta used to fly them out over the Plate River. Then they'd shoot them full of anaesthetic and drop them. Fish food.' He cleared his throat. 'Looks like our girl's taken a leaf right out of the dictatorial copybook.'

'And we know it's her, right?'

'Yeah – you won't have seen the papers this morning, I shouldn't think?'

Garner shook his head. 'No – I'm not sure where my phone ended up.'

'Well,' Rivera went on, 'Cowerman's all over the front pages condemning the brutality shown by the Foulmile protestors towards the security forces.' He shook his head. 'She's spun the whole thing. Firearms and explosions – trespassing on the fracking site. I guess she's trying to justify why she sent in Putsch Security. There's a whole load of the security guards who've gone on record claiming they were attacked.' He paused. 'You can imagine – it's all nonsense.'

'So... nothing in there that's truthful?' Garner asked.

'Not in the tabloids. And nothing about innocent protestors being smashed about with truncheons, either.' He sighed. 'This is classic stuff – if they manage to create enough public outcry, then support wanes. Jenna was right about their tactics. And, if that happens and they can prove the protest camp is dangerous, they can lobby to have it shut down. Then, if that happens...'

'...Brynworth is declared fine and they can roll out fracking elsewhere,' Garner cut in.

'Exactly. Pretty bloody bleak.'

'So what do we do?'

'Hang on,' Rivera held up a hand, raising his phone to his ear. 'It's Jenna – she was taken to hospital yesterday.'

The ex-soldier answered the call. 'How are you?' He paused as the voice spoke on the other end of the line. 'Yes... alright... OK. Yes... See you later.'

'Well?' Garner raised his eyebrows.

'Developments mate. A few of them.'

***

The news that Cowerman was travelling to Foulmile to publicly condemn the actions of the protestors had reached Cronkite through a circuitous route. The visit hadn't been officially sanctioned. It didn't class as government business. Instead, it had been masterminded by Cuthbert-Wayne, who was operating under the instruction of Chad Benning. The belief was simple: a public statement would establish GFP as being on the side of law and order. And if the visit took place unannounced, then the protestors – already in disarray after the Foulmile Rout – would be ill-prepared to respond. The journalist still had enough contacts to make her privy to the key facts once they became apparent.

When Cronkite called Rivera, she did so purely to inform him of the politician's visit. The ex-soldier didn't bother her with the details of Garner's escape; he simply told her the locum doctor was alive. He reasoned she might be able to make a story out of it sometime in the future. Laid up immobile in her hospital bed, she knew she wouldn't be able to make it to the camp, though. She hoped that Rivera might be able to disrupt the visit instead.

The ex-soldier thought the same. But he had further ideas. Ideas cemented by Garner's experience and what he'd seen the previous day. Ideas hardened by knowing that Sapphire Phoenix had effectively been sacrificed to avoid an outcry. Ideas of revenge that burned all the more brightly, knowing that Cowerman and those working with her were intent on playing God.

'I need to make a call,' Rivera replied to Garner. 'Don't you need to get checked out – at the hospital, I mean?' He paused. 'That cut looks nasty.'

'Do you have a first aid kit?'

'Yes,' the ex-soldier answered.

'A mirror?'

'Yes.'

'Well then, I'll sort myself out.'

Rivera shrugged and pointed to where he kept the medical kit, then reached his phone out of his pocket and dialled a number.

'Hoode,' he said once the call was answered. The ex-soldier paused as the man on the other end of the line expressed outrage and impotence at what had happened the previous day. 'You still want to do something positive?'

Silence.

'Black Fell Beacon,' Rivera continued. 'Bring a blue light and a spare uniform.' He hung up.

'Anything I can help with?' Garner enquired.

'Negative.' The ex-soldier shook his head. 'Anything you just heard – forget it.'

'You serious?'

'I am.' As Rivera nodded, he fixed the other man with his sniper's stare. His eyes were two cobalt discs. The locum doctor didn't feel threatened, but he understood immediately the seriousness of the other man's intentions. 'Can you drive?'

'I can.'

'Take Iris back to the parking lot under the hospital, then please – I'll see you later on.'

As he caught the keys, Garner frowned slightly and then nodded.

Chapter 49

The locum doctor had already driven the T2 away by the time Hoode arrived. The car park next to Black Fell Beacon was deserted. As the café was closed, the ramblers who usually frequented it were absent. The weather had improved slightly, and shards of sunlight threatened to break through the cloud cover. Hoode whirled the police car around, rumbling on the gravel; Rivera climbed in, and then the Sergeant drove them a couple of miles down the road to a secluded spot overlooking the moor. As he turned the engine off, a couple of disgruntled sheep stared at him in irritation before returning to munching the grass.

'You're going off grid now if you come with me – you realise that?' Rivera spoke to the policeman without looking at him. 'If you want to back out, then you need to back out now – it won't be an issue.'

'Yeah,' Hoode nodded, ignoring the utterance. 'So, this is an old car – it doesn't have all the new-fangled gadgetry.'

'Why tell me that?' the ex-soldier frowned.

'It means it doesn't automatically film everything, and there are no vehicle trackers fitted.' He paused. 'Just in case. It also has the added bonus of a load of old clothes in the back from God knows where. They don't smell too good, but what can you do?'

Rivera nodded. 'So, you're sure about this? Helping me out – I mean.'

Hoode sighed. 'I'm sure that I'm through with being fucked over and made a fool of. And I know that Cowerman's going to turn my patch into a massive slag heap by the time she's done. So, I want to stop her.' He looked hard at the other man. 'What's the plan?'

'Not a plan as such. More a hunch.'

'Go on.'

'She'll be travelling pretty incognito, right?'

'Yeah – she'll want a low profile. Then she'll just be able to spring out and address the cameras. If she brings the cavalry, then she won't have the element of surprise. The security call for things like this doesn't usually go out until about an hour before. It hasn't come through yet. Why?'

'Interception.'

Hoode whistled softly. 'Really?'

'Yeah. If we're both in uniform, they won't suspect anything. It'll be an old-fashioned stop and search.'

'And then...?'

'I'm going to ask you to trust me.'

The Sergeant sighed and shrugged. 'Why not?'

***

Rivera's hunch was correct. Cowerman's entourage was small. It consisted only of the man known as Foxtrot Delta. When Hoode flagged them down, it was he that was driving. The police officer indicated they should pull a little way up a farm track – the location was shielded from any passing traffic by a high hedge. There were few cars on the road in this location at that time of day. The incident hadn't been witnessed.

'What the fuck's going on?' demanded Cowerman angrily as she climbed out of the car. The edge of the field was muddy, and her high heels sank into it. 'Do you know who I am?'

'Yes ma'am,' Hoode nodded, gravely. 'This is for your own protection, I'm afraid.'

'This isn't acceptable!' the politician shouted. 'I'm due at the Brynworth fracking site in forty minutes.' She paused, regarding the Sergeant with disdain. 'What's the big idea? Want to get your name in the press?'

As Foxtrot Delta climbed out of the car, he looked around in suspicion. 'Quite an outmoded form of transport you have there, officer,' he announced, looking at Hoode's car in seeming amusement. He paused, the skin at the side of his mouth twitching slightly. 'How about you gentlemen show me some ID?'

Looking over, Hoode nodded at Rivera – also dressed in a police uniform - who stepped forwards. His next movement was swift. Foxtrot Delta was trained. He'd fought plenty of fights. But the butt of Rivera's pistol smashing into his face might as well have been a thunderbolt. He didn't see it coming. Instead, he sprawled across the bonnet of the car.

Cowerman screamed and reached for her phone. Hoode stepped over, smashed it out of her grasp, and quickly cuffed her hands behind her back. 'You'll go to fucking prison for this!' she snarled as Rivera pocketed her mobile.

'Shut up!' Hoode shook his head dismissively and shoved her down to a sitting position in the furrowed mud of the field. 'Try telling that to the kid who died of cholera.'

The politician laughed bitterly.

'Or those people you've injected with anaesthetic and ditched in the drink from a helicopter,' Rivera added.

For an instant, Cowerman's face crumpled. Her politician's impenetrable mask of studied indifference slipped before she recovered herself. She looked up at the ex-soldier hatefully. 'This is deception!' she spat. 'This is against the law.'

'Bingo!' Rivera announced from over his shoulder. 'Just like pretty much everything you've done here.' Going through the insensible man's pockets, he brought out a Beretta. 'Interesting,' he continued, walking over towards Cowerman. 'Does your hard man have a licence for this?'

'Of course!' the politician blustered. 'He...'

'...does not,' the ex-soldier laughed. 'Look.' He approached her and indicated a point on the edge of the barrel. 'The serial number has been filed off. That only happens if you buy your weapons in the back room of a pub.' He tutted. 'You should be a bit more careful about who you're hiring, love.'

'Fuck you! You're carrying a gun,' Cowerman shouted back. 'I doubt you have a licence for it.'

'Yeah,' Rivera sniffed. 'But I'm not a politician, am I?' He looked over as the man slumped on the hood of the car stirred. Walking back over, he slapped him awake and demanded that he unlock his phone. Groggily, the man acceded, not willing to risk another clubbing blow from Rivera's waiting gun. As the ex-soldier looked through the various apps, he paused. 'Interesting.'

'What?' Hoode asked.

'There's a dropped pin on the map.'

'Where?'

'Here.' Rivera held the phone out so the other man could see. 'LD Chopper Tours. You know it?'

'Yeah – they fly wealthy tourists over the Lake District. Sometimes along the coast. Someone told me they fly drones too. Why?'

The ex-soldier looked hard at Foxtrot Delta. 'You into helicopter tourism, are you?'

The man pushed himself off the car bonnet and looked hatefully at Rivera. 'No. Why?'

'Because...' Rivera began. 'If you're not, then you'd have no reason to be there.'

'So?' Foxtrot Delta began.

'So, I happen to know that last night, a man was flown out over Morecambe Bay, injected with a drug that temporarily paralysed him, and dumped in the sea.' He paused. 'In what I assume is your line of work, there's an old adage: dead men tell no tales.' Rivera raised his eyebrows. 'But if they miraculously survive... they might.'

'What the fuck are you telling me this for?' the man growled.

'Because I think you've been doing her bidding.' He nodded towards Cowerman. 'Anyone that speaks out too strongly against fracking, you whisk off on a helicopter and... sayonara.'

'That's preposterous!' the politician scoffed.

'Yeah? Not really,' Rivera replied. 'Number one – old face-like-a-slapped-arse over there nearly shat herself when I mentioned your little scheme. And, number two: we've got a survivor who'll testify that it's very much not bloody preposterous.'

Silence.

The ex-soldier turned to Foxtrot Delta. 'I think you've got blood on your hands, sunshine.' He paused. 'How many have you flown out there?'

The man said nothing.

Rivera pointed the pistol and cocked it. 'That man that miraculously survived last night was my friend. I'm going to ask you a very simple question: did you fly him out there?'

The man raised his two hands in a surrendering gesture, shaking his head to indicate non-comprehension.

'Last chance,' the ex-soldier said calmly. 'I'm pretty pissed off with the liberties you lot have been taking around these parts as it is. And I'm not the only one.'

Foxtrot Delta flipped him the bird.

Rivera shot him in the knee. As the man dropped to the mud and rolled around wailing, the ex-soldier turned back to Cowerman. 'What's going on at Foulmile, then?' he enquired.

'N-n-n-nothing,' she replied. The politician had crossed paths with plenty of unsavoury people on her road to Westminster. But she hadn't ever seen anyone administer violence with the gleeful disregard she'd just witnessed.

'I'm getting pretty fucking bored with people not answering my questions,' Rivera grimaced, cocking the pistol once more. 'What's going on there?'

'Press conference,' she shot back, panicked.

'And what else?' He paused. 'That alone isn't going to give you the kind of coverage you want. There were people in the crowd yesterday firing guns.' He looked hard at her. 'What the fuck else have you got planned?'

From her muddy seat, she looked up and narrowed her eyes. Stella Cowerman never had any trouble scowling – it was her resting face. But the pained expression she wore was straining under efforts to conceal her fear.

Rivera sighed and looked over at Hoode, who nodded almost imperceptibly. He then turned back to Foxtrot Delta and shot him in the head. He dragged the politician to her feet, leaned her against the car she'd arrived in, and shoved the barrel of the gun in her mouth. 'I'm going to ask you one more time,' he announced calmly. 'And if you don't give me an answer, I'll blow your fucking head off. Just like that piece of shit down there.'

Cowerman's eyes grew wide. Once the ex-soldier withdrew the gun, the words began to pour out of her in short, staccato bursts. 'Drone strike. Two o'clock. The hall there.'

The ex-soldier nodded. 'Why?'

'Make the old mines seem unsafe. So the site's cleared of crusties.'

'Clever,' Rivera nodded. 'How much of an explosion?'

The politician paused. 'Big. *Really* big,' she replied with a sharp intake of breath.

'And has it all been confirmed and authorised?'

'No, it...'

'By you, I mean.'

'Yes,' she nodded swiftly.

'Very well,' the ex-soldier nodded. 'Don't worry – you won't miss a thing. I'll get you a golden ticket. It'll be like having a front-row seat at Hiroshima.'

Rivera popped the trunk open and looked inside. He turned to face Hoode. 'I'm going to take this fucker to Foulmile,' the ex-soldier replied. 'I've got a few ideas about how we can wrap this thing up.' He paused. 'Think you can manage getting rid of that gobshite over there like we talked about?'

Hoode looked at the dead man and then nodded. 'Do you need anything else?'

Rivera frowned. 'Yeah – give me a look at those old clothes you mentioned, will you? I might need to blend in. Oh, and leave your phone on.'

The sergeant nodded.

'What about me?' the politician asked.

Rivera grabbed her by the shoulders and tipped her into the trunk of the car. A second phone clattered from her jacket pocket onto the floor. The ex-soldier took hold of it, placed it in his pocket, and then closed the lid. From inside, muffled shouts of protest were vaguely audible.

Chapter 50

Moving Stella Cowerman to Crowe Hall on the Foulmile site was less difficult than Rivera had assumed it would be. The road outside the camp was busy – both with protestors and with members of the press. Word had clearly got out via social media that the politician would be making an appearance. A couple of film crews were setting up; they weren't from national channels, but their stations were doubtless licking their lips at having their footage syndicated further afield.

The atmosphere was tense – it was an ambience borne of the previous day's memories. Representatives from Putsch Security were on hand, but they were more senior than those who'd been sent into battle. They still wore the same uniforms, but they had collars and ties visible beneath them, and they didn't sport the dehumanising black helmets that had been splashed across the front of the tabloids; any batons were carefully stored in their holsters. GFP had clearly opted for damage limitation on this occasion.

Rivera, though, didn't go anywhere near the melee. A tapestry of worn farm tracks was in existence in and around the protest site. It was a narrow one of these that he took as he veered off the main road. The road was gravelled, but its surface was broken, and tufts of thick grass spouted in the centre, where passing wheels hadn't had the chance to uproot them. On each side, the road was bordered by high hedges.

The large diplomat's car was ill-suited to its new environs – it was too wide for the road in question. Scraping its sides on thick brambles, the ex-soldier carried on, uncaring. He knew the spot he was aiming for – he'd found it on Daltrey's tour of the tunnels; the pair had exited the subterranean network a short distance away. The track split into a fork; the right lane veered off, leading to a ditch at the base of a wooded area. Rivera pulled forward into it. And, as he did, he heard a pounding noise from the boot. Cowerman clearly wasn't enjoying the off-road extravaganza.

Revving the engine, the driver moved the car further into the wooded area. Its wheels slipped and slithered as he steered between the stumps of two trees and into a deep ditch. The ground surrounding the now stationary vehicle was damp; mulched. Recent rain had turned much of the area into a quagmire – the darkened bark of the trees attested to how sodden they were. That suited the ex-soldier perfectly; he wanted to dispose of the car, but had no desire to burn the trees.

As he walked around to the back of the car, he listened. Save for the occasional thump from within the vehicle, the glade was silent. Clicking the key fob, the trunk sprung open, and the dishevelled figure of Cowerman glared back at him. Ignoring her protestations, he dragged her out and stood her on the fallen leaves.

'Here,' he said, removing some of the items of clothing he'd taken from Hoode's car. He pulled an aged woollen bobble hat onto her head. He then draped a garishly coloured shell suit jacket around her shoulders. The ex-soldier didn't bother to remove the handcuffs – he simply zipped the garment up and dragged his captive up the slope like a patch-worked mannequin.

'Why the fuck should I come with you?' she enquired. Defiant.

'Because in about twenty seconds, your car is going to turn into a fireball,' he replied coldly. 'Next question?'

Cowerman said nothing.

Rivera reached inside a briefcase on the back seat of the vehicle. He pulled out a sheaf of papers and rolled them up tightly into a tube. He then flipped the car's petrol cap off, stuffed the tube into the opening of the fuel tank, and lit the end with his cigarette lighter. Moving away, he then grabbed the politician and steered her over the broken ground and into the adjacent gully.

Ten seconds later, the pair felt a shockwave reverberate through the woods as the car exploded. Cowerman gasped involuntarily, looking back and stumbling on a root. Rivera steered her upward into an area of thicker woodland. He knew the gully and the slope beyond it would muffle most of the sound of the blast, but he also wanted to whisk the woman away lest anyone came to investigate. Pausing for a moment, he considered his bearings, knowing that the top of the incline would lead almost directly to the abandoned mine entrance.

***

Stella Cowerman wasn't suffering from Stockholm Syndrome as she made her way clumsily up the wooded slope. She had no feelings of trust or affection for her kidnapper – she'd seen him kill a man in cold blood before her eyes. But, as is human nature, she didn't expect the worst to happen to her. People rarely do. Though she realised her career as a politician was ebbing away in front of her, she reasoned she'd get through. And, once she did, she was confident that things would pick up again for her. They always did.

Rivera, on the other hand, was under no such illusions. He knew exactly what he was. And he knew exactly what was going to happen to Cowerman. He wasn't a religious man by any means, but when it came to exacting vengeance, he had a distinctly Old Testament philosophy.

The pair had reached a more level area of the path. River paused again, checking his bearings.

As he did, Cowerman's concealed phone pinged.

Rivera narrowed his eyes. He'd taken two phones from her already – that he hadn't searched her for a third felt like a rookie error.

'Where is it?' he asked, his tone icy.

'What?' the politician tried to affect a tone of innocence.

'Cut out the bullshit, Cowerman,' Rivera sighed. 'I'm getting bored of it. Phone. Now.'

Silence.

'Bottom pocket of my jacket,' she said eventually.

Rivera reached in roughly, removing the item. It was a Maraphone X1. He frowned at it. 'What the hell is this?' he demanded.

'It's African,' the politician shrugged. 'Completely untraceable.'

The ex-soldier held the phone up and squinted at the screen:

HEPHAESTOS READY.

'So... Hephaestos. I've read about him.'

Cowerman raised her eyebrows.

'Greek god of blacksmiths, carpenters – that sort of thing. Volcanoes... fire.'

The politician said nothing.

'This is to confirm the strike, isn't it?'

Silence.

'Look, love,' Rivera continued, removing the beretta from his pocket. 'You lot in Westminster are crooked as hell. But when it comes to a fight, you'll run a mile.' He paused. 'You make big claims, but when it's time to deliver, you're found wanting. All mouth and no trousers.' He shook his head. 'So, you either talk to me, or I kill you right here. I don't really give a shit either way.'

Cowerman looked back coldly. 'Can't we make a deal?'

The ex-soldier narrowed his eyes. 'Does the name Sapphire Phoenix mean anything to you?'

The politician looked back, blankly.

Rivera shook his head in disdain. 'She was the one who died of cholera a few weeks ago.'

'That's terrible!' she winced.

'Don't give me that bullshit,' he answered. 'You never knew her name. The only reason you're showing any interest now is because you think you can put a spin on it.' He paused. 'It was your fault.'

The accusation hung in the air as the wind picked up and shimmied the leaves.

'All of it's your fault,' Rivera went on. 'You don't care about anything but yourself. And your money.'

Cowerman scoffed. 'If it wasn't me, it would be someone else in the same position.' She laughed. 'Surely you're not so naïve that you don't believe that?' She shook her head. 'These people deserve what they're getting; they brought this upon themselves. Anyway, once the drone strike happens, Foulmile will be shut down. There's nothing you can do to stop it,' she went on, triumphantly. 'You're right – Hephaestos is a code. A Doomsday code. Once it's issued, there's no going back.'

'Fine. I don't want to stop it,' Rivera shrugged.

'What?' The politician frowned, uncertain.

'You heard.'

'But if Crowe Hall goes up in smoke, the camp will be closed down.'

Rivera shrugged. 'But with you out of the picture, there'll be no cheerleader to force the fracking through, anyway. It's already unpopular. And, you never know – people might wake up and start to believe that shale gas drilling in Brynworth was the cause of the explosion.'

'But that's ridiculous!' Cowerman hissed. She paused. 'Anyway, about our deal.'

'Our deal?'

'Yes – that's what you want, isn't it?'

Rivera cleared his throat and spat into the ferns. 'You see, Stella, that's the problem, isn't it? You think everyone's for sale.'

'Well, aren't they?'

'Not so much.' Rivera shrugged. 'You see, my goal in life is for it to be simple. I want to while away my days in a campervan with my cat reading books. That's it. Nothing more; nothing less. The issue is that people keep getting in my way. And, right now, I see the biggest problem here as you. And there's the fact I don't like you very much.' He paused. 'But, with you out of the picture, I see that being less of a problem.'

The politician gave a sneering laugh. 'So, what are you going to do? Kill me?'

'I don't need to,' the ex-soldier replied.

'What do you mean?'

Rivera grabbed her elbow and moved her with him along the path.

'Where are you taking me?' Cowerman pressed, a note of worry creeping into her voice.

'Crowe Hall,' the ex-soldier replied. 'Suicide by drone, sweetheart. It's almost poetic, don't you think?'

'No!' she gasped, violently bucking against his grasp. In response, he twisted her bound hand slightly, sending a spasm of pain shooting up her forearm. One of her high heels snapped off, and she hobbled as he conveyed her onwards.

'Remember,' he growled. 'You said that people around here deserve what they're getting.' He paused. 'You said they brought it upon themselves.' A forlorn tear rolled down the politician's cheek. 'This cuts both ways, Cowerman.' Rivera dragged her roughly along the path, and the pair continued up the hill. 'This is the chickens coming home to roost.'

Chapter 51

Rivera unlocked the handcuffs momentarily and then replaced them with plastic cable ties, securing the politician's wrists around a rusted, cast iron soil pipe. Cowerman remained sure the whole situation would be exposed as a bluff. A hoax. She'd spent so long getting her own way and getting away with infractions that – for the most part - she believed she operated on a higher plane to other people. That she had a right to act in whichever way she wanted. She'd spent years convincing herself of her delusions, so it didn't take much to make her believe that her captor was a chancer who was simply trying to exert leverage.

The ex-soldier didn't say much. As he'd suspected, the path out of the trees led straight to the old Nissen Hut. The Foulmile camp had been in disarray the previous day, but that was nothing compared to the state it was in now. Though he only caught glimpses, the chaotic aftermath of The Rout was abundantly clear. Many of the caravans and campervans that had been gathered around the Crowe Hall area of the site had departed. Poor sanitation and uncomfortable living conditions were one thing, but state sanctioned brutality was something else entirely. The right-wing press, predictably, had written up the incident as being a criminal enterprise; they'd decried the protestors and accused them of treasonous behaviour. However, the more liberal papers had provided a balanced view; they'd highlighted the heavy-handed tactics employed by Putsch Security and had detailed just how many hospital admissions there had been of women and children in the wake of the battle.

Cowerman cried out for help until Rivera threatened her with the beretta once more. In truth, there was nobody anywhere close. None of the camp's residents would have been inclined to assist her, anyway. But those who'd remained present had largely headed down to the road where the politician was scheduled to present her arguments. There was nothing stopping them from disrupting the filming. And nothing to prevent them from putting across their side of the story if there were any sympathetic journalists present.

Daltrey, meanwhile, was nowhere to be seen. He was the ex-soldier's only concern. That events on the road were proving such a magnet was positive – it would mean the area around Crowe Hall was clear. There was no way of getting word to the protest leader about the strike, though. Rivera didn't have time to go below ground. He simply had to hope the protest leader's tunnels were either deep enough, or remote enough, to shelter him from the blast.

'You think you'll get away with this?' Cowerman asked scornfully.

'You know that phrase, Stella – you made your bed, so lie in it?' Rivera enquired.

The politician scoffed.

Rivera looked at his watch. 'Eight minutes,' he announced. 'Let's hope your boys can tell the time.'

As he walked out of Crowe Hall, she gave a whimper. He saw no reason to gag her – he would spend the next few minutes policing the outside of the Hall. He reasoned a hundred-yard perimeter would suffice. That was if the strike was accurate. But it was a chance he would have to take.

***

The ex-soldier picked his way through the once grand hallway of Crowe Hall. Its mosaicked floor was scratched and cracked, and various tiles had been removed. Once upon a time, it would have been magnificent; that it had been ravaged by successive generations and stripped of anything valuable or useful made Rivera think of the Anglo-Saxons. They'd picked apart Roman villas when their overlords had departed and had gone back to living in primitive conditions like the protestors. Fallen plaster disrupted the patterns, and chunks of masonry had been removed from the walls. There was a hole in one section that gave a clear view from the hallway and into the dining room. The other room was in a real state of disrepair; successive seasons of storm damage had blighted its appearance, swelling its walls and peeling away paintwork and wallpaper. Many of the steps in the grandiose staircase were broken. It felt – Rivera mused – as though someone had left a demolition job half finished. It was – he reasoned – no matter. The job would be completed soon enough.

Thanks to the departure of so many of the residents, there were only a handful of vehicles parked anywhere near the former manor house. Rivera looked up at the sky a little nervously. He knew he could do nothing to prevent the strike. He didn't want to.

What he wanted was simply to stop any casualties on the ground. Other than Cowerman, of course.

Chapter 52

Rivera was just over a hundred yards away from Crowe Hall when the missiles struck. He'd looked up at the sky repeatedly while making his way around the perimeter he'd established in his head. Noise from the road had increased; it drifted on the breeze. Cloud cover was heavy once more – certainly heavy enough to obscure anything flying above it. The ex-soldier, therefore, had no way of knowing where the drone was. Or even if it really was up there. All he had to go on was what the politician had said.

He had no reason to suspect she wasn't telling the truth.

Fortunately for him, he was behind an old Ford Transit at the moment of impact. The blast was sufficient to rock the heavy vehicle on its chassis, but the van was robust enough to provide good cover. The explosion was huge – Rivera believed it to have been two separate missiles, but they hit their target so close together that it was all but impossible to judge.

The ex-soldier threw himself down on the ground and peered out from beneath the wheelbase. A fireball rose lazily up towards the sky, carrying with it the continually shifting shape of a cloud of acrid, black smoke. As it caught on the breeze, it seemed to bubble and steam like the contents of a witch's cauldron. Debris rained down on the ground nearby.

Rivera tensed himself for another explosion.

There was none.

When the smoke had cleared sufficiently, he dragged himself upright and surveyed the damage. Crowe Hall had been all but obliterated. It was – the ex-soldier mused – hardly surprising; the building had been well on the way towards dereliction, anyway. Attention had shifted from the road, and people were making their way towards the scene, talking animatedly. The TV crews, believing their luck was in, were already setting up their cameras for live-from-the-scene updates. Such a scoop was music to their ears. Rivera wished Jenna Cronkite could have been there rather than languishing in hospital; he reasoned she would have been able to weaponise the blast in her fight against GFP.

The ex-soldier rolled a cigarette. He realised the adrenalin was still pumping through his veins; it took a couple of shaky attempts before he'd managed to fashion something he could smoke.

'Need a light, buddy?' The voice addressing him came from the figure who'd just stepped around the side of the van. Its tone was familiar: Daltrey.

Rivera grinned. 'I'm glad you're here,' he began. 'I thought you were underground.' He paused. 'To be honest, I was a bit concerned you'd be underground for good.'

'Yeah. I was... underground, I mean. But I reckoned I might need to see what all the fuss was about.'

The ex-soldier laughed. 'I'm glad you made it.'

Silence.

Daltrey watched as more and more people approached the burning wreckage in wonder.

'You might want to call the police,' Rivera suggested. 'Who knows what kind of chemicals are burning there? Or if something else might blow up.'

'Way ahead of you,' the protestor grinned, waving his phone. He paused. 'So, you knew about this, then?'

The ex-soldier shrugged.

'What was it – a missile?'

'Drone strike.'

'Jesus!' Daltrey shook his head. 'This is England...'

'Yeah,' Rivera nodded. 'The England of Stella Cowerman.' He paused. 'Or, at least it was.'

The protestor narrowed his eyes for a moment until realisation dawned. 'Was she...?'

'Unfortunate accident.'

'Sonofabitch!' Daltrey marvelled. 'This is bloody brilliant! With her out of the picture, they'll lose their mojo – the frackers.'

'Yeah. Listen, you've got a whole bunch of TV crews over there. She was going to have that explosion happen in the background while she was condemning the brutality of the protestors. Then, she planned to claim it was due to the mine shafts under the camp being dangerous. After that, the next step was to condemn the place and clear you lot out.'

The protestor nodded. 'If you'll excuse me, I might go and have a word with a few journalists then – I think this explosion may just become the result of the GFP fracking organisation, don't you?'

'I think that would be a very good idea,' Rivera replied.

***

As he stood smoking, Rivera idly took out the African phone he'd confiscated from Cowerman. He cast an eye over what remained of her final resting place. It wouldn't – he mused – have been a particularly restful end. Obliteration would have been more apt. He doubted there would be anything left of her.

The phone was simplistic. It was a burner. And its screen wasn't locked; there was little evidence of it having been used. He looked at the call log and saw that the calls received hadn't come from recognisable sources; they didn't resemble conventional phone numbers. Encrypted – he assumed.

Rivera opened up the photos app. It was empty. He was about to cast the mobile aside when he pressed the deleted items. To his surprise, a short video clip remained there. Cowerman had clearly watched it and deleted it, but the security of the African phone model might not have been what she was used to. The video was blacked out, but – when the ex-soldier pressed it – he was given the option of recovering it.

Rivera felt no guilt over Cowerman's demise. It was – he knew – a case of someone getting their just desserts. She might not have pulled the trigger or put poison in the water herself, but she was behind it; she had blood on her hands. What he saw on the video made him even more convinced he'd done the right thing.

In the foreground of the screen, Rivera saw the grainy image of a car with what looked like an animal tied to the tow bar. There was no sound. As he watched, it became clear that it wasn't an animal – it was a man. It also became evident that the person filming the scene was doing so as a warning. What the intended warning was for was unclear, but the ex-soldier suspected it had to be a threat.

As he continued to regard the footage, it became clear exactly what kind of people remained for him to deal with.

The film ended. Rivera frowned, chewing his lip. In the distance, he watched as Daltrey ordered people back from the burning remains of Crowe Hall. Several questions percolated in his head. Who was it on the film? Looking at the desert scenery, he was pretty certain he was dealing with an American. Grotesque footage aside, it was the link that interested the ex-soldier. He recalled Cronkite and Daltrey talking about American capital being behind the Brynworth site, but he knew they'd had no proof. He realised that Cowerman had got into bed with some pretty bad people and there had been mention of accounts in the Caymans. Her motivation was clear: money. What wasn't clear was exactly who *they* were.

The ex-soldier resolved to press on. Removing his phone from his pocket, he called Hoode.

The phone was answered on the third ring. 'I heard there's been some drama up your way,' the Sergeant announced.

'You could say that,' Rivera replied.

'They're sending all and sundry up there by the sounds of things – and you'll be pleased to know that they're calling it a fracking accident.'

'Roger that,' the ex-soldier nodded. 'The wheels?'

Hoode paused. 'What wheels? No wheels anywhere in the vicinity.'

Silence.

'Good stuff,' Rivera went on. He sighed. 'Listen – can you get hold of another motor?'

'I'm assuming we're talking one that's off the books again, right?'

'Correct.'

Hoode paused. 'Yeah – give me a couple of hours and I'll see what I can rustle up. Do you have a lead?'

'Yeah – I thought we might pay LD Chopper Tours a visit.'

'I like your thinking.' The Sergeant paused. 'We're in pretty bloody deep here, you know?'

'We are,' Rivera nodded. 'But not so deep that we're at the bottom of Morecambe Bay.'

'Roger that,' Hoode replied. 'Anyway, I'm liking this. I think it's about time we went seeking some more justice. Where's good for you?'

'You know *Trevor's*?'

'The greasy spoon near Brynworth Hospital?'

'Yeah.'

'I do. Give me four hours.' He paused. 'If you're thinking what I'm thinking, then we'll want it to be getting dark, right?'

'You must have a crystal ball!' Rivera nodded, ending the call.

Chapter 53

'It's quite the place they have here, isn't it?' Rivera announced as he and Hoode approached LD Chopper Tours. The pair ditched the vehicle the policeman had procured at a scenic rest stop half a mile away. The car park was deserted – Hoode left the Ford in the corner furthest from the road. From there, the two men hiked to the airstrip. It was twilight by the time they reached their destination; the path cut over several steep inclines until it reached a tree-lined ridge where the ex-soldier and the policeman looked down on the space before them.

'You say this was going to be a military airfield once upon a time, right?' Rivera asked.

'Yes. During the War.' Hoode paused. 'I guess that by the time they'd started pouring concrete, things had moved on – the Allies had a foothold in France by then.'

The ex-soldier nodded. 'Not the greatest idea – sticking a base in a valley like this, though – is it? It's a bit like Dienbienphu – if it gets surrounded, then you're a sitting duck.'

Hoode shrugged. 'Yeah, maybe. But if you're running helicopter tours and you want to do some other stuff on the side with a low profile, then you're all set. Nobody will find it unless they stumble on it by accident.'

The pair hunkered down. The Sergeant took a pair of binoculars out of the small rucksack he carried, and Rivera scanned the site before them with his sniper scope.

'This all adds up,' the ex-soldier announced. 'If you wanted to keep a drone here – even a huge one – there's plenty of hangar space.'

'Roger that.'

'And if you're flying fast and low in a helicopter, Morecambe Bay isn't going to take long to reach, is it?'

Hoode nodded. 'So, what's the plan?'

Rivera paused. 'You've brought your guns, right?'

'Yeah.'

'Good.' The ex-soldier scanned the scene once more. 'Move fast and keep low. My guess is that once it gets properly dark, there will be security lights that come on, so we should get going now.'

'Agreed. And then?'

Rivera sighed. 'And then... we improvise.'

***

The pair covered the distance between the ridge and the perimeter of the LD Chopper Tours site swiftly. Neither of them knew whether to expect withering fire or just the whispering of a languid wind in their ears. There was no way of knowing if this was the small operation the business card seemed to suggest, or something much larger with plenty of back-up. Both men crouched low with their weapons drawn as they raced for the cover of the closest hangar.

They reached it without incident.

As they leaned against the corrugated iron side, Hoode panted, catching his breath. Rivera, aware of the cold night air fanning against his sweating forehead, peered around the corner. There was an open patch of ground between the hangar and what looked like an office.

'You think we can make it?' Hoode whispered.

'Kind of depends if they're expecting us,' Rivera replied. 'But let's not take any chances.'

'What about heading round the other side?' the Sergeant asked. 'There might be an easier way.'

The ex-soldier nodded, and the pair slunk off into the shadows, walking quietly alongside the wall of the hanger.

At the far end, the ground was overgrown. A door was set into the corrugated sheeting. Rivera turned the handle and pressed it.

Nothing happened.

He leaned on it again, exerting more force this time, but it refused to budge. He looked hard at the other man and drew his gun. Hoode did likewise.

'On three,' Rivera announced. 'One... two...'

There was a splintering sound as the ex-soldier's boot connected with the lock, and a clanging echo sounded out as a plank of wood landed on the concreted floor of the hanger. The two men rushed in, brandishing their weapons.

The hangar was empty save for a decommissioned Lynx helicopter.

'Nice!' Hoode exclaimed. 'No livery, I notice...'

'You reckon you could fly one of these?' Rivera asked.

'Yeah, piece of cake. I flew these back in the day.' He looked around in the half-light. 'This place is like a corrugated-iron bloody cathedral,' he remarked. 'You could fit a military-sized drone in here, couldn't you?'

'Yeah,' the ex-soldier nodded. 'You could fit a Lancaster bloody bomber in here if you wanted to. But I reckon we were never going to find the drone, were we?'

'I guess not,' Hoode shrugged. 'I should think it'll be somewhere at the bottom of the sea by now. Right?'

'Yeah,' Rivera nodded. He glanced in the other man's direction. 'Shall we?'

***

The two men moved quickly to the far end of the hangar. There was no sign of anyone else present; their boots seemed to ring out like echoing thunderclaps with each stride. The door at the far end of the structure was ajar. Peering out towards the office, the way was clear. Pausing for a moment, Rivera nodded. The pair then raced across the open ground.

Both men expected a shot to ring out. But there was no sound save for the crunching of gravel underfoot.

They reached the door of the office and waited once more. Listening.

'Right,' Rivera began, quietly. 'Either they're sitting back and waiting because they want to lure us in, or they're sitting back and waiting because they have no clue we're here.'

'Or there's nobody around,' Hoode replied. 'But I suspect the latter. Let's not take any chances, though.'

'You ready?' the ex-soldier asked, raising his eyebrows.

The Sergeant nodded. Rivera raised himself up and peered through the glass of the window that was set into the top half of the door.

'Clear,' he whispered, lowering himself. 'There's a staircase at the rear by the look of things – I'm guessing there'll be a basement.'

'Softly, softly, catchee monkey, right?' Hoode said.

'Yeah – you've got that right,' Rivera replied. He reached upwards and pulled the handle of the door.

***

The scene in the basement wasn't quite what either intruder had been expecting. It resembled a wealthy bachelor pad. Bare walls were underlit with a soft glow, and neon beer signs were tacked up at regular intervals. One man sat in a chair facing the other way. Before him, a huge computer screen was placed on a desk. The man before them was playing a video game with his back to them. A large pair of headphones covered his ears.

A second man was loudly playing on a pinball machine against the left-hand wall. The buzzers and bells of the game rang out, accompanied by assorted bleeping noises. What was more interesting to the visitors was the bound man kneeling on the floor in the centre of the room. A hessian sack was placed over his head.

Hoode and Rivera crouched down behind a pool table.

'What now?' the policeman enquired.

'I think it's time to get their attention,' the ex-soldier replied.

As Rivera stood up, the movement caught the eye of the man at the pinball machine.

Before he could speak, Rivera shot him.

***

'How much was she paying you?' Rivera enquired. Sanderson had given up his name and most of the other information the ex-soldier demanded immediately after his friend had fallen dead on the floor. He'd been further encouraged by having a beretta brandished in his face.

The pilot shrugged.

'Well,' Rivera signed. 'Whatever it was, it wasn't fucking worth it.' He looked hard at the other man. 'Innocent people died because of you.' He paused. 'How many flights did Cowerman make you take?'

'I didn't know it was her.' Sanderson shrugged. 'Not until a few days ago. Our orders came through a contact – Foxtrot Delta. She was only ever referred to as Sierra Bravo. And we were told it was a matter of national security.'

'And you swallowed that?' Hoode asked, indignant.

'Why not?' Sanderson shrugged.

'Alright then,' the ex-soldier went on. 'How many flights did this Sierra Bravo make you go on?'

'I can't remember.' The pilot's visage twitched just below his left eye. It was a clear tell.

'I'd advise you to answer,' Hoode spoke. 'This guy has a way of convincing people to do what he wants. I'm not sure you're cut out for that kind of treatment. I can only keep him on a leash for so long. Know what I mean?'

'Ball park,' Rivera demanded.

'What?' Sanderson frowned.

'Ball park figure,' the ex-soldier repeated. 'How many?'

'Ten? Twelve? Something like that.' The pilot shrugged once more. 'And the last one of them was organised by that dickhead Cuthbert-Wayne. They let that one slip.'

'Yeah?' The ex-soldier cast a glance at the policeman. 'And you still went along with it?'

'I didn't have much bloody choice,' the pilot answered.

Rivera indicated with his drawn weapon that the other man should kneel. 'What about you?' he asked, switching his attention to the man with the hessian sack over his head. 'Who the fuck are you?'

'Alexander,' the muffled voice replied. 'Brynworth Health.'

Rivera caught the policeman's eye and then frowned. 'Do you know Mark Garner?'

'I do.'

'Yeah – he's told me about you,' the ex-soldier nodded. He paused. 'How come you didn't do anything about the cholera cases?'

'I – er...'

'Yeah. Er is about right. You know that kids died because of your negligence, right?'

Silence.

The ex-soldier sighed. 'Well, at risk of déjà vu, how about this: same question, names reversed. How much was she paying you – Cowerman?' the ex-soldier pressed.

The kneeling man didn't reply. Rivera kicked him. 'I asked you a question,' he continued. 'How much was she paying you on top of your consultant's salary?'

'Twenty grand,' the physician replied.

Rivera frowned. 'Life's pretty cheap these days, isn't it?' he went on. 'And twenty grand was enough to make you look the other way?'

'Twenty grand a month,' Alexander said softly.

Hoode whistled.

'You know how people talk about blood money sometimes, right?' Rivera asked.

Silence.

'What do you reckon, then?' Hoode asked.

Rivera sighed. 'Well, we know what you've been doing here now,' he announced to the pilot. 'And we know Alexander here has been taking Cowerman's shillings to keep his mouth shut. But you didn't bank on Mark Garner being a survivor, did you? He got lucky –

extremely lucky. And he's alive and kicking.' The ex-soldier noticed how Sanderson involuntarily recoiled.

'What have you been using? Injections-wise, I mean?'

Sanderson shrugged. 'I don't know,' he replied. 'It was this guy here who gave us the stuff.'

The ex-soldier nodded. 'You're balls-deep on this one, aren't you, Alexander? A right charmer. Alright then. Spill the beans, doc.'

'I'm a consultant.' The reply was cold.

'Answer the question,' Rivera demanded. His tone was one of boredom. 'Otherwise I'll shoot you. It's pretty simple.' He paused and then added, 'Doc.'

'Pentothal,' Alexander answered.

'Where is it?' Hoode enquired.

'Why?' Sanderson asked, defensively.

'Answer the question,' Rivera said.

'Top drawer of the filing cabinet,' the answer came.

The ex-soldier nodded and then turned to Hoode. 'You really meant that you can still remember how to fly a helicopter?'

'Yeah, it's muscle memory, isn't it?' Hoode nodded, grimly. 'Like riding a bike.'

***

The protestations from Sanderson and Alexander fell on deaf ears. Rivera removed the hessian sack from the consultant's head and tied Sanderson's hands behind his back. From there, the pair of them were encouraged towards the helicopter with a series of punches and kicks.

As with Cowerman, the ex-soldier was surprised by how compliant the captives seemed to be. But then he was always amazed at people's capacity for denial in such circumstances. The pair didn't exactly cross the tarmac like lambs to the slaughter, but they certainly put up a minimal fight. They were – Rivera knew – banking on some last-minute twist to the tale; a benevolent spirit that would swoop in to deliver them.

As he secured each of them to hooks in the aircraft's fuselage, Rivera ignored their pleas.

The rumble of the engines sounded, and Hoode began to inch the helicopter forwards and through the huge doors of the hangar. He'd run through a series of checks prior to setting the rotors whirring. The death craft had been well-maintained.

'Ready?' the ex-soldier asked through the mouthpiece of his radio.

'Yeah,' Hoode nodded, his voice a crackling signal through the headsets both men had donned. 'Fast and low, right?'

'Roger that,' Rivera nodded. 'Do you have a place in mind?'

'Yeah,' the pilot nodded. 'There's a red ring drawn here.' He lifted up a laminated aviation chart that was resting on the controls. 'Any money this is a channel where they dropped the others. My guess is that the tides will be pretty strong there - I think it's a spot that'll do nicely.'

***

The flight passed without incident. True to his word, Hoode flew low – at times, it felt as though he was almost skimming the water. Rivera had done plenty of air miles, but most of it had been in the holds of cargo planes and troop transports; seeing the moonlit sea flashing beneath the cockpit made it feel as though the helicopter had gone supersonic. The distance from the hangar to the spot indicated on the map was just under twenty minutes. During that time, the aircraft encountered no other transport. Rivera kept watch below to spot any shipping, but the channel was dark.

'The fishing fleets won't be out yet,' Hoode announced over the intercom. 'At least not the ones that operate daily. And anyone else should be much further out at sea.' He paused. 'Three minutes ETA. You'll know when we're ready – I'll hit the brakes. But then I'll climb – we'll make sure these bastards don't get a soft landing.'

At this, the ex-soldier unbuckled his flight harness and clambered back into the space behind the cabin.

Both men looked up at him wide-eyed as he slid open the side door. Their pleas and protestations were lost in the sound of the wind. From his pocket, Rivera removed the two fully loaded syringes he'd taken from the filing cabinet drawer and flipped the cork stoppers off the tips of the needles. Both of the captives kicked viciously, bucking at their restraints as he approached. At the same time, the helicopter began to shoot upwards into the air, gaining altitude with every tenth of a second.

Stamping on each of their respective kneecaps with a size twelve boot stopped their vain attempts at defence. Moments after, Rivera plunged the needle through Sanderson's shirt and emptied its contents. Almost immediately, the man grew limp. His eyes blinked with increasing rapidity and then settled – his eyelids fixed open. Rivera watched as he tried to formulate a final word.

Reaching down, the ex-soldier loosened the man's restraints. Sanderson's body slipped and his head thudded onto the cold floor of the fuselage. Grabbing him by the collar, the ex-soldier dragged him to the open door and threw him out. He held onto one of the handles as he watched the dead weight plummet.

The chopper was too high up and the sea too dark for the impact to be spotted. But Rivera knew nobody could survive such a fall.

As he approached Alexander, the doctor clearly still held onto a forlorn hope of salvation. He looked up at the ex-soldier pleadingly, and silently implored the other man to spare him.

Rivera said nothing.

The doctor went through the same feeble attempts to lash out at the ex-soldier as his fallen comrade had. But it felt like pantomime. The man's spirit was crushed. He gave little reaction as the needle was plunged into his arm. His eyes rolled back in his head as the chemical hit his bloodstream; then they righted themselves as he looked fixedly up at the other man in shocked silence. As his restraints were removed, he slipped to the floor like a puppet whose strings had been cut.

Rivera was about to grab him when the helicopter lurched sharply to the left. The ex-soldier leapt, grabbing at a handle while Hoode – still in the cockpit – wrestled with the steering column to right the aircraft against the gust of wind. As he struggled to bring the helicopter back under control, Alexander's inert form began to slide slowly, irrevocably, towards the open door. His immobile arms and legs were unable to seek purchase on the smooth metal floor. Instead, momentum took over, and he slipped almost in slow motion towards the inky blackness.

As he tipped over the lip of the door, his still alert eyes locked with Rivera's.

And then he was gone.

***

'You know what they did with the choppers when Saigon fell, right?' Hoode enquired.

'Who? The Americans.'

'Yeah – they ditched them at sea.'

The ex-soldier said nothing. He listened to the thrum of the engines and the hiss of static through his headset.

'Garner surviving the Bay was a miracle,' Rivera began. 'You'd never...'

'...not in the sea, you fucking fool!' Hoode interrupted. 'There's a reservoir outside Brynworth – a huge place. We'll ditch it there.'

The ex-soldier narrowed his eyes. 'You sure?'

'Yeah – we don't want any loose ends, do we? And a helicopter's a pretty bloody big dead end, right?'

'Can't we just torch it?'

'Too risky.'

'OK,' Rivera shrugged. 'Won't they recover it?'

'No mate – there are villages that disappeared when they flooded it. In drought, you occasionally see the very tip of a church spire that was once about two hundred feet tall. There's no way anyone would waste their time. This is a Lynx helicopter – not the bloody Mary Rose!'

'Alright. How?'

'Easy,' the Sergeant smiled. 'I land. You steal a boat. I take off again and ditch the bird. Then you come and pick me up. There are life jackets under the seats with flashlights on them, so I shouldn't be hard to find.'

The ex-soldier shook his head in disbelief. 'And is it safe?'

'Absolutely not. But if I get sliced in half by a rotor blade, then I'm not going to care, am I?'

'Have you done it before?'

'What? Ditched?'

'Yeah.'

'Tonnes of times... in a simulator.' He paused. 'Twenty feet up. Nose down slightly. Ten knots ahead. Jump. Say a prayer. And Bob's your uncle!'

'And what then?'

'You swim like hell in the other direction, mate!'

Rivera puffed out his cheeks and sighed.

'What?'

'Nothing – I just can't believe that when I met you, I thought you were sane.'

Chapter 54

A week later, events in Brynworth had made their way off the front pages of the newspapers. The Foulmile camp still had an exclusion zone around it while geologists and engineers checked the remnants of the mineshaft. Military investigators were called in when fragments of the warhead were recovered from what had once been Crowe Hall. They were now attempting to piece the device back together; they believed it had been illegally sourced from a rogue state. Where it was and what the circumstances had been were secrets known only to those in the highest posts of the Secret Service.

A moratorium had been placed on drilling for shale gas in the UK. The anti-fracking movement was spinning what had happened in Lancashire as being clear evidence of the dangers of extracting the gas from underground. The tide of public opinion – it seemed – had shifted.

Word had also been leaked about the death of Sapphire Phoenix and a number of others owing to the cholera outbreak. The Environment Agency had now changed its stance; it claimed the girl's tragic demise was irrefutably down to the water table having been disturbed by the fracking.

Jenna Cronkite had appeared as a talking head on several prime-time programmes where she explained the negative effects of what GFP had been doing.

Pro-shale gas lobbyists in Westminster were strangely quiet. Without Stella Cowerman at the helm, the movement had been shorn of its most vocal cheerleader. Marley Cuthbert-Mayne, meanwhile, had taken a leave of absence from Parliament. He was, instead, focusing on Wessex Capital. As with all sensible gamblers, he'd covered his bets. That Green Fuel Prospects was seemingly self-combusting wasn't something he'd desired at all. But it was something he'd planned for, nevertheless. Ever cautious, he'd ensured that his hedge fund had moved their assets in good time. They'd made losses, but the losses weren't as calamitous as they could have been.

The politician had done everything he could to distance himself from Cowerman. And, looking at the computer screen in his office a week after the Foulmile Rout, he was pleased to see share prices associated with him and his organisation were picking up once more. He was less enamoured, though, by the continual badgering he was receiving from Chad Benning. The American had been apoplectic when he learned of what had transpired in Lancashire. He was still annoyed; it was as much at having to answer to the shareholders of Insignia TX as anything else. They weren't easily appeased, but even the surly Texan had to admit that Cuthbert-Wayne's latest olive branch was impressive: Wessex Capital had secured the drilling rights for an enormous tract of land next to the Hungarian border. With a sympathetic populist leader at the helm, there was little risk of environmental protests gaining traction. Benning had wavered, but the low wages the local labour force was prepared to work for had been the clincher.

There'd been a moment when Benning was intent on burying Cuthbert-Wayne. Now, he'd vowed to give him another six months.

Mister Alexander was still missing. The position for a new consultant was being advertised.

***

Rivera had been impressed by Hoode. The softly spoken Sergeant had proven himself to be a man of morals that aligned almost perfectly with those of the ex-soldier. Brynworth Reservoir now contained the rusting hulk of a decommissioned Lynx helicopter. Ditching the aircraft had been a textbook operation. There was only a sliver of moonlight twinkling on the water when Hoode set the chopper down for its final flight. As it was, he managed to lower it so smoothly that he'd swum well clear by the time it hit the water. An enormous spout of spray rose up – it was as if a great whale had been harpooned and was suffering its violent death throes. A dull roar sounded from beneath the surface of the water for around fifteen seconds, and then there was silence. The ex-soldier reached the policeman three minutes later; he aimed the borrowed motor launch at the pulsing light on the man's lifejacket.

Garner had collected Hoode and the ex-soldier from the reservoir a couple of hours later. Despite Rivera's assurances, Hoode had wanted to wait and see if there was any reaction to the drowned helicopter from the emergency services.

There was none.

During the drive, the locum doctor informed his passengers that he was leaving Brynworth. He'd completed his allotted number of shifts and had been offered a posting with *Médecins Sans Frontières*. It was an inauspicious farewell, considering how intense interactions had recently been between the small group.

Garner shook hands with both of the men, and then bid them goodbye.

***

The next day, Rivera ran into Daltrey.

'Fucking brilliant, isn't it, chief!' he grinned.

'What – the deaths? The destruction? Which bit?'

'All of it, mate. It's like a bloody film!'

The ex-soldier grinned. 'So – are you sticking around, or what?'

'Negative. I'm off to Hampshire.'

'Yeah?'

'Yeah. Some bastards want to build a bypass.'

'Let me guess – you're going underground?'

'Dig for victory, brother man! That's my MO.' The protestor paused and offered a hand. 'Listen, chief – we couldn't have done it without you. I mean that. We don't get to win many things in our line of work. So... thanks.'

Rivera chewed his lip and nodded slowly. 'Take it easy, Daltrey. Stay out of trouble, yeah?'

'Me?' The protestor affected a look of horror. 'No chance of that, mate!'

Chapter 55

'Well, I think things have turned out pretty well, all things considered,' said Jenna Cronkite. She was lying on the pull-out bed in the rear of Iris beneath the duvet. Rivera, propped up on one arm, turned to her.

'Yeah. Try telling that to Sapphire Phoenix's family.'

'Well – it's not like we could bring her back. But we might have gone some way to getting some kind of revenge, no?'

'Yeah, maybe.' Rivera shrugged. 'You really think fracking's dead in the water, though?'

The journalist pursed her lips. 'Maybe. They're definitely not going to be starting it up again any time soon, though.' She paused. 'There's even talk of the Foulmile camp and the area around it being designated as a wildlife sanctuary. Some twitchers have apparently found breeding pairs of some extremely rare birds.'

'Really?'

'Yes – I don't know the details, but there's already a movement – lots of support from naturalists and online organisations.'

Silence.

Rosie mewed and jumped up onto the bed. She padded across the blanket-clad forms, trying to settle herself. Rivera half-heartedly shooed her away, but she was unfazed. Instead, she nestled into the crook of his arm, and emitted a purr akin to the rumbling of a traction engine.

'What next for you then?' Cronkite enquired

Rivera shrugged. 'I have a few things I need to do.' His tone was neutral. Noncommittal.

'Do I want to know?' the journalist enquired.

'I think it's probably best that you don't,' the ex-soldier replied. 'There are a few loose ends.'

'And when will you get back?'

Rivera chewed his lip. 'I'm not sure.' He paused. 'It might be a while. Can I ask a favour?'

'You can *ask*.'

'Can you look after Rosie, please?'

Cronkite narrowed her eyes. 'When you say loose ends, do you mean loose ends overseas?'

'Maybe.'

'So, in the meantime, I'll get to use the van, right?'

'Yes.' He smiled. 'Try not to scratch her and dent her any more than she's already been scratched and dented.' He paused. 'Other than that – have some fun. See a bit of the country. Put a bit of space between you and Brynworth. Send me a postcard.'

The journalist nodded. 'Yeah, OK.'

'Just remember to feed Rosie - please!'

'Any chance of a journalistic scoop? I mean – with what you're doing now?'

'I hope not,' the ex-soldier replied. 'This will all be off the record. Way off. But that's why it might take a couple of months.'

'Won't you need help?'

'Yeah, but I've got a few irons in the fire in that regard. Don't worry.'

Cronkite lifted herself off the pillow and propped herself on an elbow to regard the ex-soldier directly. 'And what do you think when you're back? You and me?'

Rivera smiled a little. 'What? You fancy following me around and living out of a campervan like a carnival worker, do you?'

'You make it sound so glamorous!'

The ex-soldier grinned, and then his expression grew a little more serious. 'Let's just see when I get back, shall we?'

Chapter 56
London, UK.

One night, nearly a month after events in Brynworth, Marley Cuthbert-Wayne was making his way home from a heavy evening at the Ivory Club. As he wandered along a tree-lined pavement, he swayed a little en route to his exclusive apartment on Herrick Street. The street, a block away from the River Thames, was stuffed with red-bricked structures; the flats within them regularly changed hands for several million pounds. And the location – so close to the city centre – made it massively desirable. Cuthbert-Wayne's family had owned the place for several generations.

The politician's leave of absence from Westminster had been beneficial. For starters, his presence at home had placated his wife. Cuthbert-Wayne couldn't understand why she seemed so disgruntled most of the time: his children all had nannies; they were packed off to boarding schools once he considered them old enough to quietly cry themselves to sleep and not make a fuss; he was discreet about his various mistresses. And – of course – Mrs Cuthbert-Wayne had no knowledge whatsoever of the male liaisons he sometimes conducted. In the mind of the politician, he was akin to a model husband – the family lived in a Georgian mansion with grounds of several acres. They had a reasonably large staff and went skiing several times a year, as well as summering at a property they owned near Antibes. She wanted for nothing save for his company, but he reasoned that him living in

London for most of the year suited them all better. He signed the cheques, and she was largely free to do as she wished. He'd presented as loving and courteous during his last home visit; that morning she'd texted him to announce she was pregnant. Again. He placed a brief congratulatory call.

With any luck, he hoped Eton would be educating another male heir.

The only irritation in his otherwise Teflon-coated recovery was Cowerman's disappearance. He'd helped to spread the rumour that she'd defected and gone rogue, selling secrets to unfriendly nations while living in luxury under an assumed name. It was a preposterous tale – like something out of an Ian Fleming novel. He hadn't imagined it would take hold. But it did. He realised he'd underestimated the depth of hatred the nation's newspaper readers felt towards Cowerman. Through a few contacts in the press, he'd ensured she was portrayed as money-hungry and immoral, and the dailies had run with it. It meant that almost all the blame for events at Foulmile was pinned on her. That pleased him. Naturally, there were still left-wingers asking questions about who she'd been encouraged by, but he reasoned that they could be silenced if required. Besides, such questions - he knew - would dissipate soon enough; dissolved like GFP's security service.

Putsch Security had been like an army; there was no way it could have been defeated by a group of unwashed crusties. They'd had help, but nobody seemed to know *where* the help had come from. Or *who* the helper had been. The only clues they'd had were the broken and mangled frames of the guards who'd been beaten during the battle. Then there was the disappearance of the pilots. Cuthbert-Wayne had delegated ridding Green Fuel Prospects of its more vocal opponents to Cowerman. She'd proudly informed him of LD Chopper Tours and the two pilots that were prepared to do her bidding. But now they'd gone silent, as had the operative he'd provided her with. Foxtrot Delta had always proven himself extremely reliable – disappearing was out of character. At first, the politician suspected Daltrey – the charismatic protest leader – but he reasoned he wouldn't have had the expertise. Some of Putsch Security had military backgrounds that the tunnel mole wouldn't have been able to match. But whoever had attacked them clearly knew what they were doing. Jenna Cronkite – the irritating journalist – had managed to skew events in the protestors' favour, but that was hardly surprising. Cuthbert-Wayne couldn't see how she'd have any real presence in the mainstream press in the future, so she was only a minor concern.

What gave him pause was that there was, potentially, a very capable fighter still at large. Over a few sleepless nights, he'd mulled over the shadowy figure's motivation. But then he'd reassured himself; they'd gone quiet – they were hell-bent on stopping the fracking. And now it had seemingly ceased, they had no further reason to pursue their agenda.

Sometimes Cuthbert-Wayne wondered what had really become of Cowerman. He assumed she'd been killed, and he'd been certain her body would turn up. But nothing had happened. Of late, he'd adopted the mind-set that – provided she stayed buried – she'd cause him no further problems.

***

Cuthbert-Wayne crossed the marbled vestibule which was replete with palm fronds that were set in gaudy golden pots. He then began climbing the stairwell of his building; he paused for a moment, catching his breath. The evening at The Ivory Club had been celebratory – he was back in the capital. Back in the House of Commons. And – to all intents and purposes – free and single. He'd lived a life of relative sobriety while ensconced in rural England, but now the gloves were coming off once more. Being back in Westminster, he was once again exposed to the vices and temptations that underpinned his life as an MP. He violently cleared his throat a couple of times, and waited for his heart palpitations to subside.

He then began to climb once more.

The politician had been pleased with the latest deal Wessex Capital had engineered; he saw it as a feather in his cap. It had been complex and had required no small amount of patient manoeuvring. He'd financed a large shipment of arms to Novoanomyssk, where a group of Shalchik rebels had formed a breakaway republic. Using money from the sales of Soviet warheads they'd inherited upon taking over several government armouries, Cuthbert-Wayne's company had completed another deal. They'd shipped several containers filled with Kalashnikovs and had transported them on a freighter. However, since the ship had departed, government forces from Veliska had retaken Novoanomyssk. The rebel leaders were in jail awaiting trial, and the secret shipment was languishing in shipping containers on the dock at Muscat.

Wessex Capital had seized the opportunity. The money for the transaction had already been processed in the form of an untraceable series of bonds. However, one of their shell companies retained ownership of the shipment – the contract stipulated that the weapons would belong to them until the container dockets were officially switched.

Cuthbert-Wayne thought it wasteful to pass up such a gift.

So, he sold the weapons again. Rather than risking any of the fund's capital, he persuaded Chad Benning to front the money necessary to bribe port officials, and then agreed to split the profits with Insignia TX. It was a gamble that ended up being a masterstroke. Cuthbert-Wayne secured a buyer in the small Gulf emirate of Muzayaf, and suddenly both the politician and Benning received massive pay-outs. It was a short-term victory. While it didn't detract from the long-term gains that could have been made in Brynworth, it certainly took the sting out of the defeat suffered there.

***

Cuthbert-Wayne reached the doorway of his luxurious apartment and entered. Though he'd bounced back from his position of vulnerability, he'd remained edgy ever since the Foulmile Rout. He always tipped Johnson – the doorman – and instructed him to provide information about any suspicious comings and goings. To date, there had been none. Nevertheless, the politician always breathed easier once he'd done the rounds of the thickly carpeted rooms and confirmed he was alone.

***

On the roof of the Chelsea College of Arts, Rivera observed Cuthbert-Wayne through the scope of an M1 10 SASS. He'd arrived there with the sniper rifle shortly after seven o'clock that evening and made his way upwards through a service elevator. Once on the roof, he'd hunkered down; watched, and waited. In his experience, it was patience that won battles. That was something people rarely understood. The Hollywood version of warfare is all about heroic sacrifice and dramatic explosions. To the ex-soldier's mind, that was overblown nonsense. You simply needed an objective, and the wherewithal to see it through.

Cuthbert-Wayne would be complacent. At least that's what Rivera suspected. He would – the ex-soldier was pretty sure – have reasoned he'd have got away with things. People like him always did. It was a belief borne of imagining that throwing money at a problem would eradicate it.

Rivera didn't operate in the same way.

After all, there were deaths to answer for.

The ex-soldier knew there were benevolent souls in the world. The kind of people who believed in forgiving and forgetting.

But that wasn't how Rivera worked. He never forgot anything.

And forgiveness – to his mind - was a sign of weakness.

So, he lay prone and watched the world through his scope. It wasn't the same scope he used for bird-watching. He didn't want that one tainted by less salubrious activities. The sniper rifle had been sourced by Hoode; the policeman hadn't provided any details about where it had come from. Rivera hadn't asked.

At two o'clock in the morning, the ex-soldier watched from his vantage point as the figure of the Right Honourable Marley Cuthbert-Wayne tottered drunkenly towards his residence. His inebriation was made even clearer by the way he rattled at the lock of the apartment door. After thirty seconds or so, the doorman came to his assistance, placing a fatherly hand on the politician's shoulder.

A few minutes later, the lights to Cuthbert-Wayne's penthouse sprang into life. If he was living in fear – the sniper reasoned – then he wasn't showing it. Either that, or he didn't understand the nature of the threat he faced; if he had done, then he'd have been more economical with his lighting. He'd have drawn the blinds and stayed away from the windows.

But Cuthbert-Wayne did none of those things.

Rivera lined him up in the rifle sights, and then, just as he brought the crosshairs to bear, a car backfired further along the road. It spooked the politician who jerked back from the window.

The ex-soldier settled down to wait once more.

***

Satisfied he was alone, Cuthbert-Wayne sat down at the kitchen table and poured himself a large glass of Chivas Regal. Before him, his open laptop sat on the wooden surface. He opened up a private browser and accessed a secret porn site he'd grown fond of. He would – he told himself – watch for half an hour, just to still his mind before sleep. As the screen sprung into life, he reached for his whiskey.

The glass never reached his lips.

Chapter 57
Washington State, USA.

Marley Cuthbert-Wayne's untimely demise had been splashed across the tabloids in much the same way as his brains had been splashed across the kitchen of his luxury apartment. Three weeks later, Rivera crossed the Canada-US border through the Peace Arch Park in Blaine, Washington. Five days before, he'd boarded a train in Toronto and watched the prairies unfold through the window as he'd headed west through Ontario, Manitoba, Saskatchewan, Alberta and then on into British Columbia. It had been a pleasant journey – he'd spent it alternately reading, and then wondering what to do with his life. Rivera had always reasoned that he would reach a point when the world made sense. What he hadn't banked on was the disappointment he'd feel when he realised that everyone was winging everything on a daily basis.

During the journey, he'd thought of Betsy – the girl that got away. He'd also weighed up whether to make a go of things with Jenna. Pondering this, he'd realised she probably deserved better. He was – as he freely admitted to himself – shit at relationships. No sooner would he get together with someone than he'd be eyeing up her friends. As the train had drawn into Pacific Central Station, he'd texted the journalist. She'd sent him updates of her travels around the British countryside with Rosie. Her tone had been pleasant; friendly. She'd asked when he intended to return. He'd suggested he might be absent for longer than he'd previously thought.

Rivera caught took the Expo line on the SkyTrain from Pacific Central. He changed at Granville Station and then again at Bridgeport before catching a bus at White Rock Centre. The final leg of the journey – to the Peace Arch Park – took around twenty minutes on foot. He arrived right on schedule. Though there was a customs post in place, the border official seemed as disinterested in those people passing before her as was humanly possible. The scene was as different to the heavily policed boundaries between the US and Mexico as one could imagine – it harked back to what seemed like a more innocent time. There were families playing Frisbee and football; people enjoying picnics, and others simply sitting around enjoying the sunshine. The ex-soldier picked his way through them and walked south across a green expanse of well-tended lawn which was dotted with flower beds.

The parking lot he reached was half-empty. Entering it through a small gate, Rivera made his way towards an aged Toyota 4Runner. A man with a goatee was leaning against it. A plain baseball cap was pulled down low on his head, and he was sporting a pair of mirrored sunglasses. He was wearing jeans and a short-sleeved linen shirt.

Rivera narrowed his eyes. 'Quite the beard you've got there! Trying out for Hollywood, are you?'

The other man narrowed his eyes before grinning broadly. 'That's rich coming from you – you look like a fucking hobo!'

The ex-soldier laughed and the two men shook hands, before briefly bear hugging.

'Shall we?' the man in the baseball cap enquired.

'Let's,' the ex-soldier replied.

***

Larry Esposito – Lefty to his friends – had become Rivera's friend when he'd been in England. The ex-soldier was generally a solitary man, but the bond between the two men had been forged in the line of fire. It would hold firm – both of them knew that much. So, when Lefty received the British man's request for help, he didn't hesitate. San Diego to Blaine is just shy of fourteen hundred miles. The American had covered it in a day and a half.

Rivera had worked construction with Esposito's daughter Carrie, a young Californian who'd lost her life in tragic circumstances in the town of South Quay. Lefty - a retired Naval investigator - had enlisted the British man's help as he'd sought out her killers and exacted his revenge. It was a quest Rivera had been only too happy to assist with. Immediately after its completion, it had been the American who'd saved Rivera's life; the ex-soldier had caught a stray bullet fired by a corrupt constable.

'Christ!' the ex-soldier exclaimed, leaning back into the passenger seat of the 4Runner. 'This thing's a bloody antique!'

'Says the man who drives a T2 that was built before he was born!' Rivera smiled. 'How far do we have to go?'

'Twenty-five hundred miles.'

The ex-soldier gave a low whistle. 'And you think this baby will make it?'

Lefty grinned. 'Did Carrie ever mention her Uncle Jesus in Amsterdam?'

Rivera nodded, uncomfortable at the mention of the dead woman's name.

'So you know how good he is with engines?'

'Yeah,' Rivera nodded. 'He's like a Michelin-starred mechanic!'

'Exactly. Well, before he moved to Amsterdam, he rebuilt this. He took it from wreck to rock-steady in under a month.' Lefty paused. 'And he taught me to take care of it, too.' As he pulled out of the parking space, he turned to regard the other man. 'You happy enough with that, your majesty?'

'Very. Have you got the goods?'

'No.'

'No?'

'Well... yes, but not here. I don't fancy some trigger-happy state trooper taking an interest in why we're carrying hunting rifles when we're not hunting...'

'So, what's the plan, then?' Rivera pressed.

'We're going to a barbecue.' Lefty grinned.

'Are you serious?'

'Totally. We're having a stopover in Tranquillity, Texas. It's a hundred miles from Juniper, but when you're down south, that's practically next door.'

'And is Tranquillity aptly named?'

Lefty laughed. 'Amos Crenshaw lives there – he's an old buddy of mine from Naval Intelligence. And he's cooking up baby back ribs in precisely thirty-three hours. We'll take it in turns to drive: four hours at the wheel, then four hours sleep. Stops for gas, food and to hit the head. That's it. And we'll have classic rock radio all the way, baby!'

'And the guns?' Rivera pressed.

'Yeah,' the American nodded. 'Crenshaw has quite a collection. Last time I saw inside his barn, it was like he was one of those Doomsday preppers or something.'

'Nice!' The ex-soldier smiled, settled himself back into the seat once more, and closed his eyes.

Chapter 58
Texas, USA.

Nearly sixty hours after departing Blaine, Rivera was positioned on the edge of a Texas back road. The sun was dipping down behind the distant hills, casting long shadows upon the arid ground. Above, the sky was a brilliant palette of yellows and oranges. As the daylight dimmed, the temperature dropped. The sea of bluebonnets lining the asphalt quickly closed, and what had been a sapphire-coloured wash became a green-hued carpet before the blacktop gave way to sand and rock.

The Toyota 4Runner was parked in a narrow gully, invisible from the road. Two hundred yards further down the route, Lefty stood ready. In the distance, two pinpricks of light became visible through the gloom.

Chad Benning was approaching.

The businessman's home address was common knowledge. The enormous arched sign over the end of his driveway was far from subtle in its proclamation: *BENNING RANCH*. It was located a mile further along the road. Two huge Stars and Bars flags fluttered either side of the entrance.

Rivera and Lefty had arrived at their position two hours before. Since then, they'd seen no other cars. They knew there was little chance of discovery. As well as scoping out the ranch, they'd also secured details of the businessman's schedule. They knew his jet was scheduled to leave Houston at four-thirty the next morning. They also knew he was at a gala dinner that evening for a local gun club. The two men had thought long and hard about Benning's likely movements; though he was a known philanderer, they couldn't see any way he wouldn't be coming back to his house. Not when he needed to depart so early.

What Chad Benning didn't know was that he would never make it home.

***

The businessman's cream-coloured Rolls Royce was as ostentatious as it was impractical for the kind of roads he was driving on. It made it far too easy to identify whose vehicle it was. Half a mile away, Lefty was convinced it was the correct car. A quarter of a mile away, he was certain.

Just before the Rolls Royce drew level with his position, Lefty flung out the stinger. The concertinaed device flew across the surface of the road.

A second later, the high strength, hollow steel spikes penetrated the car's tyres.

The Rolls' back end slid out as its wheel rims made a screeching sound on the asphalt. It then veered onto the verge and drew noisily to a halt, throwing up gravel and uprooting a couple of hardy plants.

Seething, Benning began to climb out, brandishing a Smith & Wesson M&P Shield.

He dropped it suddenly as Rivera, springing from the scrub adjacent to the road, booted the door shut, trapping the driver's arm.

Benning swore, wincing. His eyes then grew wide as he looked at the pistol the ex-soldier was pointing at him.

'Who the fuck are you?' the American spat, rubbing at his arm.

'Want to talk about Green Fuel Prospects?'

The driver's poisonous expression was laced with contempt. As a man used to always getting his own way, he couldn't compute how someone was having the audacity to question him. He laughed in bitter indignation. 'What the fuck's it got to do with you, you Limey faggot?'

The ex-soldier sighed. 'You have blood on your hands. Quite a lot of it, in fact.'

'So who the fuck hasn't?' The American was unbowed. Unrepentant. 'Now quite wasting my time. Or...'

'...how fast can you run, Benning?' Rivera cut in.

'What?' the American frowned.

'Well, I like to think I'm a fair man, so I'll give you a five second head start.' He paused. 'Then I'll start shooting.'

Benning hesitated for a moment. He scoffed. His eyes then met those of his challenger. Looking into them, he saw his complete lack of emotion.

The American began to sprint.

The ex-soldier shot him in the back. The bullet thudded into his shoulder blade, knocking him to the floor.

A silence descended over the asphalt, broken only by the American's ragged breathing.

Rivera walked over. 'You know,' he began. 'I saw a video with you in it.' He paused before continuing calmly. 'I mean – you weren't the *only* thing in it. There was a car too. And a man being dragged behind it.' The ex-soldier cleared his throat. 'Anything to say?'

'Fuck you!' Benning grimaced.

The ex-soldier sighed. He then lowered the Smith & Wesson and shot the prone man twice in the head. A moment later, he looked up at the noise of Lefty steering the Rolls Royce into the gully at the far side of the road. 'Chuck the bastard in the ditch,' the American called out. 'They have vultures around here. With any luck, they'll have picked him clean by the start of business tomorrow. There are plenty of critters to vacuum up the blood.' He paused. 'We'll leave the car. No point torching it – the smoke will create too much interest.'

The ex-soldier nodded. 'And then?'

'The west is the best – let's head back to The Golden State and see what happens.' Lefty grinned. 'Sound good?'

***

After eleven hours of driving, Rivera and Lefty were seated at a diner outside Las Cruces, New Mexico. Each man had eaten an enormous breakfast: eggs; streaky bacon; hash browns, stacks of pancakes, and gallons of coffee. Lefty yawned.

'Can't stand the pace, old man?' Rivera asked.

The American yawned again; the question tore him out of his blank stare. He'd been idly watching traffic passing by on the freeway outside. The morning sun glinted off windscreens and chromium fenders. 'Piss off! It's been a long time since I've stayed up this long. I'm not quite the spring chicken my complexion suggests.'

The ex-soldier laughed.

Silence.

'I've been meaning to ask - are you in a hurry to head home?' the American asked.

'Not so much,' Rivera shrugged. 'Iris and Rosie are in good hands. Why?'

Lefty sighed. 'There's something I might need your help with.'

The ex-soldier nodded and rubbed at his eye with his ring finger. He studied the other man for a moment, holding his gaze. 'Come on then, Lefty,' he smiled a little. 'Talk me through it. I'm intrigued...'

Chapter 59
Next Novel Excerpt.

*T**hank you so much for reading this novel. I hope you have enjoyed it. Should you have a spare five minutes and would like to leave a short review on Amazon, I would be hugely grateful.*

Please enjoy the first chapter of the next novel in the TRENT RIVERA MYSTERIES over the next few pages.

Very best wishes.

Blake Valentine

***

SIX FATHOMS DEEP

Maria Martinez gave a start. It felt as though she was being pulled back from the brink; breathing her first breath. Panicked air rushed into her lungs. She manoeuvred her elbow to push herself upwards, but was unable to move. Straining her ears, she made out the dull mutter of hushed voices drifting in disembodied utterances. The scratchy texture of a light sheet lying across her chest was oddly comforting. She could feel a dull ache in her wrist.

Lying where she was, she knew she was only existing somewhere deep within herself; her wakefulness felt like a separate entity – her consciousness was cocooned in a dark nothingness. She was a drowning diver in the weed-strewn murky water, kicking desperately to reach a distant sun-dappled surface. But it remained tantalisingly out of reach. It was as if tendrils of vines were gripping at her feet. Dragging her down.

She tried to open her eyes, but couldn't. It was as if they were gummed shut. Her head seemed heavy – it felt as though her neck was being held in a vice. Once again, she attempted to move. But her muscles didn't obey her.

***

Access to the tunnel into which Maria Martinez had descended eight hours previously was gained via a nondescript property on the Avenida Lucrecia Toriz in Tijuana. She, and the nineteen other similarly aged members of the party who'd paid to cross the border, had been kept in a safe house above it for three days.

They'd only met Carrillo a few times. He'd come to the holding place to collect their final payments. Sitting and smoking in the lounge of what looked like a family home, he'd been all smiles. As he'd counted the cash, he'd cracked jokes and spoken confidently. Those assembled had laughed along with him. They all knew how risky it was to trust a coyote; they'd heard the horror stories. All of them had encountered deportees who'd lost everything and who'd been expelled to the south simply because the people transporting them had realised it was easier to rat them out than to make good on their promises.

It was a numbers game. And there were a million would-be migrants who were willing to take their places.

All of them were exhausted. Most carried with them the anxiety of many months of hard travelling - their constant worries were etched upon their skin. Crows' feet puckered their sun-scorched faces. Though they'd learned to be self-reliant and to live on their wits, they knew those qualities alone wouldn't be enough to get them to the Promised Land beyond the wire. For that to happen, they had to turn to other people.

But it didn't mean they had to trust them.

And Carrillo – smiles aside – was not someone they trusted at all. He was a killer: that much was clear in his eyes of flint. He comported himself in a manner that suggested despatching any of his clients would barely even register on his conscience. If he had a conscience at all.

Martinez had been taken aback by the tunnel. She'd been told that was how the group would be travelling, but she'd envisaged a sewer main at best. At worst, she'd imagined they'd be crawling through the tomb-like claustrophobia of an earth-walled excavation before being re-birthed in El Norte. It was this which terrified her most: the thought of being buried alive like an unlucky collier of old. She knew there would be no rescue party in the event of the roof collapsing - she was an undocumented traveller.

A nobody for whom a small patch of dirty ground would be grave enough for her ambitions.

The young woman had been both surprised and relieved when the party had climbed one-by-one down a steel ladder and found themselves in a well-lit gallery. The descent was long – the tunnel was perhaps fifty feet below the surface. Maybe more. When she'd reached the bottom rung, her leading foot had landed on a brick surface. The tunnel stretched ahead, its progress marked by the electric bulbs set into its ceiling. It was around eight feet in height and three feet in width.

Once the last person reached the floor, Carrillo's colleague spoke. 'You're in good hands. We have ventilation shafts built in. Over the years, we've moved thousands of people across the border through here.' He paused. 'It's perfectly safe. All you need to do is walk at a steady pace and come with me. Diego will follow from behind.' He cleared his throat. 'The US border guards have seismology machines, but they don't monitor them all the time. So you have twenty minutes to make it across.' The man paused. 'It only takes ten.'

***

Accompanied only by the steady sound of their feet falling on the floor of the passage, the group headed north. Every foot of the tunnel was uniform: earthen walls; wooden struts to protect from rock falls, and fluorescent lighting. It felt like an endless loop – a silent movie whose film spool was stuck on repeat. Had they been able to view their progress from above ground, they'd have seen themselves as pulsing icons passing beneath the Avenida Internacional; crossing the No-man's-land on either side of the border; ducking deep beneath the Tijuana River; and rising slightly upwards as they moved into the earth under the Coral Gate neighbourhood – one of the southernmost points in San Diego.

At the far end of the tunnel, an exit ladder was set into the wall; it was identical to the one which had been used to enter the subterranean passage on the Mexican side. The rungs glittered in the lights and took the group upwards. They emerged into an outhouse beside a swimming pool in the backyard of a property in San Ysidro. There, Carrillo – his scarred face cracked with a grin – welcomed them to California.

Relieved to breathe fresh air, the migrants were positive. Optimistic. It felt as though the worst was over. They even overlooked the off-putting gleam in their overseer's eye.

'Do we work here then, señor?' one of the new arrivals asked the coyote.

'No,' Carrillo laughed. 'Not here.'

When they'd made down payments for the coyote's services, they'd all been surprised by the complexity of his vetting process. They'd been promised supervisory jobs in domestic service. The coyote had talked about payment structures and promotion opportunities. His organisation – he assured them – had extremely high standards; they delivered workers to wealthy families all across the United States. It was due to this, he explained, that anyone he took on as a client needed to conform to a very definite set of criteria. Fit. Healthy. Young. Their guide stopped short of handing out questionnaires – he wouldn't have wanted a paper trail. But the questions he asked were detailed and searching, nonetheless.

Carrillo's demands had been readily acceded to. In the room where the coyote had taken their money, they'd been able to see the land beyond the border. An enormous American flag fluttered in the breeze – it looked close enough to reach out and touch. It was a masterstroke of propaganda on the part of the people smuggler. But, in truth, anyone who has travelled so far in such desperate circumstances and lost so much will take almost any risks after a while. The acceptance of terms was never going to be something they hesitated about.

***

From behind the outhouse, Martinez and her nineteen companions were loaded into panel vans. They were then driven for a short distance through San Ysidro until they reached what looked like a disused furniture warehouse. It was located on an industrial estate; the buildings adjacent to it were vacant. Once there, the group stepped out onto the asphalt of an empty parking lot.

They cast their eyes around, suddenly nervous.

Their nerves, however, were swiftly banished by the arrival of an American man. A doctor. He strode over to them from a doorway, bearing a clipboard in one hand. He looked like a physician from central casting; his manner was self-assured, and he exuded a sense of glamour that contrasted completely with the grubby, earth-streaked complexions of the new arrivals. Upon his immaculate white lab coat, he wore a photo ID bearing the logo of a company: *LAZARUS RE-HABILITATION*.

After greeting the migrants in English, he switched to Spanish. 'Welcome again,' he beamed, playing his eyes back and forth over the assembled group. 'In a few short moments, you will step through the doors of our state-of-the art medical facility.' The American man pointed towards the nearby building. 'All of you will soon have secure jobs. All of you will be able to live in prosperity.' He paused. 'This is a truly exciting time. Welcome to America!'

A warm wind wisped across the parking lot before the man continued. High above, a pair of Boeing 747s circled in a holding pattern, waiting for permission to commence their descents.

'Forgive the deception,' he smiled, casting an arm towards the nearby building. 'We can't gloss over the fact you're illegal immigrants, so we're unable to take you to a regular hospital. Nor can we outwardly advertise this place as being a medical facility. Inside, though, we'll get you cleaned up and we'll conduct some basic medical tests.' The

American man paused. 'Our clients – your new employers – have very high expectations. Therefore, we have to confirm that you're all suitably healthy to commence work.' He paused, smiling confidentially. 'Don't worry – this is a formality. Nobody could have undertaken the journeys you all have without being fighting fit. But our doctors have to sign to say that this is the case.' The American man shrugged and grinned before continuing. 'When you get inside, there are shower facilities and bathrooms divided by gender. We ask that you place your current clothes in the two red trash containers – they will be disposed of. Of course, each of you will be provided with a clothing budget by your new employers. But before we take care of that, you'll need to put on a hospital gown. They're hung up by the exit to the shower rooms for you to help yourselves. We'll hook each of you up to an IV drip to boost you full of vitamin supplements – it's standard procedure. As well as that, we'll need to administer plasma tests.' He paused. 'Though you're illegal, you'll still be able to access emergency medical coverage – we just need to ensure that your new employers have all the necessary information about blood groups and allergies – things like that.'

Silence. A low muttering was audible in certain sections of the group. Though the man addressing them was plausible, the migrants had developed an in-built mistrust of any figures in authority.

'You may enter the building right over there,' the American said. He smiled once more and indicated the door which he'd stepped out of previously.

Catching the eye of a friendly fellow traveller named Fernanda, Martinez shrugged. The pair started to make their way towards the building. The American smiled warmly at them. Once the first members had begun to make their way, the remainder would follow. Like sheep.

Silently, the rest of the group began trudging after the first pair.

***

The American looked down at the young woman. His gaze was drawn to a tiny movement; he saw her eyelids trying to flutter. They were straining at the set of skin closure strips, which had been applied to the closed eyes of all the patients when they'd first been sedated. Lowering his clipboard, he regarded her with interest. He continued to watch as two of his orderlies bustled around, busy with the tasks he'd given them. On each of the twenty beds, patients' heads were secured in position by large, elasticated bands running across their foreheads and looping beneath the frames of the gurneys. As the man watched, the woman opened her mouth, her tongue and lips forming the shape of a silent cry.

The orderlies approached, unaware of the patient's condition.

'Five hearts; eleven kidneys; two livers,' the first one announced in a strong Hispanic accent. She frowned at a clipboard.

'Yeah. And a partridge in a fucking pear tree!' orderly number two joked in response. His accent was similar to hers.

Silence.

'But that doesn't add up...' the first orderly said, her brow furrowing. She turned to the American. 'Boss?'

'They're reserves,' the man announced. His tone was one of calm authority. 'We'll sell the rest for parts.'

The woman nodded. 'Everything OK?' she asked, following the boss' gaze.

'We have a sleepwalker,' he announced, nodding at the patient before him. 'Or a *would*-be sleepwalker at any rate.'

As the two orderlies turned, Martinez's eyelids strained against the skin closure strips once more, like butterflies with clipped wings. Far behind her wall of heavy sedation, the patient understood some of what had been said. She kicked her legs fitfully, although it presented to those watching as nothing more than a slight flexing of her toes.

'What do we do, boss?' The second orderly's voice was a little hesitant.

'Jab her again,' the American instructed tonelessly. 'Double dose. Triple if required.'

Before the darkness of oblivion descended, Maria Martinez felt a pinch in her left forearm. It was followed by a slight feeling of discomfort as a burning sensation began spreading.

And then there was nothing.

Chapter 60
TRENT RIVERA NOVELS.

ONE BAD APPLE
TWO'S COMPANY
THREE BAGS FULL
FOUR-LEAF CLOVER

If you fancy reading a few books in one go (and saving a little money in the process) then why not grab a boxset?
THE TRENT RIVERA MYSTERY SERIES: BOOKS 1 - 3

Chapter 61
Get Exclusive Blake Valentine Material.

Hello!
I really hope you've enjoyed this book and that you want to continue following Trent Rivera on his journey.

If so, then why not sign up to my reader group? As well as regular updates and a monthly newsletter, there are regular polls and competitions. You will receive a FREE prequel novella – ZERO HOUR – which sees Trent involved in an investigation back in the days when he was still in uniform.

You can get your FREE book by signing up HERE.

Chapter 62
About the Author.

Blake Valentine is the author of the TRENT RIVERA MYSTERY SERIES. Prior to becoming a writer, he worked in the music industry as both performer and producer before moving into various roles in education. He has lived in Osaka, Japan and San Diego, California, and now resides on the south coast of England with his wife, 2 children, and a cat.

For more information:
www.blakevalentine.com
blake@blakevalentine.com
You can also connect with Blake on Facebook.

Printed in Great Britain
by Amazon